THE EDITOR

Franklin Walker is Professor Emeritus of American Literature, Mills College, and the author and editor of numerous books, including FRANK NORRIS: A BIOGRAPHY, AMBROSE BIERCE, and THE LETTERS OF FRANK NORRIS, as well as several studies in the literary history of the American West. A former Rhodes Scholar, Professor Walker has also held a Rockefeller Fellowship and a Guggenheim Fellowship.

BANTAM LITERATURE

Heart of Darkness
and
The Secret Sharer
Joseph Conrad

With an introduction, biographical sketch, and a selection of background materials and commentaries by

FRANKLIN WALKER
Mills College

HEART OF DARKNESS *and*
THE SECRET SHARER
A Bantam Book / published by arrangement with
Doubleday & Company, Inc. and
J. M. Dent & Sons Ltd.

Bantam Critical edition / August 1969
2nd printing .... October 1970
Bantam edition / December 1971
9 printings through August 1978
10th printing
11th printing

ACKNOWLEDGMENTS

From Joseph Conrad: A Critical Biography *by Jocelyn Baines.*
Copyright © 1960 by Jocelyn Baines. Used by permission of the
McGraw-Hill Book Company and George Weidenfeld and
Nicolson Ltd.   From Joseph Conrad: The Making of a Novel-
ist *by John Dozier Gordan (Cambridge, Mass.: Harvard Uni-*
versity Press). Copyright, 1940, by the President and Fellows of
Harvard College. Reprinted by permission of the publishers.
From The Twentieth Century Novel: Studies in Technique *by*
Joseph Warren Beach. Copyright, 1932, by The Century Com-
pany. Reprinted by permission of Appleton-Century-Crofts, Divi-
sion of Meredith Corporation.   From The Great Tradition *by*
F. R. Leavis. Copyright © 1963 by New York University Press.
Reprinted by permission of New York University Press and
Chatto and Windus Ltd.   From Conrad the Novelist *by Albert*
J. Guerard (Cambridge, Mass.: Harvard University Press); Copy-
right, 1958, by the President and Fellows of Harvard College.
Reprinted by permission of the publishers.   From "Kurtz, the
Cannibals, and the Second-Rate Helmsman" *by Harold R. Col-*
lins, Copyright, 1954, by the University of Utah. Reprinted from
THE WESTERN HUMANITIES REVIEW *(Autumn, 1954), by permis-*
sion of THE WESTERN HUMANITIES REVIEW *and Harold R. Col-*
lins.   From Joseph Conrad: Giant in Exile *by Leo Gurko.*
Copyright © 1962 by Leo Gurko. Reprinted with permission of
The Macmillan Company.

ISBN 0-553-12426-9

Published simultaneously in the United States and Canada

Bantam Books are published by Bantam Books, Inc. Its trade-
mark, consisting of the words "Bantam Books" and the por-
trayal of a bantam, is registered in the United States Patent
Office and in other countries. Marca Registrada. Bantam
Books, Inc., 666 Fifth Avenue, New York, New York 10019.

PRINTED IN THE UNITED STATES OF AMERICA

CONTENTS

INTRODUCTION

In his famous preface to *The Nigger of the "Narcissus"*, Conrad stated that: "Art itself may be defined as a single-minded attempt to render the highest kind of justice to the visible universe, by bringing to light the truth, manifold and one, underlying its every aspect." But what *was* the truth for Conrad? Was he basically an observer of life or a moralist commenting on it? H. L. Mencken wrote in 1917, "Conrad makes war on nothing; he is pre-eminently *not* a moralist. He swings, indeed, as far from revolt and moralizing as is possible, for he does not even criticize God." While Douglas Hewitt asserted in 1952, "The most cursory glance at Conrad's work is enough to convince us that he has a conception of a transcendental evil, embodying itself in individuals—a sense of evil as great as that of any avowedly Catholic or Calvinist writer." These judgments obviously reflect a radical shift in critical fashion, but Conrad's intentions themselves may be complex enough to support such a double reading.

A similar quandary presents itself in any discussion of Conrad's technique. Early readers of his fiction felt that his appeal lay in the surface level of his writing—in his handling of plot, setting, and characters. But today critics delve into its deeper levels of symbol and myth. Conrad clearly supports both views in his comments on his writing. At one time he stated: "My task which I am trying to achieve is, by the power of the written word to make you hear, to make you feel—it is, before all, to make you *see*." But at another time he wrote to a reader who had inquired about the meaning of one of his stories: "Coming to the subject of your inquiry, I wish first to put before you a general proposition: that a work of art is very seldom limited to one exclusive meaning and not necessarily tending to a definite conclusion. And this for the reason that the nearer it approaches art, the more it acquires a symbolic character."

Certainly there can be no doubt about the authenticity of the adventures and settings in *The Secret Sharer* and *Heart of Darkness*. Like much of Conrad's fiction, they are autobiographical in that they make use of the author's own experiences and reflect characters he had met and events he had heard about in his far-flung voyages. Conrad was prompted to write *The Secret Sharer* by the visit of a sea captain from Penang who reminded Conrad of his own sailing days in the Malay Archipelago twenty years before, when he had assumed his first and only sea command on the sailing ship *Otago* in Bangkok after the death of its captain. Such an initiation into the awesome responsibility of commanding a ship is at the heart of Conrad's story.

The crime and escape of Leggatt were based on the experiences of a first mate known as Sidney Smith who had killed a rebellious seaman and was given an opportunity to escape by his skipper. Conrad noted in his preface that the story was widely known in the Far East at the time, and he may have heard it when he was in Singapore. For the purposes of his tale, he made Leggatt a much more sympathetic character than the hard-fibered, despotic Smith, who had killed his man with an iron capstan-bar. Conrad's sailor is a younger man, son of an English parson (like Lord Jim), and he kills in a desperate act of self-defense while trying to save his ship. Thus, in helping Leggatt, the young skipper in *The Secret Sharer* is put in the position of favoring Christian humanism over the harsh maritime letter-of-the-law attitude represented by the commander of the *Sephora*.

It is the emphasis that Conrad puts on Leggatt as the protagonist's double which has puzzled many readers and encouraged a number of moralistic or psychological interpretations. The controversy over this element in the story is well illustrated by the difference in opinion between

Albert J. Guerard, perhaps the most influential interpreter of Conrad's fiction and Jocelyn Baines, who has written the best biography of Conrad. Guerard looks upon the story as a symbolist masterpiece, in which Leggatt, "criminally impulsive," represents the lower elements in the narrator's nature and the action iself becomes a psychological "night journey" into the captain's unconscious. Baines, on the other hand, feels that the work has little psychological or moral content. One "symbolist" critic finds the sleeping suits worn by both characters represent "the garb of unconscious life" (in spite of our knowledge that Conrad frequently wore his pajamas on the deck of the becalmed *Otago* because of the heat). Another claims that *The Secret Sharer* reflects not only the archetypal Cain–Abel story but also the Jonah myth, with Leggatt reaching a state of repentance in the sail-locker such as Jonah experienced in the whale's belly. To the present writer, the captain's predicament most resembles the moral dilemma of Captain Vere in Herman Melville's *Billy Budd*.

Conrad was himself much annoyed with a critic who referred to Leggatt as "a murderous ruffian." Moreover, Leggatt, unlike the double in Poe's "William Wilson," is not a typical "doppelgänger," that is, "an apparitional double or counterpart of a living person"; on the contrary, he is a very real person. Perhaps the best clue to the meaning of the story lies in Conrad's statement that it "deals with what might be called the 'esprit de corps,' the deep fellowship of two young seamen meeting for the first time." The young captain's successful protection of Leggatt gives him confidence in *himself*—both in his ability to make difficult moral decisions, and in the brilliant navigational skill that finally assures Leggatt's escape. In assuming responsibility for Leggatt, he has proven himself worthy of command.

In 1889, when Conrad was thirty-one, he resigned his command of the *Otago* in Australia, for reasons that are not entirely clear, and returned to England. A few

months later he went out to Africa to command a river-
boat for the Belgian Company for Commerce on the
Upper Congo. His motives for this venture were mixed;
he was out of a job and had spent his savings, he could
not find another sea command, he had connections who
could help him with the company authorities in Brussels,
and, most of all, he had wanted since boyhood, to journey
to the little explored center of the dark continent. He
spent six months in the Congo, two of them learning the
river as first mate of a small steamer which went up as
far as the end of navigation at Stanley Falls. There, at the
company's inner station, the boat picked up a sick agent
named Klein, who died on the return trip—a trip during
which Conrad took command of the boat for a few days
because of the captain's illness. After returning to Kinshasa and learning that he was not to have charge of the
steamer he had been promised, ill and thoroughly disturbed at the Belgians' crass imperialism, he left for home,
visiting Brussels *en route*, where he saw his aunt and possibly called on Klein's "Intended."

Although he never fully recovered from his sickness
picked up on the Congo, Conrad was still able to say to
a friend, "Before the Congo I was a mere animal."
There is no question but that the experience affected him
deeply. He drew on it for two stories: first "The Outpost of Progress," concerning two misfits among the "pilgrims" or agents, and then, eight years after he came back
to London, *Heart of Darkness*, which deals with the
Congo without ever mentioning it by name. Like *Lord
Jim*, which started to be 20,000 words long and ended
up 140,000, *Heart of Darkness* began as a short story
and ended as a novelette. Before he wrote it, Conrad had
published three novels and a collection of tales. He had
emerged from his apprentice period.

Conrad once stated that *Heart of Darkness* was "experience pushed a little (and very little) beyond the facts
of the case"; perhaps this is the reason for the sense of
immediacy that makes most readers feel with F. R. Leavis

that the "details and circumstances of the voyage to and up the Congo are present to us as if we were making the journey ourselves." By his mastery of tone as well, Conrad gave his "somber theme" a "sinister resonance" and "continued vibration"; as T. S. Eliot put it, "we are continually reminded of the power and terror of Nature, and the isolation and feebleness of Man."

But what more was Conrad doing in the story? The common assumption when it came out was that, unlike Kipling, he was attacking imperialism. Certainly imperialism was at its worst in the Congo despoliation by Leopold II, whose heritage is still with us, and the tale amply illustrates that "merry dance of death and trade." As Conrad wrote elsewhere, the Congo venture was "the vilest scramble for loot that ever disfigured the history of human conscience and geographical exploration." Kurtz's collapse also exemplified a related theme popular with Conrad and other writers of the period—the perils of going native, whether it be on an island in the Indies, a South Seas atoll, or a wild part of Africa.

More recent interpretations of the story stress the role of Marlow, the narrator. Marlow was Conrad, but he was also a character in himself. He had appeared as the protagonist of *Youth* and was to tell most of the story in *Lord Jim* and *Chance.* Probably he is the narrator in *The Secret Sharer,* although he is not identified there. The use of Marlow as narrator allowed the author to comment on his story without using old devices like Thackeray's "dear reader" asides. It also preserved a sense of immediacy and enabled Conrad to manipulate time almost as freely as later practitioners of the stream-of-consciousness technique. Above all, the use of Marlow controlled aesthetic "point of view"—the camera angle, as it were, from which the story is recorded.

Today it is widely accepted that Marlow, not Kurtz, is the principal character, and that *Heart of Darkness* deals with his maturing through an arduous and soul-searching initiation, for it is clear that Conrad was writing about the impact of Africa on himself. This emphasis on Marlow has also led to much discussion of the "frame," that portion of the narrative which takes place on the yacht at the mouth of the Thames. Here Conrad emphasizes the play of light and dark first over London and then out at sea, and he anticipates the situation in Africa with Marlow's comments on the days when Romans were invading primitive Britain. As one critic has pointed out, the yacht swings with the tide between the beginning and end of the story, so that Marlow first faces upstream towards the "mournful gloom" of "the monstrous town" (London) and later, down the Thames waterway leading to "the uttermost ends of the earth . . . into the heart of an immense darkness." Thus the present is linked to the moral universe of the story.

The action of *Heart of Darkness* has also been related to the theories of Freud and Jung, though it is unlikely that Conrad read either psychologist. Most bizarre is the suggestion that Kurtz is like the *id*, the unharnessed primal forces, with the manager representing the timid repression of the *superego* and Marlow the awareness and control of the *ego*. More persuasive is Albert J. Guerard's thesis that, whether he knew it or not, Conrad was writing of "a night journey" or a discovery below the level of consciousness of the evil innate in all men. This concept is based in part on the generally accepted theory that writers tell more than they realize. Corollary to this view are the several suggestions that *Heart of Darkness* reflects archetypal myths, some found in folklore and religion, others in literary works which build on them. Thus, Marlow's journey becomes a descent into Hell, the main question being whether Conrad echoed Virgil, Dante or the Orpheus legend. Biblical analogies have also been applied: the story reflects the myth of the fall; Kurtz is driven out of Eden; Kurtz is a Christian Satan; the story is a disguised retelling of the Passion Week; it is an "epiphany" or discovery story in Joyce's terms. Readers interested in medieval literature have suggested that *Heart of Darkness* parallels the quest for the Holy Grail and that there is an Arthurian echo in the manager's round table at the Central Station. Drawing on anthropology, Harold R. Collins has argued persuasively that a main element in the story is the "detribalization" of the helmsman and Kurtz; both succumb because they have abandoned their tribal views and customs.

Not only the meaning of Marlow's experience, but also his reaction to it is open to a wide variety of interpretations. As Marlow tells his story, is he still suffering from a nervous breakdown, or has he gained serenity by glimpsing the nature of evil? Or does he show that even he is unchanged, strangely unaffected by his journey into the heart of darkness? What about his puzzling interview with Kurtz's "Intended"? Does Marlow lie to her in order to defend Kurtz's memory, because he has always over-idealized women, because he wants to balance evil with good, or because he has become a relativist, willing to go against his own pronounced dislike of lying? Is Marlow an "isolato" in existentialist terms, who lives as he dreams —alone? Has he come to realize that he lives in an irrational universe, or has he simply revolted against conformity? That might explain his ironic view of life.

It seems to me, however, that the emphasis on Marlow has resulted in neglect of Kurtz and in a distorted interpretation of his character. He is surely more than Marlow's evil inner self or his depraved double; he, like Leggatt, is very much a man in his own right. It is well to remember Conrad's own description of his story as a "histoire farouche d'un journaliste qui devient chef de station à l'intérieur et se fait adorer par une tribu de sauvages" [a wild story about a journalist who became a chief of station in the interior and made himself adored by a tribe of savages]. From the time Marlow first hears of him from the Accountant to the occasion when he tells Kurtz's fiancée that he died with her name on his lips, Kurtz remains the focal point of *Heart of Darkness*.

There is some justification for assuming, with most

critics, that Kurtz had become a completely depraved man. Even Conrad called him "hollow at the core." No doubt Kurtz was self-centered, power-mad, and lacked the "restraint" exhibited principally by the cannibals in the story. But, as Marlow points out, "whatever he was he was not common," as the other traders were common. It is significant that Marlow remains loyal "to the nightmare of his choice." Even after he learns of Kurtz's violent acts, Marlow is still drawn to him, risks his life for him, lies for him. He recognizes a kindred spirit.

An "emissary of pity, of science, and progress, and devil knows what else," Kurtz was idealistic even though his ideals proved of little help to him in the jungle. In this quality, as in others, he is contrasted with the opportunistic, tepid-blooded agents whom Marlow (and Conrad) so much disliked. He had initiative and was fearless. He had "the gift of expression"; even to the end he retained his voice. But most commendable (and dangerous) of all, he was imaginative and hence inordinately curious. The other agents, who represent much the worst of nightmares, were "too dull even to know you are being assaulted by the heart of darkness."

Conrad was constantly interested in the effect of imagination in men. As he wrote of Lord Jim, "your imaginative people swing farther in any direction, as if given a longer scope of cable in the uneasy anchorage of life." Certainly, Kurtz swung to extremes: to his idealistic paper on the "Suppression of Savage Customs," he added a postscript in an unsteady hand, "Exterminate all of the brutes." It is these extremes of vision, and the path of Kurtz's career from the most enlightened European traditions to the most primitive human instincts, which give Conrad's vivid story of his African adventure its immense range and lasting resonance as a work of art.

FRANKLIN WALKER

HEART OF
DARKNESS

I

The *Nellie*, a cruising yawl, swung to her anchor without a flutter of the sails, and was at rest. The flood had made, the wind was nearly calm, and being bound down the river, the only thing for it was to come to and wait for the turn of the tide.

The sea-reach of the Thames stretched before us like the beginning of an interminable waterway. In the offing the sea and the sky were welded together without a joint, and in the luminous space the tanned sails of the barges drifting up with the tide seemed to stand still in red clusters of canvas sharply peaked, with gleams of varnished sprits. A haze rested on the low shores that ran out to sea in vanishing flatness. The air was dark above Gravesend, and farther back still seemed condensed into a mournful gloom, brooding motionless over the biggest, and the greatest, town on earth.

The Director of Companies was our captain and our host. We four affectionately watched his back as he stood in the bows looking to seaward. On the whole river there was nothing that looked half so nautical. He resembled a pilot, which to a seaman is trustworthiness personified. It was difficult to realize his work was not out there in the luminous estuary, but behind him, within the brooding gloom.

Between us there was, as I have already said somewhere, the bond of the sea. Besides holding our hearts

together through long periods of separation, it had
the effect of making us tolerant of each other's yarns
—and even convictions. The Lawyer—the best of old
fellows—had, because of his many years and many
virtues, the only cushion on deck, and was lying on the
only rug. The Accountant had brought out already a
box of dominoes, and was toying architecturally with
the bones. Marlow sat cross-legged right aft, leaning
against the mizzenmast. He had sunken cheeks, a
yellow complexion, a straight back, an ascetic aspect,
and, with his arms dropped, the palms of hands outwards, resembled an idol. The Director, satisfied the
anchor had good hold, made his way aft and sat down
amongst us. We exchanged a few words lazily. Afterwards there was silence on board the yacht. For some
reason or other we did not begin that game of dominoes. We felt meditative, and fit for nothing but
placid staring. The day was ending in a serenity of
still and exquisite brilliance. The water shone pacifi-
cally; the sky, without a speck, was a benign immensity of unstained light; the very mist on the Essex
marsh was like a gauzy and radiant fabric, hung from
the wooded rises inland, and draping the low shores
in diaphanous folds. Only the gloom to the west,
brooding over the upper reaches, became more sombre
every minute, as if angered by the approach of the sun.

And at last, in its curved and imperceptible fall, the
sun sank low, and from glowing white changed to a
dull red without rays and without heat, as if about to
go out suddenly, stricken to death by the touch of
that gloom brooding over a crowd of men.

Forthwith a change came over the waters, and the

serenity became less brilliant but more profound. The old river in its broad reach rested unruffled at the decline of day, after ages of good service done to the race that peopled its banks, spread out in the tranquil dignity of a waterway leading to the uttermost ends of the earth. We looked at the venerable stream not in the vivid flush of a short day that comes and departs for ever, but in the august light of abiding memories. And indeed nothing is easier for a man who has, as the phrase goes, "followed the sea" with reverence and affection, than to evoke the great spirit of the past upon the lower reaches of the Thames. The tidal current runs to and fro in its unceasing service, crowded with memories of men and ships it had borne to the rest of home or to the battles of the sea. It had known and served all the men of whom the nation is proud, from Sir Francis Drake to Sir John Franklin, knights all, titled and untitled—the great knights-errant of the sea. It had borne all the ships whose names are like jewels flashing in the night of time, from the *Golden Hind* returning with her round flanks full of treasure, to be visited by the Queen's Highness and thus pass out of the gigantic tale, to the *Erebus* and *Terror*, bound on other conquests—and that never returned. It had known the ships and the men. They had sailed from Deptford, from Greenwich, from Erith—the adventurers and the settlers; kings' ships and the ships of men on 'Change; captains, admirals, the dark "interlopers" of the Eastern trade, and the commissioned "generals" of East India fleets. Hunters for gold or pursuers of fame, they all had gone out on that stream, bearing the sword, and often the torch, messengers of the might within the land, bearers of a spark from the sacred fire. What greatness had not floated on the ebb of that river into the mystery of an unknown earth! . . . The dreams of men, the seed of commonwealths, the germs of empires.

The sun set; the dusk fell on the stream, and lights began to appear along the shore. The Chapman light-house, a three-legged thing erect on a mud-flat, shone strongly. Lights of ships moved in the fairway—a great stir of lights going up and going down. And farther west on the upper reaches the place of the monstrous town was still marked ominously on the sky, a brooding gloom in sunshine, a lurid glare under the stars.

"And this also," said Marlow suddenly, "has been one of the dark places of the earth."

He was the only man of us who still "followed the sea." The worst that could be said of him was that he did not represent his class. He was a seaman, but he was a wanderer, too, while most seamen lead, if one may so express it, a sedentary life. Their minds are of the stay-at-home order, and their home is always with them—the ship; and so is their country—the sea. One ship is very much like another, and the sea is always the same. In the immutability of their sur-roundings the foreign shores, the foreign faces, the changing immensity of life, glide past, veiled not by a sense of mystery but by a slightly disdainful igno-rance; for there is nothing mysterious to a seaman unless it be the sea itself, which is the mistress of his existence and as inscrutable as Destiny. For the rest, after his hours of work, a casual stroll or a casual spree on shore suffices to unfold for him the secret of a whole continent, and generally he finds the secret not worth knowing. The yarns of seamen have a direct simplicity, the whole meaning of which lies within the shell of a cracked nut. But Marlow was not typical (if his propensity to spin yarns be excepted), and to him the meaning of an episode was not inside like a kernel but outside, enveloping the tale which brought it out only as a glow brings out a haze, in the likeness of one of these misty halos that sometimes are made visible by the spectral illuminination of moonshine.

His remark did not seem at all surprising. It was just like Marlow. It was accepted in silence. No one took the trouble to grunt even; and presently he said, very slow—

"I was thinking of very old times, when the Romans first came here, nineteen hundred years ago— the other day. . . . Light came out of this river since—you say Knights? Yes; but it is like a running blaze on a plain, like a flash of lightning in the clouds. We live in the flicker—may it last as long as the old earth keeps rolling! But darkness was here yesterday. Imagine the feelings of a commander of a fine—what d'ye call 'em?—trireme in the Mediterranean, ordered suddenly to the north run overland across the Gauls in a hurry; put in charge of one of these craft the legionaries—a wonderful lot of handy men they must have been, too—used to build, apparently by the hundred, in a month or two, if we may believe what we read. Imagine him here—the very end of the world, a sea the colour of lead, a sky the colour of smoke, a kind of ship about as rigid as a concertina—

and going up this river with stores, or orders, or what you like. Sand-banks, marshes, forests, savages,— precious little to eat fit for a civilized man, nothing but Thames water to drink. No Falernian wine here, no going ashore. Here and there a military camp lost in a wilderness, like a needle in a bundle of hay—cold, fog, tempests, disease, exile, and death—death skulking in the air, in the water, in the bush. They must have been dying like flies here. Oh, yes—he did it. Did it very well, too, no doubt, and without thinking much about it either, except afterwards to brag of what he had gone through in his time, perhaps. They were men enough to face the darkness. And perhaps he was cheered by keeping his eye on a chance of promotion to the fleet at Ravenna by and by, if he had good friends in Rome and survived the awful climate. Or think of a decent young citizen in a toga—perhaps too much dice, you know—coming out here in the train of some prefect, or tax-gatherer, or trader even, to mend his fortunes. Land in a swamp, march through the woods, and in some inland post feel the savagery, the utter savagery, had closed round him— all that mysterious life of the wilderness that stirs in the forest, in the jungles, in the hearts of wild men. There's no initiation either into such mysteries. He has to live in the midst of the incomprehensible, which is also detestable. And it has a fascination, too, that goes to work upon him. The fascination of the abomination—you know, imagine the growing regrets, the longing to escape, the powerless disgust, the surrender, the hate."

He paused.

"Mind," he began again, lifting one arm from the elbow, the palm of the hand outwards, so that, with his legs folded before him, he had the pose of a Buddha preaching in European clothes and without a lotus-flower—"Mind, none of us would feel exactly like this. What saves us is efficiency—the devotion to efficiency. But these chaps were not much account, really. They were no colonists; their administration was merely a squeeze, and nothing more, I suspect. They were conquerors, and for that you want only brute force—nothing to boast of, when you have it, since your strength is just an accident arising from the weakness of others. They grabbed what they could get for the sake of what was to be got. It was just robbery with violence, aggravated murder on a great scale, and men going at it blind—as is very proper for those who tackle a darkness. The conquest of the earth, which mostly means the taking it away from those who have a different complexion or slightly flatter noses than ourselves, is not a pretty thing when you look into it too much. What redeems it is the idea only. An idea at the back of it; not a sentimental pretence but an idea; and an unselfish belief in the idea—something you can set up, and bow down before, and offer a sacrifice to. . . ."

He broke off. Flames glided in the river, small green flames, red flames, white flames, pursuing, overtaking, joining, crossing each other—then separating slowly or hastily. The traffic of the great city went on in the deepening night upon the sleepless river. We looked on, waiting patiently—there was nothing else to do till the end of the flood; but it was only after a

long silence, when he said, in a hesitating voice, "I
suppose you fellows remember I did once turn fresh-
water sailor for a bit," that we knew we were fated,
before the ebb began to run, to hear about one of
Marlow's inconclusive experiences.

"I don't want to bother you much with what happened to me personally," he began, showing in this
remark the weakness of many tellers of tales who
seem so often unaware of what their audience would
best like to hear; "yet to understand the effect of it on
me you ought to know how I got out there, what I
saw, how I went up that river to the place where I
first met the poor chap. It was the farthest point of
navigation and the culminating point of my experience. It seemed somehow to throw a kind of light on
everything about me—and into my thoughts. It was
sombre enough, too—and pitiful—not extraordinary
in any way—not very clear either. No, not very clear.
And yet it seemed to throw a kind of light.

"I had then, as you remember, just returned to
London after a lot of Indian Ocean, Pacific, China
Seas—a regular dose of the East—six years or so, and
I was loafing about, hindering you fellows in your
work and invading your homes, just as though I had
got a heavenly mission to civilize you. It was very fine
for a time, but after a bit I did get tired of resting.
Then I began to look for a ship—I should think the
hardest work on earth. But the ships wouldn't even
look at me. And I got tired of that game, too.

"Now when I was a little chap I had a passion for
maps. I would look for hours at South America, or
Africa, or Australia, and lose myself in all the glories

of exploration. At that time there were many blank
spaces on the earth, and when I saw one that looked
particularly inviting on a map (but they all look that)
I would put my finger on it and say, 'When I grow
up I will go there.' The North Pole was one of these
places, I remember. Well, I haven't been there yet,
and shall not try now. The glamour's off. Other places
were scattered about the Equator, and in every sort of
latitude all over the two hemispheres. I have been in
some of them, and . . . well, we won't talk about
that. But there was one yet—the biggest, the most
blank, so to speak—that I had a hankering after.

"True, by this time it was not a blank space any
more. It had got filled since my boyhood with rivers
and lakes and names. It had ceased to be a blank space
of delightful mystery—a white patch for a boy to
dream gloriously over. It had become a place of darkness. But there was in it one river especially, a mighty
big river, that you could see on the map, resembling
an immense snake uncoiled, with its head in the sea, its
body at rest curving afar over a vast country, and its
tail lost in the depths of the land. And as I looked at
the map of it in a shop-window, it fascinated me as a
snake would a bird—a silly little bird. Then I remembered there was a big concern, a Company for trade
on that river. Dash it all! I thought to myself, they
can't trade without using some kind of craft on that lot
of fresh water—steamboats! Why shouldn't I try to
get charge of one? I went on along Fleet Street, but
could not shake off the idea. The snake had charmed
me.

"You understand it was a Continental concern, that

Trading society; but I have a lot of relations living on the Continent, because it's cheap and not so nasty as it looks, they say.

"I am sorry to own I began to worry them. This was already a fresh departure for me. I was not used to get things that way, you know. I always went my own road and on my own legs where I had a mind to go. I wouldn't have believed it of myself; but, then—you see—I felt somehow I must get there by hook or by crook. So I worried them. The men said 'My dear fellow,' and did nothing. Then—would you believe it?—I tried the women. I, Charlie Marlow, set the women to work—to get a job. Heavens! Well, you see, the notion drove me. I had an aunt, a dear enthusiastic soul. She wrote: 'It will be delightful. I am ready to do anything, anything for you. It is a glorious idea. I know the wife of a very high personage in the Administration, and also a man who has lots of influence with,' etc., etc. She was determined to make no end of fuss to get me appointed skipper of a river steamboat, if such was my fancy.

"I got my appointment—of course; and I got it very quick. It appears the Company had received news that one of their captains had been killed in a scuffle with the natives. This was my chance, and it made me the more anxious to go. It was only months and months afterwards, when I made the attempt to recover what was left of the body, that I heard the original quarrel arose from a misunderstanding about some hens. Yes, two black hens. Fresleven—that was the fellow's name, a Dane—thought himself wronged somehow in the bargain, so he went ashore and started to hammer the chief of the village with a stick. Oh, it didn't surprise me in the least to hear this, and at the same time to be told that Fresleven was the gentlest, quietest creature that ever walked on two legs. No doubt he was; but he had been a couple of years already out there engaged in the noble cause, you know, and he probably felt the need at last of asserting his self-respect in some way. Therefore he whacked the old nigger mercilessly, while a big crowd of his people watched him, thunderstruck, till some man—I was told the chief's son—in desperation at hearing the old chap yell, made a tentative jab with a spear at the white man—and of course it went quite easy between the shoulder-blades. Then the whole population cleared into the forest, expecting all kinds of calamities to happen, while, on the other hand, the steamer Fresleven commanded left also in a bad panic, in charge of the engineer, I believe. Afterwards nobody seemed to trouble much about Fresleven's remains, till I got out and stepped into his shoes. I couldn't let it rest, though; but when an opportunity offered at last to meet my predecessor, the grass growing through his ribs was tall enough to hide his bones. They were all there. The supernatural being had not been touched after he fell. And the village was deserted, the huts gaped black, rotting, all askew within the fallen enclosures. A calamity had come to it, sure enough. The people had vanished. Mad terror had scattered them, men, women, and children, through the bush, and they had never returned. What became of the hens I don't know either. I should think the cause of progress got them, anyhow. However, through this glorious affair I got my appointment, before I had fairly begun to hope for it.

"I flew around like mad to get ready, and before forty-eight hours I was crossing the Channel to show myself to my employers, and sign the contract. In a very few hours I arrived in a city that always makes me think of a whited sepulchre. Prejudice no doubt. I had no difficulty in finding the Company's offices. It was the biggest thing in the town, and everybody I met was full of it. They were going to run an over-sea empire, and make no end of coin by trade.

"A narrow and deserted street in deep shadow, high houses, innumerable windows with venetian blinds, a dead silence, grass sprouting between the stones, imposing carriage archways right and left, immense double doors standing ponderously ajar. I slipped through one of these cracks, went up a swept and ungarnished staircase, as arid as a desert, and opened the first door I came to. Two women, one fat and the other slim, sat on straw-bottomed chairs, knitting black wool. The slim one got up and walked straight at me —still knitting with downcast eyes—and only just as I began to think of getting out of her way, as you would for a somnambulist, stood still, and looked up. Her dress was as plain as an umbrella-cover, and she turned round without a word and preceded me into a waiting-room. I gave my name, and looked about. Deal table in the middle, plain chairs all round the walls, on one end a large shining map, marked with all the colours of a rainbow. There was a vast amount of red—good to see at any time, because one knows that some real work is done in there, a deuce of a lot of blue, a little green, smears of orange, and, on the East Coast, a purple patch, to show where the jolly pioneers of progress drink the jolly lager-beer. However, I wasn't going into any of these. I was going into the yellow. Dead in the centre. And the river was there—fascinating—deadly—like a snake. Ough! A door opened, a white-haired secretarial head, but wearing a compassionate expression, appeared, and a skinny forefinger beckoned me into the sanctuary. Its light was dim, and a heavy writing-desk squatted in the middle. From behind that structure came out an impression of pale plumpness in a frock-coat. The great man himself. He was five feet six, I should judge, and had his grip on the handle-end of ever so many millions. He shook hands, I fancy, murmured vaguely, was satisfied with my French. *Bon voyage.*

"In about forty-five seconds I found myself again in the waiting-room with the compassionate secretary, who, full of desolation and sympathy, made me sign some document. I believe I undertook amongst other things not to disclose any trade secrets. Well, I am not going to.

"I began to feel slightly uneasy. You know I am not used to such ceremonies, and there was something ominous in the atmosphere. It was just as though I had been let into some conspiracy—I don't know—something not quite right; and I was glad to get out. In the outer room the two women knitted black wool feverishly. People were arriving, and the younger one was walking back and forth introducing them. The old one sat on her chair. Her flat cloth slippers were propped up on a foot-warmer, and a cat reposed on her lap. She wore a starched white affair on her head, had a wart on one cheek, and silver-rimmed spectacles hung on the tip of her nose. She glanced at me above the glasses. The swift and indifferent placidity of that look troubled me. Two youths with foolish and cheery countenances were being piloted over, and she threw at them the same quick glance of unconcerned wisdom. She seemed to know all about them and about me, too. An eerie feeling came over me. She seemed uncanny and fateful. Often far away there I thought of these two, guarding the door of Darkness, knitting black wool as for a warm pall, one introducing, introducing continuously to the unknown, the other scrutinizing the cheery and foolish faces with unconcerned old eyes. *Ave!* Old knittter of black wool. *Morituri te salutant*. Not many of those she looked at ever saw her again—not half, by a long way.

"There was yet a visit to the doctor. 'A simple formality,' assured me the secretary, with an air of taking an immense part in all my sorrows. Accordingly a young chap wearing his hat over the left eyebrow, some clerk I suppose—there must have been clerks in the business, though the house was as still as a house in a city of the dead—came from somewhere up-stairs, and led me forth. He was shabby and careless, with inkstains on the sleeves of his jacket, and his cravat was large and billowy, under a chin shaped like the toe of an old boot. It was a little too early for the doctor, so I proposed a drink, and thereupon he developed a vein of joviality. As we sat over our vermouths he glorified the Company's business, and by and by I expressed casually my surprise at him not going out there. He became very cool and collected all at once. 'I am not such a fool as I look, quoth Plato to his disciples,' he said sententiously, emptied his glass with great resolution, and we rose.

"The old doctor felt my pulse, evidently thinking of something else the while. 'Good, good for there,' he mumbled, and then with a certain eagerness asked me whether I would let him measure my head. Rather surprised, I said Yes, when he produced a thing like calipers and got the dimensions back and front and every way, taking notes carefully. He was an un-shaven little man in a threadbare coat like a gaberdine, with his feet in slippers, and I thought him a harmless fool. 'I always ask leave, in the interests of science, to measure the crania of those going out there,' he said. 'And when they come back, too?' I asked. 'Oh, I never see them,' he remarked; 'and, moreover, the changes take place inside, you know.' He smiled, as if at some quiet joke. 'So you are going out there. Famous. Interesting, too.' He gave me a searching glance, and made another note. 'Ever any madness in your fam-ily?' he asked, in a matter-of-fact tone. I felt very annoyed. 'Is that question in the interests of science, too?' 'It would be,' he said, without taking notice of my irritation, 'interesting for science to watch the mental changes of individuals, on the spot, but . . .' 'Are you an alienist?' I interrupted. 'Every doctor should be—a little,' answered that original, imperturb-ably. 'I have a little theory which you messieurs who go out there must help me to prove. This is my share in the advantages my country shall reap from the possession of such a magnificent dependency. The

mere wealth I leave to others. Pardon my questions,
but you are the first Englishman coming under my
observation . . .' I hastened to assure him I was not
in the least typical. 'If I were,' said I, 'I wouldn't be
talking like this with you.' 'What you say is rather
profound, and probably erroneous,' he said, with a
laugh. 'Avoid irritation more than exposure to the
sun. Adieu. How do you English say, eh? Good-bye.
Ah! Good-bye. Adieu. In the tropics one must before
everything keep calm.' . . . He lifted a warning
forefinger. . . 'Du calme, du calme, Adieu.'

"One thing more remained to do—say good-bye to
my excellent aunt. I found her triumphant. I had a
cup of tea—the last decent cup of tea for many days—
and in a room that most soothingly looked just as you
would expect a lady's drawing-room to look, we had a
long quiet chat by the fireside. In the course of these
confidences it became quite plain to me I had been
represented to the wife of the high dignitary, and
goodness knows to how many more people besides, as
an exceptional and gifted creature—a piece of good
fortune for the Company—a man you don't get hold
of every day. Good heavens! and I was going to take
charge of a two-penny-half-penny river-steamboat with
a penny whistle attached! It appeared, however, I
was also one of the Workers, with a capital—you
know. Something like an emissary of light, something
like a lower sort of apostle. There had been a lot of
such rot let loose in print and talk just about that time,
and the excellent woman, living right in the rush of
all that humbug, got carried off her feet. She talked
about 'weaning those ignorant millions from their

horrid ways,' till, upon my word, she made me quite uncomfortable. I ventured to hint that the Company was run for profit.

" 'You forget, dear Charlie, that the labourer is worthy of his hire,' she said, brightly. It's queer how out of touch with truth women are. They live in a world of their own, and there has never been anything like it, and never can be. It is too beautiful altogether, and if they were to set it up it would go to pieces before the first sunset. Some confounded fact we men have been living contentedly with ever since the day of creation would start up and knock the whole thing over.

"After this I got embraced, told to wear flannel, be sure to write often, and so on—and I left. In the street—I don't know why—a queer feeling came to me that I was an impostor. Odd thing that I, who used to clear out for any part of the world at twenty-four hours' notice, with less thought than most men give to the crossing of a street, had a moment—I won't say of hesitation, but of startled pause, before this commonplace affair. The best way I can explain it to you is by saying that, for a second or two, I felt as though, instead of going to the centre of a continent, I were about to set off for the centre of the earth.

"I left in a French steamer, and she called in every blamed port they have out there, for, as far as I could see, the sole purpose of landing soldiers and custom-house officers. I watched the coast. Watching a coast as it slips by the ship is like thinking about an enigma. There it is before you—smiling, frowning, inviting, grand, mean, insipid, or savage, and always

mute with an air of whispering, 'Come and find out.'
This one was almost featureless, as if still in the making, with an aspect of monotonous grimness. The edge
of a colossal jungle, so dark-green as to be almost
black, fringed with white surf, ran straight, like a
ruled line, far, far away along a blue sea whose glitter
was blurred by a creeping mist. The sun was fierce,
the land seemed to glisten and drip with steam. Here
and there greyish-whitish specks showed up clustered
inside the white surf, with a flag flying above them
perhaps. Settlements some centuries old, and still no
bigger than pinheads on the untouched expanse of
their background. We pounded along, stopped, landed
soldiers; went on, landed custom-house clerks to
levy toll in what looked like a God-forsaken wilderness, with a tin shed and a flag-pole lost in it; landed
more soldiers—to take care of the custom-house clerks,
presumably. Some, I heard, got drowned in the surf;
but whether they did or not, nobody seemed particularly to care. They were just flung out there, and on
we went. Every day the coast looked the same, as
though we had not moved; but we passed various
places—trading places—with names like Gran' Bas-
sam, Little Popo; names that seemed to belong to
some sordid farce acted in front of a sinister back-cloth.
The idleness of a passenger, my isolation amongst all
these men with whom I had no point of contact, the
oily and languid sea, the uniform sombreness of the
coast, seemed to keep me away from the truth of things,
within the toil of a mournful and senseless delusion.
The voice of the surf heard now and then was a positive pleasure, like the speech of a brother. It was some-

thing natural, that had its reason, that had a meaning. Now and then a boat from the shore gave one a momentary contact with reality. It was paddled by black fellows. You could see from afar the white of their eyeballs glistening. They shouted, sang; their bodies streamed with perspiration; they had faces like grotesque masks—these chaps; but they had bone, muscle, a wild vitality, an intense energy of movement, that was as natural and true as the surf along their coast. They wanted no excuse for being there. They were a great comfort to look at. For a time I would feel I belonged still to a world of straightforward facts; but the feeling would not last long. Something would turn up to scare it away. Once, I remember, we came upon a man-of-war anchored off the coast. There wasn't even a shed there, and she was shelling the bush. It appears the French had one of their wars going on thereabouts. Her ensign dropped limp like a rag; the muzzles of the long six-inch guns stuck out all over the low hull; the greasy, slimy swell swung her up lazily and let her down, swaying her thin masts. In the empty immensity of earth, sky, and water, there she was, incomprehensible, firing into a continent. Pop, would go one of the six-inch guns; a small flame would dart and vanish, a little white smoke would disappear, a tiny projectile would give a feeble screech—and nothing happened. Nothing could happen. There was a touch of insanity in the proceeding, a sense of lugubrious drollery in the sight; and it was not dissipated by somebody on board assuring me earnestly there was a camp of natives—he called them enemies!—hidden out of sight somewhere.

"We gave her her letters (I heard the men in that lonely ship were dying of fever at the rate of three a day) and went on. We called at some more places with farcical names, where the merry dance of death and trade goes on in a still and earthy atmosphere as of an overheated catacomb; all along the formless coast bordered by dangerous surf, as if Nature herself had tried to ward off intruders; in and out of rivers, streams of death in life, whose banks were rotting into mud, whose waters, thickened into slime, invaded the contorted mangroves, that seemed to writhe at us in the extremity of an impotent despair. Nowhere did we stop long enough to get a particularized impression, but the general sense of vague and oppressive wonder grew upon me. It was like a weary pilgrimage amongst hints for nightmares.

"It was upward of thirty days before I saw the mouth of the big river. We anchored off the seat of the government. But my work would not begin till some two hundred miles farther on. So as soon as I could I made a start for a place thirty miles higher up.

"I had my passage on a little sea-going steamer. Her captain was a Swede, and knowing me for a seaman, invited me on the bridge. He was a young man, lean, fair, and morose, with lanky hair and a shuffling gait. As we left the miserable little wharf, he tossed his head contemptuously at the shore. 'Been living there?' he asked. I said, 'Yes.' 'Fine lot these government chaps—are they not?' he went on, speaking English with great precision and considerable bitterness. 'It is funny what some people will do for a few francs a month. I wonder what becomes of that

kind when it goes upcountry?' I said to him I expected
to see that soon. 'So-o-o!' he exclaimed. He shuffled
athwart, keeping one eye ahead vigilantly. 'Don't be
too sure,' he continued. 'The other day I took up a
man who hanged himself on the road. He was a
Swede, too.' 'Hanged himself! Why, in God's name?'
I cried. He kept on looking out watchfully. 'Who
knows? The sun too much for him, or the country
perhaps.'

"At last we opened a reach. A rocky cliff appeared,
mounds of turned-up earth by the shore, houses on a
hill, others with iron roofs, amongst a waste of exca-
vations, or hanging to the declivity. A continuous noise
of the rapids above hovered over this scene of inhabited devastation. A lot of people, mostly black
and naked, moved about like ants. A jetty projected
into the river. A blinding sunlight drowned all this
at times in a sudden recrudescence of glare. 'There's
your Company's station,' said the Swede, pointing to
three wooden barrack-like structures on the rocky
slope. 'I will send your things up. Four boxes did you
say? So. Farewell.'

"I came upon a boiler wallowing in the grass, then
found a path leading up the hill. It turned aside for
the boulders, and also for an undersized railway-truck
lying there on its back with its wheels in the air. One
was off. The thing looked as dead as the carcass of
some animal. I came upon more pieces of decaying
machinery, a stack of rusty rails. To the left a clump
of trees made a shady spot, where dark things seemed
to stir feebly. I blinked, the path was steep. A horn
tooted to the right, and I saw the black people run. A

heavy and dull detonation shook the ground, a puff of smoke came out of the cliff, and that was all. No change appeared on the face of the rock. They were building a railway. The cliff was not in the way or anything; but this objectless blasting was all the work going on.

"A slight clinking behind me made me turn my head. Six black men advanced in a file, toiling up the path. They walked erect and slow, balancing small baskets full of earth on their heads, and the clink kept time with their footsteps. Black rags were wound round their loins, and the short ends behind waggled to and fro like tails. I could see every rib, the joints of their limbs were like knots in a rope; each had an iron collar on his neck, and all were connected together with a chain whose bights swung between them, rhythmically clinking. Another report from the cliff made me think suddenly of that ship of war I had seen firing into a continent. It was the same kind of ominous voice; but these men could by no stretch of imagination be called enemies. They were called criminals, and the outraged law, like the bursting shells, had come to them, an insoluble mystery from the sea. All their meagre breasts panted together, the violently dilated nostrils quivered, the eyes stared stonily uphill. They passed me within six inches, without a glance, with that complete, deathlike indifference of unhappy savages. Behind this raw matter one of the reclaimed, the product of the new forces at work, strolled despondently, carrying a rifle by its middle. He had a uniform jacket with one button off, and seeing a white man on the path, hoisted his weapon to his shoulder with alacrity. This was simple prudence, white men being so much alike at a distance that he could not tell who I might be. He was speedily reassured, and with a large, white, rascally grin, and a glance at his charge, seemed to take me into partnership in his exalted trust. After all, I also was a part of the great cause of these high and just proceedings.

"Instead of going up, I turned and descended to the left. My idea was to let that chain-gang get out of sight before I climbed the hill. You know I am not particularly tender; I've had to strike and to fend off. I've had to resist and to attack sometimes—that's only one way of resisting—without counting the exact cost, according to the demands of such sort of life as I had blundered into. I've seen the devil of violence, and the devil of greed, and the devil of hot desire; but, by all the stars! these were strong, lusty, red-eyed devils, that swayed and drove men—men, I tell you. But as I stood on this hillside, I foresaw that in the blinding sunshine of that land I would become acquainted with a flabby, pretending, weak-eyed devil of a rapacious and pitiless folly. How insidious he could be, too, I was only to find out several months later and a thousand miles farther. For a moment I stood appalled, as though by a warning. Finally I descended the hill, obliquely, towards the trees I had seen.

"I avoided a vast artificial hole somebody had been digging on the slope, the purpose of which I found it impossible to divine. It wasn't a quarry or a sandpit, anyhow. It was just a hole. It might have been connected with the philanthropic desire of giving the criminals something to do. I don't know. Then I nearly fell into a very narrow ravine, almost no more than a scar in the hillside. I discovered that a lot of imported drainage-pipes for the settlement had been tumbled in there. There wasn't one that was not broken. It was a wanton smash-up. At last I got under the trees. My purpose was to stroll into the shade for a moment; but no sooner within than it seemed to me I had stepped into the gloomy circle of some Inferno. The rapids were near, and an uninterrupted, uniform, headlong, rushing noise filled the mournful stillness of the grove, where not a breath stirred, not a leaf moved, with a mysterious sound—as though the tearing pace of the launched earth had suddenly become audible.

"Black shapes crouched, lay, sat between the trees leaning against the trunks, clinging to the earth, half coming out, half effaced within the dim light, in all the attitudes of pain, abandonment, and despair. Another mine on the cliff went off, followed by a slight shudder of the soil under my feet. The work was going on. The work! And this was the place where some of the helpers had withdrawn to die.

"They were dying slowly—it was very clear. They were not enemies, they were not criminals, they were nothing earthly now—nothing but black shadows of disease and starvation, lying confusedly in the greenish gloom. Brought from all the recesses of the coast in all the legality of time contracts, lost in uncongenial surroundings, fed on unfamiliar food, they sickened, became inefficient, and were then allowed to crawl away and rest. These moribund shapes were

free as air—and nearly as thin. I began to distinguish
the gleam of the eyes under the trees. Then, glancing
down, I saw a face near my hand. The black bones
reclined at full length with one shoulder against the
tree, and slowly the eyelids rose and the sunken eyes
looked up at me, enormous and vacant, a kind of
blind, white flicker in the depths of the orbs, which
died out slowly. The man seemed young—almost a
boy—but you know with them it's hard to tell. I
found nothing else to do but to offer him one of my
good Swede's ship's biscuits I had in my pocket. The
fingers closed slowly on it and held—there was no
other movement and no other glance. He had tied a
bit of white worsted round his neck—Why? Where
did he get it? Was it a badge—an ornament—a charm
—a propitiatory act? Was there any idea at all connected with it? It looked startling round his black
neck, this bit of white thread from beyond the seas.

"Near the same tree two more bundles of acute
angles sat with their legs drawn up. One, with his
chin propped on his knees, stared at nothing, in an
intolerable and appalling manner: his brother phantom rested its forehead, as if overcome with a great
weariness; and all about others were scattered in
every pose of contorted collapse, as in some picture of
a massacre or a pestilence. While I stood horror-
struck, one of these creatures rose to his hands and
knees, and went off on all-fours towards the river to
drink. He lapped out of his hand, then sat up in the
sunlight, crossing his shins in front of him, and after
a time let his woolly head fall on his breastbone.

"I didn't want any more loitering in the shade, and

I made haste towards the station. When near the
buildings I met a white man, in such an unexpected
elegance of getup that in the first moment I took him
for a sort of vision. I saw a high starched collar,
white cuffs, a light alpaca jacket, snowy trousers, a
clean necktie, and varnished boots. No hat. Hair
parted, brushed, oiled, under a green-lined parasol
held in a big white hand. He was amazing, and had a
penholder behind his ear.

"I shook hands with this miracle, and I learned he
was the Company's chief accountant, and that all the
bookkeeping was done at this station. He had come
out for a moment, he said, 'to get a breath of fresh
air.' The expression sounded wonderfully odd, with
its suggestion of sedentary desk-life. I wouldn't have
mentioned the fellow to you at all, only it was from
his lips that I first heard the name of the man who is
so indissolubly connected with the memories of that
time. Moreover, I respected the fellow. Yes; I respected his collars, his vast cuffs, his brushed hair. His
appearance was certainly that of a hairdresser's
dummy; but in the great demoralization of the land
he kept up his appearance. That's backbone. His
starched collars and got-up shirt-fronts were achieve-
ments of character. He had been out nearly three
years; and later, I could not help asking him how he
managed to sport such linen. He had just the faintest
blush, and said modestly, 'I've been teaching one of
the native women about the station. It was difficult.
She had a distaste for the work.' Thus this man had
verily accomplished something. And he was devoted
to his books, which were in apple-pie order.

"Everything else in the station was in a muddle—heads, things, buildings. Strings of dusty niggers with splay feet arrived and departed; a stream of manufactured goods, rubbishy cottons, beads, and brass-wire set into the depths of darkness, and in return came a precious trickle of ivory.

"I had to wait in the station for ten days—an eternity. I lived in a hut in the yard, but to be out of the chaos I would sometimes get into the accountant's office. It was built of horizontal planks, and so badly put together that, as he bent over his high desk, he was barred from neck to heels with narrow strips of sunlight. There was no need to open the big shutter to see. It was hot there, too; big flies buzzed fiendishly, and did not sting, but stabbed. I sat generally on the floor, while, of faultless appearance (and even slightly scented), perching on a high stool, he wrote, he wrote. Sometimes he stood up for exercise. When a truckle-bed with a sick man (some invalid agent from up-country) was put in there, he exhibited a gentle annoyance. 'The groans of this sick person,' he said, 'distract my attention. And without that it is extremely difficult to guard against clerical errors in this climate.'

"One day he remarked, without lifting his head, 'In the interior you will no doubt meet Mr. Kurtz.' On my asking who Mr. Kurtz was, he said he was a first-class agent; and seeing my disappointment at this information, he added slowly, laying down his pen, 'He is a very remarkable person.' Further questions elicited from him that Mr. Kurtz was at present in charge of a trading-post, a very important one, in

the true ivory-country, at 'the very bottom of there.
Sends in as much ivory as all the others put together
. . .' He began to write again. The sick man was too
ill to groan. The flies buzzed in a great peace.

"Suddenly there was a growing murmur of voices
and a great tramping of feet. A caravan had come in.
A violent babble of uncouth sounds burst out on the
other side of the planks All the carriers were speaking
together, and in the midst of the uproar the lamentable voice of the chief agent was heard 'giving it up'
tearfully for the twentieth time that day. . . . He
rose slowly. 'What a frightful row,' he said. He
crossed the room gently to look at the sick man, and
returning, said to me, 'He does not hear.' 'What!
Dead?' I asked, startled. 'No, not yet,' he answered,
with great composure. Then, alluding with a toss of
the head to the tumult in the station-yard, 'When one
has got to make correct entries, one comes to hate
those savages—hate them to the death.' He remained
thoughtful for a moment. 'When you see Mr. Kurtz'
he went on, 'tell him from me that everything here'—
he glanced at the deck—'is very satisfactory. I don't
like to write to him—with those messengers of ours
you never know who may get hold of your letter—at
that Central Station.' He stared at me for a moment
with his mild, bulging eyes. 'Oho, he will go far, very
far,' he began again. 'He will be a somebody in the
Administration before long. They, above—the Council in Europe, you know—mean him to be.'

"He turned to his work. The noise outside had
ceased, and presently in going out I stopped at the
door. In the steady buzz of flies the homeward-bound

agent was lying flushed and insensible; the other, bent over his books, was making correct entries of perfectly correct transactions; and fifty feet below the doorstep I could see the still treetops of the grove of death.

"Next day I left that station at last, with a caravan of sixty men, for a two-hundred-mile tramp.

"No use telling you much about that. Paths, paths, everywhere; a stamped-in network of paths spreading over the empty land, through the long grass, through burnt grass, through thickets, down and up chilly ravines, up and down stony hills ablaze with heat; and a solitude, a solitude, nobody, not a hut. The population had cleared out a long time ago. Well, if a lot of mysterious niggers armed with all kinds of fearful weapons suddenly took to travelling on the road between Deal and Gravesend, catching the yokels right and left to carry heavy loads for them, I fancy every farm and cottage thereabouts would get empty very soon. Only here the dwellings were gone, too. Still I passed through several abandoned villages. There's something pathetically childish in the ruins of grass walls. Day after day, with the stamp and shuffle of sixty pair of bare feet behind me, each pair under a 60-lb. load. Camp, cook, sleep, strike camp, march. Now and then a carrier dead in harness, at rest in the long grass near the path, with an empty water-gourd and his long staff lying by his side. A great silence around and above. Perhaps on some quiet night the tremor of far-off drums, sinking, swelling, a tremor vast, faint; a sound weird, appealing, suggestive, and wild—and perhaps with as profound

a meaning as the sound of bells in a Christian country.
Once a white man in an unbuttoned uniform, camping
on the path with an armed escort of lank Zanzibaris,
very hospitable and festive—not to say drunk. Was
looking after the upkeep of the road, he declared.
Can't say I saw any road or any upkeep, unless the
body of a middle-aged negro, with a bullet-hole in the
forehead, upon which I absolutely stumbled three
miles farther on, may be considered as a permanent
improvement. I had a white companion, too, not a bad
chap, but rather too fleshy and with the exasperating
habit of fainting on the hot hillsides, miles away from
the least bit of shade and water. Annoying, you know,
to hold your own coat like a parasol over a man's
head while he is coming to. I couldn't help asking him
once what he meant by coming there at all. 'To make
money, of course. What do you think?' he said, scorn-
fully. Then he got fever, and had to be carried in a
hammock slung under a pole. As he weighed sixteen
stone I had no end of rows with the carriers. They
jibbed, ran away, sneaked off with their loads in the
night—quite a mutiny. So, one evening, I made a
speech in English with gestures, not one of which was
lost to the sixty pairs of eyes before me, and the next
morning I started the hammock off in front all right.
An hour afterwards I came upon the whole concern
wrecked in a bush—man, hammock, groans, blankets,
horrors. The heavy pole had skinned his poor nose.
He was very anxious for me to kill somebody, but
there wasn't the shadow of a carrier near. I remembered the old doctor—'It would be interesting for
science to watch the mental changes of individuals, on

the spot.' I felt I was becoming scientifically interest-ing. However, all that is to no purpose. On the fif-teenth day I came in sight of the big river again, and hobbled into the Central Station. It was on a back water surrounded by scrub and forest, with a pretty border of smelly mud on one side, and on the three others enclosed by a crazy fence of rushes. A ne-glected gap was all the gate it had, and the first glance at the place was enough to let you see the flabby devil was running that show. White men with long staves in their hands appeared languidly from amongst the buildings, strolling up to take a look at me, and then retired out of sight somewhere. One of them, a stout, excitable chap with black moustaches, informed me with great volubility and many digressions, as soon as I told him who I was, that my steamer was at the bottom of the river. I was thunderstruck. What, how, why? Oh, it was 'all right.' The 'manager himself' was there. All quite correct. 'Everybody had behaved splendidly! splendidly!'—'you must,' he said in agi-tation, 'go and see the general manager at once. He is waiting!'

"I did not see the real significance of that wreck at once. I fancy I see it now, but I am not sure—not at all. Certainly the affair was too stupid—when I think of it—to be altogether natural. Still . . . But at the moment it presented itself simply as a confounded nuisance. The steamer was sunk. They had started two days before in a sudden hurry up the river with the manager on board, in charge of some volunteer skipper, and before they had been out three hours they tore the bottom out of her on stones, and she sank near the south bank. I asked myself what I was to do there, now my boat was lost. As a matter of fact, I had plenty to do in fishing my command out of the river. I had to set about it the very next day. That, and the repairs when I brought the pieces to the station, took some months.

"My first interview with the manager was curious. He did not ask me to sit down after my twenty-mile walk that morning. He was commonplace in complexion, in feature, in manners, and in voice. He was of middle size and of ordinary build. His eyes, of the usual blue, were perhaps remarkably cold, and he certainly could make his glance fall on one as trenchant and heavy as an axe. But even at these times the rest of his person seemed to disclaim the intention. Otherwise there was only an indefinable, faint expression of his lips, something stealthy—a smile—not a smile—I remember it, but I can't explain. It was unconscious, this smile was, though just after he had said something it got intensified for an instant. It came at the end of his speeches like a seal applied on the words to make the meaning of the commonest phrase appear absolutely inscrutable. He was a common trader, from his youth up employed in these parts—nothing more. He was obeyed, yet he inspired neither love nor fear, nor even respect. He inspired uneasiness. That was it! Uneasiness. Not a definite mistrust—just uneasiness—nothing more. You have no idea how effective such a . . . a . . . faculty can be. He had no genius for organizing, for initiative, or for order even. That was evident in such things as the deplorable state of the station. He had no learn-

ing, and no intelligence. His position had come to him
—why? Perhaps because he was never ill . . . He
had served three terms of three years out there . . .
Because triumphant health in the general rout of con-
stitutions is a kind of power in itself. When he went
home on leave he rioted on a large scale—pompously.
Jack ashore—with a difference—in externals only.
This one could gather from his casual talk. He origi-
nated nothing, he could keep the routine going—
that's all. But he was great. He was great by this little
thing that it was impossible to tell what could control
such a man. He never gave that secret away. Perhaps
there was nothing within him. Such a suspicion made
one pause—for out there there were no external
checks. Once when various tropical diseases had laid
low almost every 'agent' in the station, he was heard
to say, 'Men who come out here should have no en-
trails.' He sealed the utterance with that smile of his,
as though it had been a door opening into a darkness
he had in his keeping. You fancied you had seen
things—but the seal was on. When annoyed at meal-
times by the constant quarrels of the white men about
precedence, he ordered an immense round table to be
made, for which a special house had to be built. This
was the station's mess-room. Where he sat was the
first place—the rest were nowhere. One felt this to be
his unalterable conviction. He was neither civil nor
uncivil. He was quiet. He allowed his 'boy'—an overfed young negro from the coast—to treat the white
men, under his very eyes, with provoking insolence.

"He began to speak as soon as he saw me. I had
been very long on the road. He could not wait. Had

to start without me. The up-river stations had to be relieved. There had been so many delays already that he did not know who was dead and who was alive, and how they got on—and so on, and so on. He paid no attention to my explanation, and, playing with a stick of sealing-wax, repeated several times that the situation was 'very grave, very grave.' There were rumours that a very important station was in jeopardy, and its chief, Mr. Kurtz, was ill. Hoped it was not true. Mr. Kurtz was . . . I felt weary and irritable. Hang Kurtz, I thought. I interrupted him by saying I had heard of Mr. Kurtz on the coast. 'Ah! So they talk of him down there,' he murmured to himself. Then he began again, assuring me Mr. Kurtz was the best agent he had, an exceptional man, of the greatest importance to the Company; therefore I could understand his anxiety. He was, he said, 'very, very uneasy.' Certainly he fidgeted on his chair a good deal, exclaimed, 'Ah, Mr. Kurtz!' broke the stick of sealing-wax and seemed dumfounded by the accident. Next thing he wanted to know 'how long it would take to' . . . I interrupted him again. Being hungry, you know, and kept on my feet too, I was getting savage. 'How can I tell?' I said. 'I haven't even seen the wreck yet—some months, no doubt.' All this talk seemed to me so futile. 'Some months,' he said. 'Well, let us say three months before we can make a start. Yes. That ought to do the affair.' I flung out of his hut (he lived all alone in a clay hut with a sort of verandah) muttering to myself my opinion of him. He was a chattering idiot. Afterwards I took it back when it was borne in upon me startlingly with what extreme nicety he had estimated the time requisite for the 'affair.'

"I went to work the next day, turning, so to speak, my back on that station. In that way only it seemed to me I could keep my hold on the redeeming facts of life. Still, one must look about sometimes; and then I saw this station, these men strolling aimlessly about in the sunshine of the yard. I asked myself sometimes what it all meant. They wandered here and there with their absurd long staves in their hands, like a lot of faithless pilgrims bewitched inside a rotten fence. The word 'ivory' rang in the air, was whispered, was sighed. You would think they were praying to it. A taint of imbecile rapacity blew through it all, like a whiff from some corpse. By Jove! I've never seen anything so unreal in my life. And outside, the silent wilderness surrounding this cleared speck on the earth struck me as something great and invincible, like evil or truth, waiting patiently for the passing away of this fantastic invasion.

"Oh, these months! Well, never mind. Various things happened. One evening a grass shed full of calico, cotton prints, beads, and I don't know what else, burst into a blaze so suddenly that you would have thought the earth had opened to let an avenging fire consume all that trash. I was smoking my pipe quietly by my dismantled steamer, and saw them all cutting capers in the light, with their arms lifted high, when the stout man with moustaches came tearing down to the river, a tin pail in his hand, assured me that everybody was 'behaving splendidly, splendidly,' dipped about a quart of water and tore back again. I noticed there was a hole in the bottom of his pail.

"I strolled up. There was no hurry. You see the thing had gone off like a box of matches. It had been hopeless from the very first. The flame had leaped high, driven everybody back, lighted up everything—and collapsed. The shed was already a heap of embers glowing fiercely. A nigger was being beaten near by. They said he had caused the fire in some way; be that as it may, he was screeching most horribly. I saw him, later, for several days, sitting in a bit of shade looking very sick and trying to recover himself: afterwards he arose and went out—and the wilderness without a sound took him into its bosom again. As I approached the glow from the dark I found myself at the back of two men, talking. I heard the name of Kurtz pronounced, then the words, 'take advantage of this unfortunate accident.' One of the men was the manager. I wished him a good evening. 'Did you ever see anything like it—eh? it is incredible,' he said, and walked off. The other man remained. He was a first-class agent, young, gentlemanly, a bit reserved, with a forked little beard and a hooked nose. He was stand-offish with the other agents, and they on their side said he was the manager's spy upon them. As to me, I had hardly ever spoken to him before. We got into talk, and by and by we strolled away from the hissing ruins. Then he asked me to his room, which was in the main building of the station. He struck a match, and I perceived that this young aristocrat had not only a silver-mounted dressing-case but also a whole candle all to himself. Just at that time the manager was the only man supposed to have any right to candles.

Native mats covered the clay walls; a collection of spears, assegais, shields, knives was hung up in trophies. The business intrusted to this fellow was the making of bricks—so I had been informed; but there wasn't a fragment of a brick anywhere in the station, and he could not make bricks without something, I don't know what—straw maybe. Anyway, it could not be found there and as it was not likely to be sent from Europe, it did not appear clear to me what he was waiting for. An act of special creation perhaps. However, they were all waiting—all the sixteen or twenty pilgrims of them—for something; and upon my word it did not seem an uncongenial occupation, from the way they took it, though the only thing that ever came to them was disease—as far as I could see. They beguiled the time by backbiting and intriguing against each other in a foolish kind of way. There was an air of plotting about that station, but nothing came of it, of course. It was as unreal as everything else—as the philanthropic pretence of the whole concern, as their talk, as their government, as their show of work. The only real feeling was a desire to get appointed to a trading-post where ivory was to be had, so that they could earn percentages. They intrigued and slandered and hated each other only on that account—but as to effectually lifting a little finger—oh, no. By heavens! there is something after all in the world allowing one man to steal a horse while another must not look at a halter. Steal a horse straight out. Very well. He has done it. Perhaps he can ride. But there is a way of looking at a halter that would provoke the most charitable of saints into a kick.

"I had no idea why he wanted to be sociable, but as
we chatted in there it suddenly occurred to me the
fellow was trying to get at something—in fact, pump-
ing me. He alluded constantly to Europe, to the people I was supposed to know there—putting leading
questions as to my acquaintances in the sepulchral city,
and so on. His little eyes glittered like mica discs—
with curiosity—though he tried to keep up a bit of
superciliousness. At first I was astonished, but very
soon I became awfully curious to see what he would
find out from me. I couldn't possibly imagine what I
had in me to make it worth his while. It was very pretty
to see how he baffled himself, for in truth my body was
full only of chills, and my head had nothing in it but
that wretched steamboat business. It was evident he
took me for a perfectly shameless prevaricator. At last
he got angry, and, to conceal a movement of furious
annoyance, he yawned. I rose. Then I noticed a small
sketch in oils, on a panel, representing a woman,
draped and blindfolded, carrying a lighted torch. The
background was sombre—almost black. The movement of the woman was stately, and the effect of the
torchlight on the face was sinister.

"It arrested me, and he stood by civilly, holding an
empty half-pint champagne bottle (medical comforts)
with the candle stuck in it. To my question he said
Mr. Kurtz had painted this—in this very station more
than a year ago—while waiting for means to go to his
trading-post. 'Tell me, pray,' said I, 'who is this Mr.
Kurtz?'

" 'The chief of the Inner Station,' he answered in a
short tone, looking away. 'Much obliged,' I said,

laughing. 'And you are the brickmaker of the Central Station. Every one knows that.' He was silent for a while. 'He is a prodigy,' he said at last. 'He is an emissary of pity and science and progress, and devil knows what else. We want,' he began to declaim suddenly, 'for the guidance of the cause intrusted to us by Europe, so to speak, higher intelligence, wide sympathies, a singleness of purpose.' 'Who says that?' I asked. 'Lots of them,' he replied. 'Some even write that; and so *he* comes here, a special being, as you ought to know.' 'Why ought I to know?' I interrupted, really surprised. He paid no attention. 'Yes. Today he is chief of the best station, next year he will be assistant-manager, two years more and . . . but I daresay you know what he will be in two years' time. You are of the new gang—the gang of virtue. The same people who sent him specially also recommended you. Oh, don't say no. I've my own eyes to trust.' Light dawned upon me. My dear aunt's influential acquaintances were producing an unexpected effect upon that young man. I nearly burst into a laugh. 'Do you read the Company's confidential correspondence?' I asked. He hadn't a word to say. It was great fun. 'When Mr. Kurtz,' I continued, severely, 'is General Manager, you won't have the opportunity.'

"He blew the candle out suddenly, and we went outside. The moon had risen. Black figures strolled about listlessly, pouring water on the glow, whence proceeded a sound of hissing; steam ascended in the moonlight, the beaten nigger groaned somewhere. 'What a row the brute makes!' said the indefatigable man with the moustaches, appearing near us. 'Serve him right. Transgression—punishment—bang! Pitiless, pitiless. That's the only way. This will prevent all conflagrations for the future. I was just telling the manager . . .' He noticed my companion, and became crestfallen all at once. 'Not in bed yet,' he said, with a kind of servile heartiness; 'it's so natural. Ha! Danger—agitation.' He vanished. I went on to the riverside, and the other followed me. I heard a scathing murmur at my ear, 'Heap of muffs—go to.' The pilgrims could be seen in knots gesticulating, discussing. Several had still their staves in their hands. I verily believe they took these sticks to bed with them. Beyond the fence the forest stood up spectrally in the moonlight, and through the dim stir, through the faint sounds of that lamentable courtyard, the silence of the land went home to one's very heart—its mystery, its greatness, the amazing reality of its concealed life. The hurt nigger moaned feebly somewhere near by, and then fetched a deep sigh that made me mend my pace away from there. I felt a hand introducing itself under my arm. 'My dear sir,' said the fellow, 'I don't want to be misunderstood, and especially by you, who will see Mr. Kurtz long before I can have that pleasure. I wouldn't like him to get a false idea of my disposition. . . .'

"I let him run on, this papier-maché Mephistopheles, and it seemed to me that if I tried I could poke my forefinger through him, and would find nothing inside but a little loose dirt, maybe. He, don't you see, had been planning to be assistant-manager by and by under the present man, and I could see that the coming of that Kurtz had upset them both not a little. He talked precipitately, and I did not try to stop him. I had my shoulders against the wreck of my steamer, hauled up on the slope like a carcass of some big river animal. The smell of mud, of primeval mud, by Jove! was in my nostrils, the high stillness of primeval forest was before my eyes; there were shiny patches on the black creek. The moon had spread over everything a thin layer of silver—over the rank grass, over the mud, upon the wall of matted vegetation standing higher than the wall of a temple, over the great river I could see through a sombre gap glittering, glittering, as it flowed broadly by without a murmur. All this was great, expectant, mute, while the man jabbered about himself. I wondered whether the stillness on the face of the immensity looking at us two were meant as an appeal or as a menace. What were we who had strayed in here? Could we handle that dumb thing, or would it handle us? I felt how big, how confoundedly big, was that thing that couldn't talk, and perhaps was deaf as well. What was in there? I could see a little ivory coming out from there, and I had heard Mr. Kurtz was in there. I had heard enough about it, too—God knows! Yet somehow it didn't bring any image with it—no more than if I had been told an angel or a fiend was in there. I believed it in the same way one of you might believe there are inhabitants in the planet Mars. I knew once a Scotch sailmaker who was certain, dead sure, there were people in Mars. If you asked him for some idea how they looked and behaved, he would get shy and mutter something about 'walking on all-fours.' If you as

much as smiled, he would—though a man of sixty—
offer to fight you. I would not have gone so far as to
fight for Kurtz, but I went for him near enough to
lie. You know I hate, detest, and can't bear a lie, not
because I am straighter than the rest of us, but simply
because it appalls me. There is a taint of death, a
flavour of mortality in lies—which is exactly what I
hate and detest in the world—what I want to forget.
It makes me miserable and sick, like biting something
rotten would do. Temperament, I suppose. Well, I
went near enough to it by letting the young fool there
believe anything he liked to imagine as to my influence in Europe. I became in an instant as much of a
pretence as the rest of the bewitched pilgrims. This
simply because I had a notion it somehow would be of
help to that Kurtz whom at the time I did not see—
you understand. He was just a word for me. I did
not see the man in the name any more than you
do. Do you see him? Do you see the story? Do you
see anything? It seems to me I am trying to tell you
a dream—making a vain attempt, because no relation
of a dream can convey the dream-sensation, that commingling of absurdity, surprise, and bewilderment in
a tremor of struggling revolt, that notion of being
captured by the incredible which is of the very essence
of dreams. . . ."

He was silent for a while.

". . . No, it is impossible; it is impossible to convey the life-sensation of any given epoch of one's existence—that which makes its truth, its meaning—its
subtle and penetrating essence. It is impossible. We
live, as we dream—alone. . . ."

He paused again as if reflecting, then added:

"Of course in this you fellows see more than I could then. You see me, whom you know. . . ."

It had become so pitch dark that we listeners could hardly see one another. For a long time already he, sitting apart, had been no more to us than a voice. There was not a word from anybody. The others might have been asleep, but I was awake. I listened, I listened on the watch for the sentence, for the word, that would give me the clue to the faint uneasiness inspired by this narrative that seemed to shape itself without human lips in the heavy night-air of the river.

". . . Yes—I let him run on," Marlow began again, "and think what he pleased about the powers that were behind me. I did! And there was nothing behind me! There was nothing but that wretched, old, mangled steamboat I was leaning against, while he talked fluently about 'the necessity for every man to get on.' 'And when one comes out here, you conceive, it is not to gaze at the moon.' Mr. Kurtz was a 'universal genius,' but even a genius would find it easier to work with 'adequate tools—intelligent men.' He did not make bricks—why, there was a physical impossibility in the way—as I was well aware; and if he did secretarial work for the manager, it was because 'no sensible man rejects wantonly the confidence of his superiors.' Did I see it? I saw it. What more did I want? What I really wanted was rivets, by heaven! Rivets. To get on with the work—to stop the hole. Rivets I wanted. There were cases of them down at the coast—cases—piled up—burst—split! You kicked a loose rivet at every second step in that station-yard on the hillside. Rivets had rolled into the grove of death. You could fill your pockets with rivets for the trouble of stooping down—and there wasn't one rivet to be found where it was wanted. We had plates that would do, but nothing to fasten them with. And every week the messenger, a lone negro, letter-bag on shoulder and staff in hand, left our station for the coast. And several times a week a coast caravan came in with trade goods—ghastly glazed calico that made you shudder only to look at it, glass beads value about a penny a quart, confounded spotted cotton handkerchiefs. And no rivets. Three carriers could have brought all that was wanted to set that steamboat afloat.

"He was becoming confidential now, but I fancy my unresponsive attitude must have exasperated him at last, for he judged it necessary to inform me he feared neither God nor devil, let alone any mere man. I said I could see that very well, but what I wanted was a certain quantity of rivets—and rivets were what really Mr. Kurtz wanted, if he had only known it. Now letters went to the coast every week. . . . 'My dear sir,' he cried, 'I write from dictation.' I demanded rivets. There was a way—for an intelligent man. He changed his manner; became very cold, and suddenly began to talk about a hippopotamus; wondered whether sleeping on board the steamer (I stuck to my salvage night and day) I wasn't disturbed. There was an old hippo that had the bad habit of getting out on the bank and roaming at night over the station grounds. The pilgrims used to turn out in a body and

empty every rifle they could lay hands on at him.
Some even had sat up o' nights for him. All this
energy was wasted, though. 'That animal has a
charmed life,' he said; 'but you can say this only of
brutes in this country. No man—you apprehend me?
—no man here bears a charmed life.' He stood there
for a moment in the moonlight with his delicate
hooked nose set a little askew, and his mica eyes
glittering without a wink, then, with a curt Good-
night, he strode off. I could see he was disturbed and
considerably puzzled, which made me feel more hope-
ful than I had been for days. It was a great comfort
to turn from that chap to my influential friend, the
battered, twisted, ruined, tin-pot steamboat. I clam-
bered on board. She rang under my feet like an empty
Huntley & Palmer biscuit-tin kicked along a gutter;
she was nothing so solid in make, and rather less pretty
in shape, but I had expended enough hard work on
her to make me love her. No influential friend would
have served me better. She had given me a chance to
come out a bit—to find out what I could do. No, I
don't like work. I had rather laze about and think of
all the fine things that can be done. I don't like work
—no man does—but I like what is in the work—the
chance to find yourself. Your own reality—for yourself, not for others—what no other man can ever
know. They can only see the mere show, and never
can tell what it really means.

"I was not surprised to see somebody sitting aft, on
the deck, with his legs dangling over the mud. You
see I rather chummed with the few mechanics there
were in that station, whom the other pilgrims natur-

ally despised—on account of their imperfect manners,
I suppose. This was the foreman—a boiler-maker by
trade—a good worker. He was a lank, bony, yellow-
faced man, with big intense eyes. His aspect was
worried, and his head was as bald as the palm of my
hand; but his hair in falling seemed to have stuck to
his chin, and had prospered in the new locality, for
his beard hung down to his waist. He was a widower
with six young children (he had left them in charge
of a sister of his to come out there), and the passion of
his life was pigeon-flying. He was an enthusiast and
a connoisseur. He would rave about pigeons. After
work hours he used sometimes to come over from his
hut for a talk about his children and his pigeons; at
work, when he had to crawl in the mud under the
bottom of the steamboat, he would tie up that beard
of his in a kind of white serviette he brought for the
purpose. It had loops to go over his ears. In the evening he could be seen squatted on the bank rinsing that
wrapper in the creek with great care, then spreading
it solemnly on a bush to dry.

"I slapped him on the back and shouted, 'We shall
have rivets!' He scrambled to his feet exclaiming,
'No! Rivets!' as though he couldn't believe his ears.
Then in a low voice, 'You . . . eh?' I don't know
why we behaved like lunatics. I put my finger to the
side of my nose and nodded mysteriously. 'Good for
you!' he cried, snapped his fingers above his head,
lifting one foot. I tried a jig. We capered on the iron
deck. A frightful clatter came out of that hulk, and
the virgin forest on the other bank of the creek sent
it back in a thundering roll upon the sleeping station.

It must have made some of the pilgrims sit up in their hovels. A dark figure obscured the lighted doorway of the manager's hut, vanished, then, a second or so after, the doorway itself vanished, too. We stopped, and the silence driven away by the stamping of our feet flowed back again from the recesses of the land. The great wall of vegetation, an exuberant and entangled mass of trunks, branches, leaves, boughs, festoons, motionless in the moonlight, was like a rioting invasion of soundless life, a rolling wave of plants, piled up, crested, ready to topple over the creek, to sweep every little man of us out of his little existence. And it moved not. A deadened burst of mighty splashes and snorts reached us from afar, as though an ichthyosaurus had been taking a bath of glitter in the great river. 'After all,' said the boiler-maker in a reasonable tone, 'why shouldn't we get the rivets?' Why not, indeed! I did not know of any reason why we shouldn't. 'They'll come in three weeks,' I said, confidently.

"But they didn't. Instead of rivets there came an invasion, an infliction, a visitation. It came in sections during the next three weeks, each section headed by a donkey carrying a white man in new clothes and tan shoes, bowing from that elevation right and left to the impressed pilgrims. A quarrelsome band of footsore sulky niggers trod on the heels of the donkey; a lot of tents, campstools, tin boxes, white cases, brown bales would be shot down in the court-yard, and the air of mystery would deepen a little over the muddle of the station. Five such instalments came, with their absurd air of disorderly flight with the loot of innumerable outfit shops and provision stores, that, one would think, they were lugging, after a raid, into the wilderness for equitable division. It was an inextricable mess of things decent in themselves but that human folly made look like the spoils of thieving.

"This devoted band called itself the Eldorado Exploring Expedition, and I believe they were sworn to secrecy. Their talk, however, was the talk of sordid buccaneers: it was reckless without hardihood, greedy without audacity, and cruel without courage; there was not an atom of foresight or of serious intention in the whole batch of them, and they did not seem aware these things are wanted for the work of the world. To tear treasure out of the bowels of the land was their desire, with no more moral purpose at the back of it than there is in burglars breaking into a safe. Who paid the expenses of the noble enterprise I don't know; but the uncle of our manager was leader of that lot.

"In exterior he resembled a butcher in a poor neighbourhood, and his eyes had a look of sleepy cunning. He carried his fat paunch with ostentation on his short legs, and during the time his gang infested the station spoke to no one but his nephew. You could see these two roaming about all day long with their heads close together in an everlasting confab.

"I had given up worrying myself about the rivets. One's capacity for that kind of folly is more limited than you would suppose. I said Hang!—and let things slide. I had plenty of time for meditation, and now and then I would give some thought to Kurtz.

I wasn't very interested in him. No. Still, I was curious to see whether this man, who had come out equipped with moral ideas of some sort, would climb to the top after all and how he would set about his work when there."

II

"One evening as I was lying flat on the deck of my steamboat, I heard voices approaching—and there were the nephew and the uncle strolling along the bank. I laid my head on my arm again, and had nearly lost myself in a doze, when somebody said in my ear, as it were: 'I am as harmless as a little child, but I don't like to be dictated to. Am I the manager—or am I not? I was ordered to send him there. It's incredible.'. . . I became aware that the two were standing on the shore alongside the forepart of the steamboat, just below my head. I did not move; it did not occur to me to move: I was sleepy. 'It *is* unpleasant,' grunted the uncle. 'He has asked the Administration to be sent there,' said the other, 'with the idea of showing what he could do; and I was instructed accordingly. Look at the influence that man must have. Is it not frightful?' They both agreed it was frightful, then made several bizarre remarks: 'Make rain and fine weather—one man—the Council—by the nose'—bits of absurd sentences that got the better of my drowsiness, so that I had pretty near the whole of my

wits about me when the uncle said, 'The climate may
do away with this difficulty for you. Is he alone there?'
'Yes,' answered the manager; 'he sent his assistant
down the river with a note to me in these terms:
"Clear this poor devil out of the country, and don't
bother sending more of that sort. I had rather be
alone than have the kind of men you can dispose of
with me." It was more than a year ago. Can you imagine such impudence!' 'Anything since then?' asked
the other hoarsely. 'Ivory,' jerked the nephew; 'lots
of it—prime sort—lots—most annoying, from him.'
'And with that?' questioned the heavy rumble. 'In-
voice,' was the reply fired out, so to speak. Then silence. They had been talking about Kurtz.

"I was broad awake by this time, but, lying perfectly at ease, remained still, having no inducement to
change my position. 'How did that ivory come all
this way?' growled the elder man, who seemed very
vexed. The other explained that it had come with a
fleet of canoes in charge of an English half-caste
clerk Kurtz had with him; that Kurtz had apparently
intended to return himself, the station being by that
time bare of goods and stores, but after coming three
hundred miles, had suddenly decided to go back,
which he started to do alone in a small dugout with
four paddlers, leaving the half-caste to continue down
the river with the ivory. The two fellows there seemed
astounded at anybody attempting such a thing. They
were at a loss for an adequate motive. As to me, I
seemed to see Kurtz for the first time. It was a distinct
glimpse: the dugout, four paddling savages, and the
lone white man turning his back suddenly on the

headquarters, on relief, on thoughts of home—perhaps; setting his face towards the depths of the wilderness, towards his empty and desolate station. I did not know the motive. Perhaps he was just simply a fine fellow who stuck to his work for its own sake. His name, you understand, had not been pronounced once. He was 'that man.' The half-caste, who, as far as I could see, had conducted a difficult trip with great prudence and pluck, was invariably alluded to as 'that scoundrel.' The 'scoundrel' had reported that the 'man' had been very ill—had recovered imperfectly. . . . The two below me moved away then a few paces, and strolled back and forth at some little distance. I heard: 'Military post—doctor—two hundred miles—quite alone now—unavoidable delays—nine months—no news—strange rumours.' They approached again, just as the manager was saying, 'No one, as far as I know, unless a species of wandering trader—a pestilential fellow, snapping ivory from the natives.' Who was it they were talking about now? I gathered in snatches that this was some man supposed to be in Kurtz's district, and of whom the manager did not approve. 'We will not be free from unfair competition till one of these fellows is hanged for an example,' he said. 'Certainly,' grunted the other; 'get him hanged! Why not? Anything—anything can be done in this country. That's what I say; nobody here, you understand, *here*, can endanger your position. And why? You stand the climate—you outlast them all. The danger is in Europe; but there before I left I took care to——' They moved off and whispered, then their voices rose again. 'The extraordinary series

of delays is not my fault. I did my best.' The fat man
sighed. 'Very sad.' 'And the pestiferous absurdity of
his talk,' continued the other; 'he bothered me enough
when he was here. "Each station should be like a
beacon on the road towards better things, a centre for
trade of course, but also for humanizing, improving,
instructing." Conceive you—that ass! And he wants
to be manager! No, it's——' Here he got choked by
excessive indignation, and I lifted my head the least
bit. I was surprised to see how near they were—
right under me. I could have spat upon their hats.
They were looking on the ground, absorbed in
thought. The manager was switching his leg with a
slender twig: his sagacious relative lifted his head.
'You have been well since you came out this time?' he
asked. The other gave a start. 'Who? I? Oh! Like a
charm—like a charm. But the rest—oh, my goodness!
All sick. They die so quick, too, that I haven't the
time to send them out of the country—it's incredible!'
'H'm. Just so,' grunted the uncle. 'Ah! my boy, trust
to this—I say, trust to this.' I saw him extend his
short flipper of an arm for a gesture that took in the
forest, the creek, the mud, the river—seemed to
beckon with a dishonouring flourish before the sunlit
face of the land a treacherous appeal to the lurking
death, to the hidden evil, to the profound darkness of
its heart. It was so startling that I leaped to my feet
and looked back at the edge of the forest, as though
I had expected an answer of some sort to that black
display of confidence. You know the foolish notions
that come to one sometimes. The high stillness con-

fronted these two figures with its ominous patience, waiting for the passing away of a fantastic invasion.

"They swore aloud together—out of sheer fright, I believe—then pretending not to know anything of my existence, turned back to the station. The sun was low; and leaning forward side by side, they seemed to be tugging painfully uphill their two ridiculous shadows of unequal length, that trailed behind them slowly over the tall grass without bending a single blade.

"In a few days the Eldorado Expedition went into the patient wilderness, that closed upon it as the sea closes over a diver. Long afterwards the news came that all the donkeys were dead. I know nothing as to the fate of the less valuable animals. They, no doubt, like the rest of us, found what they deserved. I did not inquire. I was then rather excited at the prospect of meeting Kurtz very soon. When I say very soon I mean it comparatively. It was just two months from the day we left the creek when we came to the bank below Kurtz's station.

"Going up that river was like travelling back to the earliest beginnings of the world, when vegetation rioted on the earth and the big trees were kings. An empty stream, a great silence, an impenetrable forest. The air was warm, thick, heavy, sluggish. There was no joy in the brilliance of sunshine. The long stretches of the waterway ran on, deserted, into the gloom of over-shadowed distances. On silvery sand-banks hippos and alligators sunned themselves side by side. The broadening waters flowed through a mob of wooded islands; you lost your way on that river as you would in a desert, and butted all day long against shoals, trying to find the channel, till you thought yourself bewitched and cut off for ever from everything you had known once—somewhere—far away—in another existence perhaps. There were moments when one's past came back to one, as it will sometimes when you have not a moment to spare to yourself; but it came in the shape of an unrestful and noisy dream, remembered with wonder amongst the overwhelming realities of this strange world of plants, and water, and silence. And this stillness of life did not in the least resemble a peace. It was the stillness of an implacable force brooding over an inscrutable intention. It looked at you with a vengeful aspect. I got used to it afterwards; I did not see it any more; I had no time. I had to keep guessing at the channel; I had to discern, mostly by inspiration, the signs of hidden banks; I watched for sunken stones; I was learning to clap my teeth smartly before my heart flew out, when I shaved by a fluke some infernal sly old snag that would have ripped the life out of the tin-pot steamboat and drowned all the pilgrims; I had to keep a lookout for the signs of dead wood we could cut up in the night for next day's steaming. When you have to attend to things of that sort, to the mere incidents of the surface, the reality— the reality, I tell you—fades. The inner truth is hid- den—luckily, luckily. But I felt it all the same; I felt often its mysterious stillness watching me at my monkey tricks, just as it watches you fellows perform- ing on your respective tight-ropes for—what is it? half-a-crown a tumble——"

"Try to be civil, Marlow," growled a voice, and I knew there was at least one listener awake besides myself.

"I beg your pardon. I forgot the heartache which makes up the rest of the price. And indeed what does the price matter, if the trick be well done? You do your tricks very well. And I didn't do badly either, since I managed not to sink that steamboat on my first trip. It's a wonder to me yet. Imagine a blindfolded man set to drive a van over a bad road. I sweated and shivered over that business considerably, I can tell you. After all, for a seaman, to scrape the bottom of the thing that's supposed to float all the time under his care is the unpardonable sin. No one may know of it, but you never forget the thump—eh? A blow on the very heart. You remember it, you dream of it, you wake up at night and think of it—years after—and go hot and cold all over. I don't pretend to say that steamboat floated all the time. More than once she had to wade for a bit, with twenty cannibals splashing around and pushing. We had enlisted some of these chaps on the way for a crew. Fine fellows—cannibals —in their place. They were men one could work with, and I am grateful to them. And, after all, they did not eat each other before my face: they had brought along a provision of hippo-meat which went rotten, and made the mystery of the wilderness stink in my nostrils. Phoo! I can sniff it now. I had the manager on board and three or four pilgrims with their staves —all complete. Sometimes we came upon a station close by the bank, clinging to the skirts of the un- known, and the white men rushing out of a tumble-

down hovel, with great gestures of joy and surprise
and welcome, seemed very strange—had the appearance of being held there captive by a spell. The word
ivory would ring in the air for a while—and on we
went again into the silence, along empty reaches,
round the still bends, between the high walls of our
winding way, reverberating in hollow claps the ponderous beat of the stern-wheel. Trees, trees, millions
of trees, massive, immense, running up high; and
at their foot, hugging the bank against the stream,
crept the little begrimed steamboat, like a sluggish
beetle crawling on the floor of a lofty portico. It made
you feel very small, very lost, and yet it was not altogether depressing, that feeling. After all, if you were
small, the grimy beetle crawled on—which was just
what you wanted it to do. Where the pilgrims imagined it crawled to I don't know. To some place
where they expected to get something. I bet! For me
it crawled towards Kurtz—exclusively; but when the
steam-pipes started leaking we crawled very slow.
The reaches opened before us and closed behind, as if
the forest had stepped leisurely across the water to
bar the way for our return. We penetrated deeper and
deeper into the heart of darkness. It was very quiet
there. At night sometimes the roll of drums behind
the curtain of trees would run up the river and remain
sustained faintly, as if hovering in the air high over
our heads, till the first break of day. Whether it meant
war, peace, or prayer we could not tell. The dawns
were heralded by the descent of a chill stillness; the
wood-cutters slept, their fires burned low; the snapping of a twig would make you start. We were wan-

derers on a prehistoric earth, on an earth that wore the aspect of an unknown planet. We could have fancied ourselves the first of men taking possession of an accursed inheritance, to be subdued at the cost of profound anguish and of excessive toil. But suddenly, as we struggled round a bend, there would be a glimpse of rush walls, of peaked grass-roofs, a burst of yells, a whirl of black limbs, a mass of hands clapping, of feet stamping, of bodies swaying, of eyes rolling, under the droop of heavy and motionless foliage. The steamer toiled along slowly on the edge of a black and incomprehensible frenzy. The prehistoric man was cursing us, praying to us, welcoming us —who could tell? We were cut off from the comprehension of our surroundings; we glided past like phantoms, wondering and secretly appalled, as sane men would be before an enthusiastic outbreak in a madhouse. We could not understand because we were too far and could not remember because we were travelling in the night of first ages, of those ages that are gone, leaving hardly a sign—and no memories.

"The earth seemed unearthly. We are accustomed to look upon the shackled form of a conquered monster, but there—there you could look at a thing monstrous and free. It was unearthly, and the men were —— No, they were not inhuman. Well, you know, that was the worst of it—this suspicion of their not being inhuman. It would come slowly to one. They howled and leaped, and spun, and made horrid faces; but what thrilled you was just the thought of their humanity—like yours—the thought of your remote kinship with this wild and passionate uproar. Ugly.

Yes, it was ugly enough; but if you were man enough you would admit to yourself that there was in you just the faintest trace of a response to the terrible frankness of that noise, a dim suspicion of there being a meaning in it which you—you so remote from the night of first ages—could comprehend. And why not? The mind of man is capable of anything—because everything is in it, all the past as well as all the future. What was there after all? Joy, fear, sorrow, devotion, valour, rage—who can tell?—but truth—truth stripped of its cloak of time. Let the fool gape and shudder—the man knows, and can look on without a wink. But he must at least be as much of a man as these on the shore. He must meet that truth with his own true stuff—with his own inborn strength. Principles won't do. Acquisitions, clothes, pretty rags—rags that would fly off at the first good shake. No; you want a deliberate belief. An appeal to me in this fiendish row—is there? Very well; I hear; I admit, but I have a voice, too, and for good or evil mine is the speech that cannot be silenced. Of course, a fool, what with sheer fright and fine sentiments, is always safe. Who's that grunting? You wonder I didn't go ashore for a howl and a dance? Well, no—I didn't. Fine sentiments, you say? Fine sentiments, be hanged! I had no time. I had to mess about with white-lead and strips of woolen blanket helping to put bandages on those leaky steampipes—I tell you. I had to watch the steering, and circumvent those snags, and get the tin-pot along by hook or by crook. There was surface-truth enough in these things to save a wiser man. And between whiles I had to look after the savage who was fireman. He was an improved specimen; he could fire up a vertical boiler. He was there below me, and, upon my word, to look at him was as edifying as seeing a dog in a parody of breeches and a feather hat, walking on his hind-legs. A few months of training had done for that really fine chap. He squinted at the steam-gauge and at the water-guage with an evident effort of intrepidity—and he had filed teeth, too, the poor devil, and the wool of his pate shaved into queer patterns, and three ornamental scars on each of his cheeks. He ought to have been clapping his hands and stamping his feet on the bank, instead of which he was hard at work, a thrall to strange witchcraft, full of improving knowledge. He was useful because he had been instructed; and what he knew was this—that should the water in that transparent thing disappear, the evil spirit inside the boiler would get angry through the greatness of his thirst, and take a terrible vengeance. So he sweated and watched the glass fearfully (with an impromptu charm, made of rags, tied to his arm, and a piece of polished bone, as big as a watch, stuck flatways through his lower lip), while the wooded banks slipped past us slowly, the short noise was left behind, the interminable miles of silence—and we crept on, towards Kurtz. But the snags were thick, the water was treacherous and shallow, the boiler seemed indeed to have a sulky devil in it, and thus neither that fireman nor I had any time to peer into our creepy thoughts.

"Some fifty miles below the Inner Station we came upon a hut of reeds, an inclined and melancholy pole, with the unrecognizable tatters of what had been a flag of some sort flying from it, and a neatly stacked woodpile. This was unexpected. We came to the bank, and on the stack of firewood found a flat piece of board with some faded pencil-writing on it. When deciphered it said: 'Wood for you. Hurry up. Approach cautiously.' There was a signature, but it was illegible —not Kurtz—a much longer word. 'Hurry up.' Where? Up the river? 'Approach cautiously.' We had not done so. But the warning could not have been meant for the place where it could be only found after approach. Something was wrong above. But what—and how much? That was the question. We commented adversely upon the imbecility of that telegraphic style. The bush around said nothing, and would not let us look very far either. A torn curtain of red twill hung in the doorway of the hut, and flapped sadly in our faces. The dwelling was dismantled; but we could see a white man had lived there not very long ago. There remained a rude table —a plank on two posts; a heap of rubbish reposed in a dark corner, and by the door I picked up a book. It had lost its covers, and the pages had been thumbed into a state of extremely dirty softness; but the back had been lovingly stitched afresh with white cotton thread, which looked clean yet. It was an extraordinary find. Its title was, *An Inquiry into some Points of Seamanship*, by a man Towser, Towson—some such name—Master in his Majesty's Navy. The matter looked dreary reading enough, with illustrative diagrams and repulsive tables of figures, and the copy was sixty years old. I handled this amazing antiquity with the greatest possible tenderness, lest it should dissolve in my hands. Within, Towson or Towser was inquiring earnestly into the breaking strain of ships' chains and tackle, and other such matters. Not a very enthralling book; but at the first glance you could see there a singleness of intention, an honest concern for the right way of going to work, which made these humble pages, thought out so many years ago, luminous with another than a professional light. The simple old sailor, with his talk of chains and purchases, made me forget the jungle and the pilgrims in a delicious sensation of having come upon something unmistakably real. Such a book being there was wonderful enough but still more astounding were the notes pencilled in the margin, and plainly referring to the text. I couldn't believe my eyes! They were in cipher! Yes, it looked like cipher. Fancy a man lugging with him a book of that description into this nowhere and studying it—and making notes—in cipher at that! It was an extravagant mystery.

"I had been dimly aware for some time of a worrying noise, and when I lifted my eyes I saw the woodpile was gone, and the manager, aided by all the pilgrims, was shouting at me from the riverside. I slipped the book into my pocket. I assure you to leave off reading was like tearing myself away from the shelter of an old and solid friendship.

"I started the lame engine ahead. 'It must be this miserable trader—this intruder,' exclaimed the manager, looking back malevolently at the place we had left. 'He must be English,' I said. 'It will not save him from getting into trouble if he is not careful,' muttered the manager darkly. I observed with assumed innocence that no man was safe from trouble in this world.

"The current was more rapid now, the steamer seemed at her last gasp, the stern-wheel flopped languidly, and I caught myself listening on tiptoe for the next beat of the boat, for in sober truth I expected the wretched thing to give up every moment. It was like watching the last flickers of a life. But still we crawled. Sometimes I would pick out a tree a little way ahead to measure our progress towards Kurtz by, but I lost it invariably before we got abreast. To keep the eyes so long on one thing was too much for human patience. The manager displayed a beautiful resignation. I fretted and fumed and took to arguing with myself whether or no I would talk openly with Kurtz; but before I could come to any conclusion it occurred to me that my speech or my silence, indeed any action of mine, would be a mere futility. What did it matter what any one knew or ignored? What did it matter who was manager? One gets sometimes such a flash of insight. The essentials of this affair lay deep under the surface, beyond my reach, and beyond my power of meddling.

"Towards the evening of the second day we judged ourselves about eight miles from Kurtz's station. I wanted to push on; but the manager looked grave, and told me the navigation up there was so dangerous that it would be advisable, the sun being very low already, to wait where we were till next morning. Moreover, he pointed out that if the warning to approach cautiously were to be followed, we must approach in daylight—not at dusk or in the dark. This was sensible enough. Eight miles meant nearly three hours' steaming for us, and I could also see suspicious ripples at the upper end of the reach. Nevertheless, I was annoyed beyond expression at the delay, and most unreasonably, too, since one night more could not matter much after so many months. As we had plenty of wood, and caution was the word, I brought up in the middle of the stream. The reach was narrow, straight, with high sides like a railway cutting. The dusk came gliding into it long before the sun had set. The current ran smooth and swift, but a dumb immobility sat on the banks. The living trees, lashed together by the creepers and every living bush of the undergrowth, might have been changed into stone, even to the slenderest twig, to the lightest leaf. It was not sleep—it seemed unnatural, like a state of trance. Not the faintest sound of any kind could be heard. You looked on amazed, and began to suspect yourself of being deaf—then the night came suddenly, and struck you blind as well. About three in the morning some large fish leaped, and the loud splash made me jump as though a gun had been fired. When the sun rose there was a white fog, very warm and clammy, and more blinding than the night. It did not shift or drive; it was just there, standing all round you like something solid. At eight or nine, perhaps, it lifted as a shutter lifts. We had a glimpse of the towering multitude of trees, of the immense matted jungle, with the blazing little ball of the sun hanging over it—all perfectly still—and then the white shutter came down again, smoothly, as if sliding in greased grooves. I ordered the chain, which we had begun to

heave in, to be paid out again. Before it stopped running with a muffled rattle, a cry, a very loud cry, as of
infinite desolation, soared slowly in the opaque air. It
ceased. A complaining clamour, modulated in savage
discords, filled our ears. The sheer unexpectedness of
it made my hair stir under my cap. I don't know how
it struck the others: to me it seemed as though the
mist itself had screamed, so suddenly, and apparently
from all sides at once, did this tumultuous and mournful uproar arise. It culminated in a hurried outbreak
of almost intolerably excessive shrieking, which
stopped short, leaving us stiffened in a variety of silly
attitudes, and obstinately listening to the nearly as
appalling and excessive silence. 'Good God! What is
the meaning——' stammered at my elbow one of the
pilgrims—a little fat man, with sandy hair and red
whiskers, who wore sidespring boots, and pink pyjamas tucked into his socks. Two others remained
open-mouthed a whole minute, then dashed into the
little cabin, to rush out incontinently and stand dart-
ing scared glances, with Winchesters at 'ready' in
their hands. What we could see was just the steamer
we were on, her outlines blurred as though she had
been on the point of dissolving, and a misty strip of
water, perhaps two feet broad, around her—and that
was all. The rest of the world was nowhere, as far as
our eyes and ears were concerned. Just nowhere.
Gone, disappeared; swept off without leaving a
whisper or a shadow behind.

"I went forward, and ordered the chain to be
hauled in short, so as to be ready to trip the anchor
and move the steamboat at once if necessary. 'Will

they attack?' whispered an awed voice. 'We will be all butchered in this fog,' murmured another. The faces twitched with the strain, the hands trembled slightly, the eyes forgot to wink. It was very curious to see the contrast of expressions of the white men and of the black fellows of our crew, who were as much strangers to that part of the river as we, though their homes were only eight hundred miles away. The whites, of course greatly discomposed, had besides a curious look of being painfully shocked by such an outrageous row. The others had an alert, naturally interested expression; but their faces were essentially quiet, even those of the one or two who grinned as they hauled at the chain. Several exchanged short, grunting phrases, which seemed to settle the matter to their satisfaction. Their headman, a young, broad-chested black, severely draped in dark-blue fringed cloths, with fierce nostrils and his hair all done up artfully in oily ringlets, stood near me. 'Aha!' I said, just for good fellowship's sake. 'Catch 'im,' he snapped, with a bloodshot widening of his eyes and a flash of sharp teeth—'catch 'im. Give 'im to us.' 'To you, eh?' I asked; 'what would you do with them?' 'Eat 'im!' he said curtly, and, leaning his elbow on the rail, looked out into the fog in a dignified and profoundly pensive attitude. I would no doubt have been properly horrified, had it not occurred to me that he and his chaps must be very hungry: that they must have been growing increasingly hungry for at least this month past. They had been engaged for six months (I don't think a single one of them had any clear idea of time, as we at the end of countless ages

have. They still belonged to the beginnings of time—
had no inherited experience to teach them as it were),
and of course, as long as there was a piece of paper
written over in accordance with some farcical law or
other made down the river, it didn't enter anybody's
head to trouble how they would live. Certainly they
had brought with them some rotten hippo-meat, which
couldn't have lasted very long, anyway, even if the
pilgrims hadn't, in the midst of a shocking hullabaloo,
thrown a considerable quantity of it overboard. It
looked like a high-handed proceeding; but it was
really a case of legitimate self-defence. You can't
breathe dead hippo waking, sleeping, and eating, and
at the same time keep your precarious grip on existence. Besides that, they had given them every week
three pieces of brass wire, each about nine inches long;
and the theory was they were to buy their provisions
with that currency in riverside villages. You can see
how *that* worked. There were either no villages, or
the people were hostile, or the director, who like the
rest of us fed out of tins, with an occasional old he-goat
thrown in, didn't want to stop the steamer for some
more or less recondite reason. So, unless they swallowed the wire itself, or made loops of it to snare the
fishes with, I don't see what good their extravagant
salary could be to them. I must say it was paid with a
regularity worthy of a large and honourable trading
company. For the rest, the only thing to eat—though
it didn't look eatable in the least—I saw in their possession was a few lumps of some stuff like half-cooked
dough, of a dirty lavender colour, they kept wrapped
in leaves, and now and then swallowed a piece of,

but so small that it seemed done more for the looks of
the thing than for any serious purpose of sustenance.
Why in the name of all the gnawing devils of hunger
they didn't go for us—they were thirty to five—and
have a good tuck-in for once, amazes me now when I
think of it. They were big powerful men, with not
much capacity to weigh the consequences, with courage, with strength, even yet, though their skins were
no longer glossy and their muscles no longer hard.
And I saw that something restraining, one of those
human secrets that baffle probability, had come into
play there. I looked at them with a swift quickening of
interest—not because it occurred to me I might be
eaten by them before very long, though I own to you
that just then I perceived—in a new light, as it were
—how unwholesome the pilgrims looked, and I
hoped, yes, I positively hoped, that my aspect was not
so—what shall I say?—so—unappetizing: a touch of
fantastic vanity which fitted well with the dream-sensation that pervaded all my days at that time. Perhaps
I had a little fever, too. One can't live with one's finger
everlastingly on one's pulse. I had often 'a little
fever,' or a little touch of other things—the playful
paw-strokes of the wilderness, the preliminary trifling
before the more serious onslaught which came in due
course. Yes; I looked at them as you would on any
human being, with a curiosity of their impulses,
motives, capacities, weaknesses, when brought to the
test of an inexorable physical necessity. Restraint!
What possible restraint? Was it superstition, disgust,
patience, fear—or some kind of primitive honour? No
fear can stand up to hunger, no patience can wear it out,

disgust simply does not exist where hunger is; and as to superstition, beliefs, and what you may call principles, they are less than chaff in a breeze. Don't you know the devilry of lingering starvation, its exasperating torment, its black thoughts, its sombre and brooding ferocity? Well, I do. It takes a man all his inborn strength to fight hunger properly. It's really easier to face bereavement, dishonour, and the perdition of one's soul—than this kind of prolonged hunger. Sad, but true. And these chaps, too, had no earthly reason for any kind of scruple. Restraint! I would just as soon have expected restraint from a hyena prowling amongst the corpses of a battlefield. But there was the fact facing me—the fact dazzling, to be seen, like the foam on the depths of the sea, like a ripple on an unfathomable enigma, a mystery greater—when I thought of it—than the curious, inexplicable note of desperate grief in this savage clamour that had swept by us on the river-bank, behind the blind whiteness of the fog.

"Two pilgrims were quarrelling in hurried whispers as to which bank. 'Left.' 'No, no; how can you? Right, right, of course.' 'It is very serious,' said the manager's voice behind me; 'I would be desolated if anything should happen to Mr. Kurtz before we came up.' I looked at him, and had not the slightest doubt he was sincere. He was just the kind of man who would wish to preserve appearances. That was his restraint. But when he muttered something about going on at once, I did not even take the trouble to answer him. I knew, and he knew, that it was impossible. Were we to let go our hold of the bottom, we would be absolutely in the air—in space. We wouldn't be able to tell where we were going to—whether up or down stream, or across—till we fetched against one bank or the other—and then we wouldn't know at first which it was. Of course I made no move. I had no mind for a smash-up. You couldn't imagine a more deadly place for a shipwreck. Whether drowned at once or not, we were sure to perish speedily in one way or another. 'I authorize you to take all the risks,' he said, after a short silence. 'I refuse to take any,' I said shortly; which was just the answer he expected, though its tone might have surprised him. 'Well, I must defer to your judgment. You are captain,' he said with marked civility. I turned my shoulder to him in sign of my appreciation, and looked into the fog. How long would it last? It was the most hopeless lookout. The approach to this Kurtz grubbing for ivory in the wretched bush was beset by as many dangers as though he had been an enchanted princess sleeping in a fabulous castle. 'Will they attack, do you think?' asked the manager, in a confidential tone.

"I did not think they would attack, for several obvious reasons. The thick fog was one. If they left the bank in their canoes they would get lost in it, as we would be if we attempted to move. Still, I had also judged the jungle of both banks quite impenetrable—and yet eyes were in it, eyes that had seen us. The riverside bushes were certainly very thick; but the undergrowth behind was evidently penetrable. However, during the short lift I had seen no canoes anywhere in the reach—certainly not abreast of the steamer. But what made the idea of attack inconceivable to me was the nature of the noise—of the cries we had heard. They had not the fierce character boding immediate hostile intention. Unexpected, wild, and violent as they had been, they had given me an irresistible impression of sorrow. The glimpse of the steamboat had for some reason filled those savages with unrestrained grief. The danger, if any, I expounded, was from our proximity to a great human passion let loose. Even extreme grief may ultimately vent itself in violence—but more generally takes the form of apathy. . . .

"You should have seen the pilgrims stare! They had no heart to grin, or even to revile me: but I believe they thought me gone mad—with fright, maybe. I delivered a regular lecture. My dear boys, it was no good bothering. Keep a lookout? Well, you may guess I watched the fog for the signs of lifting as a cat watches a mouse; but for anything else our eyes were of no more use to us than if we had been buried miles deep in a heap of cotton-wool. It felt like it, too— choking, warm, stifling. Besides, all I said, though it sounded extravagant, was absolutely true to fact. What we afterwards alluded to as an attack was really an attempt at repulse. The action was very far from being aggressive—it was not even defensive, in the usual sense: it was undertaken under the stress of desperation, and in its essence was purely protective.

"It developed itself, I should say, two hours after the fog lifted, and its commencement was at a spot, roughly speaking, about a mile and a half below Kurtz's station. We had just floundered and flopped round a bend, when I saw an islet, a mere grassy hum-

mock of bright green, in the middle of the stream.
It was the only thing of the kind; but as we opened
the reach more, I perceived it was the head of a long
sand-bank, or rather of a chain of shallow patches
stretching down the middle of the river. They were
discoloured, just awash, and the whole lot was seen
just under the water, exactly as a man's backbone is
seen running down the middle of his back under the
skin. Now, as far as I did see, I could go to the right
or to the left of this. I didn't know either channel, of
course. The banks looked pretty well alike, the depth
appeared the same; but as I had been informed the
station was on the west side, I naturally headed for
the western passage.

"No sooner had we fairly entered it than I became
aware it was much narrower than I had supposed. To
the left of us there was the long uninterrupted shoal,
and to the right a high, steep bank heavily overgrown
with bushes. Above the bush the trees stood in serried
ranks. The twigs overhung the current thickly, and
from distance to distance a large limb of some tree
projected rigidly over the stream. It was then well on
in the afternoon, the face of the forest was gloomy,
and a broad strip of shadow had already fallen on the
water. In this shadow we steamed up—very slowly, as
you may imagine. I sheered her well inshore—the
water being deepest near the bank, as the sounding-
pole informed me.

"One of my hungry and forbearing friends was
sounding in the bows just below me. This steamboat
was exactly like a decked scow. On the deck, there
were two little teakwood houses, with doors and win-

dows. The boiler was in the fore-end, and the machinery right astern. Over the whole there was a light roof, supported on stanchions. The funnel projected through that roof, and in front of the funnel a small cabin built of light planks served for a pilot-house. It contained a couch, two camp-stools, a loaded Martini-Henry leaning in one corner, a tiny table, and the steering-wheel. It had a wide door in front and a broad shutter at each side. All these were always thrown open, of course. I spent my days perched up there on the extreme fore-end of that roof, before the door. At night I slept, or tried to, on the couch. An athletic black belonging to some coast tribe and educated by my poor predecessor, was the helmsman. He sported a pair of brass earrings, wore a blue cloth wrapper from the waist to the ankles, and thought all the world of himself. He was the most unstable kind of fool I had ever seen. He steered with no end of a swagger while you were by; but if he lost sight of you, he became instantly the prey of an abject funk, and would let that cripple of a steamboat get the upper hand of him in a minute.

"I was looking down at the sounding-pole, and feeling much annoyed to see at each try a little more of it stick out of that river, when I saw my poleman give up the business suddenly, and stretch himself flat on the deck, without even taking the trouble to haul his pole in. He kept hold on it though, and it trailed in the water. At the same time the fireman, whom I could also see below me, sat down abruptly before his furnace and ducked his head. I was amazed. Then I had to look at the river mighty quick, because there was a snag in the fairway. Sticks, little sticks, were flying about—thick: they were whizzing before my nose, dropping below me, striking behind me against my pilot-house. All this time the river, the shore, the woods, were very quiet—perfectly quiet. I could only hear the heavy splashing thump of the stern-wheel and the patter of these things. We cleared the snag clumsily. Arrows, by Jove! We were being shot at! I stepped in quickly to close the shutter on the land-side. That fool-helmsman, his hands on the spokes, was lifting his knees high, stamping his feet, champing his mouth, like a reined-in horse. Confound him! And we were staggering within ten feet of the bank. I had to lean right out to swing the heavy shutter, and I saw a face amongst the leaves on the level with my own, looking at me very fierce and steady; and then suddenly, as though a veil had been removed from my eyes, I made out, deep in the tangled gloom, naked breasts, arms, legs, glaring eyes—the bush was swarming with human limbs in movement, glistening, of bronze colour. The twigs shook, swayed, and rustled, the arrows flew out of them, and then the shutter came to. 'Steer her straight,' I said to the helmsman. He held his head rigid, face forward; but his eyes rolled, he kept on lifting and setting down his feet gently, his mouth foamed a little. 'Keep quiet!' I said in a fury. I might just as well have ordered a tree not to sway in the wind. I darted out. Below me there was a great scuffle of feet on the iron deck; confused exclamations; a voice screamed, 'Can you turn back?' I caught sight of a V-shaped ripple on the water ahead. What? Another snag! A fusillade burst out under my feet. The pilgrims had opened with their Winchesters, and were simply squirting lead into that bush. A deuce of a lot of smoke came up and drove slowly forward. I swore at it. Now I couldn't see the ripple or the snag either. I stood in the doorway, peering, and the arrows came in swarms. They might have been poisoned, but they looked as though they wouldn't kill a cat. The bush began to howl. Our wood-cutters raised a warlike whoop; the report of a rifle just at my back deafened me. I glanced over my shoulder, and the pilot-house was yet full of noise and smoke when I made a dash at the wheel. The fool-nigger had dropped everything, to throw the shutter open and let off that Martini-Henry. He stood before the wide opening, glaring, and I yelled at him to come back, while I straightened the sudden twist out of that steamboat. There was no room to turn even if I had wanted to, the snag was somewhere very near ahead in that confounded smoke, there was no time to lose, so I just crowded her into the bank—right into the bank, where I knew the water was deep.

"We tore slowly along the overhanging bushes in a whirl of broken twigs and flying leaves. The fusil-lade below stopped short, as I had foreseen it would when the squirts got empty. I threw my head back to a glinting whizz that traversed the pilot-house, in at one shutter-hole and out at the other. Looking past that mad helmsman, who was shaking the empty rifle and yelling at the shore, I saw vague forms of men running bent double, leaping, gliding, distinct, incomplete, evanescent. Something big appeared in the air before the shutter, the rifle went overboard, and the man stepped back swiftly, looked at me over his shoulder in an extraordinary, profound, familiar manner, and fell upon my feet. The side of his head hit the wheel twice, and the end of what appeared a long cane clattered round and knocked over a little campstool. It looked as though after wrenching that thing from somebody ashore he had lost his balance in the effort. The thin smoke had blown away, we were clear of the snag, and looking ahead I could see that in another hundred yards or so I would be free to sheer off, away from the bank; but my feet felt so very warm and wet that I had to look down. The man had rolled on his back and stared straight up at me; both his hands clutched that cane. It was the shaft of a spear that, either thrown or lunged through the opening, had caught him in the side just below the ribs; the blade had gone in out of sight, after making a frightful gash; my shoes were full; a pool of blood lay very still, gleaming dark-red under the wheel; his eyes shone with an amazing lustre. The fusillade burst out again. He looked at me anxiously, gripping the spear like something precious, with an air of being afraid I would try to take it away from him. I had to make an effort to free my eyes from his gaze and attend to the steering. With one hand I felt above my head for the line of the steam whistle, and jerked out screech after screech hurriedly. The tumult of angry and warlike yells was checked instantly, and then from the depths of the woods went out such a tremulous and prolonged wail of mournful fear and utter despair as may be imagined to follow the flight of the last hope from the earth. There was a great commotion in the bush; the shower of arrows stopped, a few dropping shots rang out sharply—then silence, in which the languid beat of the stern-wheel came plainly to my ears. I put the helm hard a-starboard at the moment when the pilgrim in pink pyjamas, very hot and agitated, appeared in the doorway. 'The manager sends me——' he began in an official tone, and stopped short. 'Good God!' he said, glaring at the wounded man. —

"We two whites stood over him, and his lustrous and inquiring glance enveloped us both. I declare it looked as though he would presently put to us some question in an understandable language; but he died without uttering a sound, without moving a limb, without twitching a muscle. Only in the very last moment, as though in response to some sign we could not see, to some whisper we could not hear, he frowned heavily, and that frown gave to his black death-mask an inconceivably sombre, brooding, and menacing expression. The lustre of inquiring glance faded swiftly into vacant glassiness. 'Can you steer?' I asked the agent eagerly. He looked very dubious; but I made a grab at his arm, and he understood at once I meant him to steer whether or no. To tell you the truth, I was morbidly anxious to change my shoes and socks. 'He is dead,' murmured the fellow, immensely impressed. 'No doubt about it,' said I, tugging like mad at the shoe-laces. 'And by the way, I suppose Mr. Kurtz is dead as well by this time.'

"For the moment that was the dominant thought. There was a sense of extreme disappointment, as though I had found out I had been striving after some-

thing altogether without a substance. I couldn't have
been more disgusted if I had travelled all this way
for the sole purpose of talking with Mr. Kurtz. Talking with . . . I flung one shoe overboard, and became
aware that that was exactly what I had been looking
forward to—a talk with Kurtz. I made the strange
discovery that I had never imagined him as doing,
you know, but as discoursing. I didn't say to myself,
'Now I will never see him,' or 'Now I will never shake
him by the hand,' but, 'Now I will never hear him.'
The man presented himself as a voice. Not of course
that I did not connect him with some sort of action.
Hadn't I been told in all the tones of jealousy and
admiration that he had collected, bartered, swindled,
or stolen more ivory than all the other agents together? That was not the point. The point was in his
being a gifted creature, and that of all his gifts the
one that stood out preëminently, that carried with it
a sense of real presence, was his ability to talk, his
words—the gift of expression, the bewildering, the
illuminating, the most exalted and the most con-
temptible, the pulsating stream of light, or the deceit-
ful flow from the heart of an impenetrable darkness.

"The other shoe went flying unto the devil-god of
that river. I thought, 'By Jove! it's all over. We are
too late; he has vanished—the gift has vanished, by
means of some spear, arrow, or club. I will never hear
that chap speak after all'—and my sorrow had a startling extravagance of emotion, even such as I had
noticed in the howling sorrow of these savages in the
bush. I couldn't have felt more of lonely desolation
somehow, had I been robbed of a belief or had missed

my destiny in life. . . . Why do you sigh in this beastly way, somebody? Absurd? Well, absurd. Good Lord! mustn't a man ever—— Here, give me some tobacco." . . .

There was a pause of profound stillness, then a match flared, and Marlow's lean face appeared, worn, hollow, with downward folds and dropped eyelids, with an aspect of concentrated attention; and as he took vigorous draws at his pipe, it seemed to retreat and advance out of the night in the regular flicker of tiny flame. The match went out.

"Absurd!" he cried. "This is the worst of trying to tell. . . . Here you all are, each moored with two good addresses, like a hulk with two anchors, a butcher round one corner, a policeman round another, excellent appetites, and temperature normal—you hear—normal from year's end to year's end. And you say, Absurd! Absurd be—exploded! Absurd! My dear boys, what can you expect from a man who out of sheer nervousness had just flung overboard a pair of new shoes! Now I think of it, it is amazing I did not shed tears. I am, upon the whole, proud of my fortitude. I was cut to the quick at the idea of having lost the inestimable privilege of listening to the gifted Kurtz. Of course I was wrong. The privilege was waiting for me. Oh, yes, I heard more than enough. And I was right, too. A voice. He was very little more than a voice. And I heard—him—it—this voice—other voices—all of them were so little more than voices—and the memory of that time itself lingers around me, impalpable, like a dying vibration of one immense jabber, silly, atrocious, sordid, savage, or simply mean, without any kind of sense. Voices, voices—even the girl herself—now——"

He was silent for a long time.

"I laid the ghost of his gifts at last with a lie," he began, suddenly. "Girl! What? Did I mention a girl? Oh, she is out of it—completely. They—the women I mean—are out of it—should be out of it. We must help them to stay in that beautiful world of their own, lest ours gets worse. Oh, she had to be out of it. You should have heard the disinterred body of Mr. Kurtz saying, 'My Intended.' You would have perceived directly then how completely she was out of it. And the lofty frontal bone of Mr. Kurtz! They say the hair goes on growing sometimes, but this—ah—specimen, was impressively bald. The wilderness had patted him on the head, and, behold, it was like a ball —an ivory ball; it had caressed him, and—lo!—he had withered; it had taken him, loved him, embraced him, got into his veins, consumed his flesh, and sealed his soul to its own by the inconceivable ceremonies of some devilish initiation. He was its spoiled and pampered favourite. Ivory? I should think so. Heaps of it, stacks of it. The old mud shanty was bursting with it. You would think there was not a single tusk left either above or below the ground in the whole country. 'Mostly fossil,' the manager had remarked, disparagingly. It was no more fossil than I am; but they call it fossil when it is dug up. It appears these niggers do bury the tusks sometimes—but evidently they couldn't bury this parcel deep enough to save the gifted Mr. Kurtz from his fate. We filled the steamboat with it, and had to pile a lot on the deck. Thus he could see and enjoy as long as he could see, because the appreciation of this favour had remained with him to the last. You should have heard him say, 'My ivory.' Oh, yes, I heard him. 'My Intended, my ivory, my station, my river, my——' everything belonged to him. It made me hold my breath in expectation of hearing the wilderness burst into a prodigious peal of laughter that would shake the fixed stars in their places. Everything belonged to him—but that was a trifle. The thing was to know what he belonged to, how many powers of darkness claimed him for their own. That was the reflection that made you creepy all over. It was impossible—it was not good for one either —trying to imagine. He had taken a high seat amongst the devils of the land—I mean literally. You can't understand. How could you?—with solid pavement under your feet, surrounded by kind neighbours ready to cheer you or to fall on you, stepping delicately between the butcher and the policeman, in the holy terror of scandal and gallows and lunatic asylums—how can you imagine what particular region of the first ages a man's untrammelled feet may take him into by the way of solitude—utter solitude without a policeman—by the way of silence—utter silence, where no warning voice of a kind neighbour can be heard whispering of public opinion? These little things make all the great difference. When they are gone you must fall back upon your own innate strength, upon your own capacity for faithfulness. Of course you may be too much of a fool to go wrong— too dull even to know you are being assulted by the powers of darkness. I take it, no fool ever made a bargain for his soul with the devil; the fool is too much of a fool, or the devil too much of a devil —I don't know which. Or you may be such a thunderingly exalted creature as to be altogether deaf and blind to anything but heavenly sights and sounds. Then the earth for you is only a standing place—and whether to be like this is your loss or your gain I won't pretend to say. But most of us are neither one nor the other. The earth for us is a place to live in, where we must put up with sights, with sounds, with smells, too, by Jove!—breathe dead hippo, so to speak, and not be contaminated. And there, don't you see? Your strength comes in, the faith in your ability for the digging of unostentatious holes to bury the stuff in—your power of devotion, not to yourself, but to an obscure, back-breaking business. And that's difficult enough. Mind, I am not trying to excuse or even explain—I am trying to account to myself for—for—Mr. Kurtz—for the shade of Mr. Kurtz. This initiated wraith from the back of Nowhere honoured me with its amazing confidence before it vanished altogether. This was because it could speak English to me. The original Kurtz had been educated partly in England, and—as he was good enough to say himself—his sympathies were in the right place. His mother was half-English, his father was half-French. All Europe contributed to the making of Kurtz; and by and by I learned that, most appropriately, the International Society for the Suppression of Savage Customs had intrusted him with the making of a report, for its future guidance. And he had written it, too. I've seen it. I've read it. It was eloquent, vibrating with eloquence, but too high-strung, I think. Seventeen pages of close writing he had found time for! But this must have been before his—let us say—nerves, went wrong, and caused him to preside at certain midnight dances ending with unspeakable rites, which—as far as I reluctantly gathered from what I heard at various times—were offered up to him—do you understand?—to Mr. Kurtz himself. But it was a beautiful piece of writing. The opening paragraph, however, in the light of later information, strikes me now as ominous. He began with the argument that we whites, from the point of development we had arrived at, 'must necessarily appear to them [savages] in the nature of supernatural beings—we approach them with the might as of a deity,' and so on, and so on. 'By the simple exercise of our will we can exert a power for good practically unbounded,' etc., etc. From that point he soared and took me with him. The peroration was magnificent, though difficult to remember, you know. It gave me the notion of an exotic Immensity ruled by an august Benevolence. It made me tingle with enthusiasm. This was the unbounded power of eloquence—of words—of burning noble words. There were no practical hints to interrupt the magic current of phrases, unless a kind of note at the foot of the last page, scrawled evidently much later, in an unsteady hand, may be regarded as the exposition of a method. It was very simple, and at the end of that moving appeal to every altruistic sentiment it blazed at you, luminous and terrifying, like a flash of lightning in a serene sky: 'Exterminate all the brutes!' The curious part was that he had apparently forgotten all about that valuable postscriptum, because, later on, when he in a sense came to himself, he repeatedly entreated me to take good care of 'my pamphlet' (he called it), as it was sure to have in the future a good influence upon his career. I had full information about all these things, and, besides, as it turned out, I was to have the care of his memory. I've done enough for it to give me the indisputable right to lay it, if I choose, for an everlasting rest in the dust-bin of progress, amongst all the sweepings and, figuratively speaking, all the dead cats of civilization. But then, you see, I can't choose. He won't be forgotten. Whatever he was, he was not common. He had the power to charm or frighten rudimentary souls into an aggravated witch-dance in his honour; he could also fill the small souls of the pilgrims with bitter misgivings: he had one devoted friend at least, and he had conquered one soul in the world that was neither rudimentary nor tainted with self-seeking. No; I can't forget him, though I am not prepared to affirm the fellow was exactly worth the life we lost in getting to him. I missèd my late helmsman awfully—I missed him even while his body was still lying in the pilot-house. Perhaps you will think it passing strange this regret for a savage who was no more account than a grain of sand in a black Sahara. Well, don't you see, he had done something, he had steered; for months I had him at my back—a help—an instrument. It was a kind of partnership. He steered for me—I had to look after him, I worried about his deficiencies, and thus a subtle bond had been created, of which I only became aware

when it was suddenly broken. And the intimate profundity of that look he gave me when he received his
hurt remains to this day in my memory—like a claim
of distant kinship affirmed in a supreme moment.

"Poor fool! If he had only left that shutter alone.
He had no restraint, no restraint—just like Kurtz—a
tree swayed by the wind. As soon as I had put on a dry
pair of slippers, I dragged him out, after first jerking
the spear out of his side, which operation I confess I
performed with my eyes shut tight. His heels leaped
together over the little doorstep; his shoulders were
pressed to my breast; I hugged him from behind desperately. Oh! he was heavy, heavy; heavier than any
man on earth, I should imagine. Then without more
ado I tipped him overboard. The current snatched
him as though he had been a wisp of grass, and I saw
the body roll over twice before I lost sight of it for
ever. All the pilgrims and the manager were then
congregated on the awning-deck about the pilot-house,
chattering at each other like a flock of excited magpies,
and there was a scandalized murmur at my heartless
promptitude. What they wanted to keep that body
hanging about for I can't guess. Embalm it, maybe.
But I had also heard another, and a very ominous,
murmur on the deck below. My friends the wood-
cutters were likewise scandalized, and with a better
show of reason—though I admit that the reason itself
was quite inadmissible. Oh, quite! I had made up my
mind that if my late helmsman was to be eaten, the
fishes alone should have him. He had been a very
second-rate helmsman while alive, but now he was
dead he might have become a first-class temptation,

and possibly cause some startling trouble. Besides, I was anxious to take the wheel, the man in pink pyjamas showing himself a hopeless duffer at the business.

"This I did directly the simple funeral was over. We were going half-speed, keeping right in the middle of the stream, and I listened to the talk about me. They had given up Kurtz, they had given up the station; Kurtz was dead, and the station had been burnt—and so on—and so on. The red-haired pilgrim was beside himself with the thought that at least this poor Kurtz had been properly avenged. 'Say! We must have made a glorious slaughter of them in the bush. Eh? What do you think? Say?' He positively danced, the bloodthirsty little gingery beggar. And he had nearly fainted when he saw the wounded man! I could not help saying, 'You made a glorious lot of smoke, anyhow.' I had seen, from the way the tops of the bushes rustled and flew, that almost all the shots had gone too high. You can't hit anything unless you take aim and fire from the shoulder; but these chaps fired from the hip with their eyes shut. The retreat, I maintained—and I was right—was caused by the screeching of the steam whistle. Upon this they forgot Kurtz, and began to howl at me with indignant protests.

"The manager stood by the wheel murmuring confidentially about the necessity of getting well away down the river before dark at all events, when I saw in the distance a clearing on the riverside and the outlines of some sort of building. 'What's this?' I asked. He clapped his hands in wonder. 'The station!'

he cried. I edged in at once, still going half-speed.

"Through my glasses I saw the slope of a hill inter-
spersed with rare trees and perfectly free from undergrowth. A long decaying building on the summit was
half buried in the high grass; the large holes in the
peaked roof gaped black from afar; the jungle and
the woods made a background. There was no en-
closure or fence of any kind; but there had been one
apparently, for near the house half-a-dozen slim posts
remained in a row, roughly trimmed, and with their
upper ends ornamented with round carved balls. The
rails, or whatever there had been between, had disappeared. Of course the forest surrounded all that.
The river-bank was clear, and on the waterside I saw
a white man under a hat like a cartwheel beckoning
persistently with his whole arm. Examining the edge
of the forest above and below, I was almost certain I
could see movements—human forms gliding here and
there. I steamed past prudently, then stopped the
engines and let her drift down. The man on the shore
began to shout, urging us to land. 'We have been at-
tacked,' screamed the manager. 'I know—I know. It's
all right,' yelled back the other, as cheerful as you
please. 'Come along. It's all right. I am glad.'

"His aspect reminded me of something I had seen
—something funny I had seen somewhere. As I
manoeuvred to get alongside, I was asking myself,
'What does this fellow look like?' Suddenly I got it.
He looked like a harlequin. His clothes had been
made of some stuff that was brown holland probably,
but it was covered with patches all over, with bright
patches, blue, red, and yellow—patches on the back,

patches on the front, patches on elbows, on knees; coloured binding around his jacket, scarlet edging at the bottom of his trousers; and the sunshine made him look extremely gay and wonderfully neat withal, because you could see how beautifully all this patching had been done. A beardless, boyish face, very fair, no features to speak of, nose peeling, little blue eyes, smiles and frowns chasing each other over that open countenance like sunshine and shadow on a wind-swept plain. 'Look out, captain!' he cried; 'there's a snag lodged in here last night.' What! Another snag? I confess I swore shamefully. I had nearly holed my cripple, to finish off that charming trip. The harlequin on the bank turned his little pug-nose up to me. 'You English?' he asked, all smiles. 'Are you?' I shouted from the wheel. The smiles vanished, and he shook his head as if sorry for my disappointment. Then he brightened up. 'Never mind!' he cried encouragingly. 'Are we in time?' I asked. 'He is up there,' he replied, with a toss of the head up the hill, and becoming gloomy all of a sudden. His face was like the autumn sky, overcast one moment and bright the next.

"When the manager, escorted by the pilgrims, all of them armed to the teeth, had gone to the house this chap came on board. 'I say, I don't like this. These natives are in the bush,' I said. He assured me earnestly it was all right. 'They are simple people,' he added; 'well, I am glad you came. It took me all my time to keep them off.' 'But you said it was all right,' I cried. 'Oh, they meant no harm,' he said; and as I stared he corrected himself, 'Not exactly.' Then vivaciously, 'My faith, your pilot-house wants a clean-up!'

In the next breath he advised me to keep enough steam on the boiler to blow the whistle in case of any trouble. 'One good screech will do more for you than all your rifles. They are simple people,' he repeated. He rattled away at such a rate he quite overwhelmed me. He seemed to be trying to make up for lots of silence, and actually hinted, laughing, that such was the case. 'Don't you talk with Mr. Kurtz?' I said. 'You don't talk with that man—you listen to him,' he exclaimed with severe exaltation. 'But now——' He waved his arm, and in the twinkling of an eye was in the uttermost depths of despondency. In a moment he came up again with a jump, possessed himself of both my hands, shook them continuously, while he gabbled: 'Brother sailor . . . honour . . . pleasure . . . delight . . . introduce myself . . . Russian . . . son of an arch-priest . . . Government of Tambov . . . What? Tobacco! English tobacco; the excellent English tobacco! Now, that's brotherly. Smoke? Where's a sailor that does not smoke?'

"The pipe soothed him, and gradually I made out he had run away from school, had gone to sea in a Russian ship; ran away again; served some time in English ships; was now reconciled with the arch-priest. He made a point of that. 'But when one is young one must see things, gather experience, ideas; enlarge the mind.' 'Here!' I interrupted. 'You can never tell! Here I met Mr. Kurtz,' he said, youthfully solemn and reproachful. I held my tongue after that. It appears he had persuaded a Dutch trading-house on the coast to fit him out with stores and goods, and had started for the interior with a light heart and no more idea of what would happen to him than a baby. He had been wandering about that river for nearly two years alone, cut off from everybody and everything. 'I am not so young as I look. I am twenty-five,' he said. 'At first old Van Shuyten would tell me to go to the devil,' he narrated with keen enjoyment; 'but I stuck to him, and talked and talked, till at last he got afraid I would talk the hind-leg off his favourite dog, so he gave me some cheap things and a few guns, and told me he hoped he would never see my face again. Good old Dutchman, Van Shuyten. I've sent him one small lot of ivory a year ago, so that he can't call me a little thief when I get back. I hope he got it. And for the rest I don't care. I had some wood stacked for you. That was my old house. Did you see?'

"I gave him Towson's book. He made as though he would kiss me, but restrained himself. 'The only book I had left, and I thought I had lost it,' he said, looking at it ecstatically. 'So many accidents happen to a man going about alone, you know. Canoes get upset sometimes—and sometimes you've got to clear out so quick when the people get angry.' He thumbed the pages. 'You made notes in Russian?' I asked. He nodded. 'I thought they were written in cipher,' I said. He laughed, then became serious. 'I had lots of trouble to keep these people off,' he said. 'Did they want to kill you?' I asked. 'Oh, no!' he cried, and checked himself. 'Why did they attack us?' I pursued. He hesitated, then said shamefacedly, 'They don't want him to go.' 'Don't they?' I said curiously. He nodded a nod full of mystery and wisdom. 'I tell you,' he cried, 'this man has enlarged my mind.' He opened his arms wide, staring at me with his little blue eyes that were perfectly round."

III

"I looked at him, lost in astonishment. There he was before me, in motley, as though he had absconded from a troupe of mimes, enthusiastic, fabulous. His very existence was improbable, inexplicable, and altogether bewildering. He was an insoluble problem. It was inconceivable how he had existed, how he had succeeded in getting so far, how he had managed to remain—why he did not instantly disappear. 'I went a little farther,' he said, 'then still a little farther—till I had gone so far that I don't know how I'll ever get back. Never mind. Plenty time. I can manage. You take Kurtz away quick—quick—I tell you.' The glamour of youth enveloped his parti-coloured rags, his destitution, his loneliness, the essential desolation of his futile wanderings. For months—for years—his life hadn't been worth a day's purchase; and there he was gallantly, thoughtlessly alive, to all appearance indestructible solely by the virtue of his few years and of his unreflecting audacity. I was seduced into something like admiration—like envy. Glamour urged him on, glamour kept him unscathed. He surely wanted nothing from the wilderness but space to breathe in and to push on through. His need was to exist, and to move onwards at the greatest possible risk, and with a maximum of privation. If the absolutely pure, uncalculating, unpractical spirit of adventure had ever ruled a human being, it ruled this bepatched youth. I almost envied him the possession of this modest and clear flame. It seemed to have consumed all thought of self so completely, that even while he was talking to you, you forgot that it was he—the man before your eyes—who had gone through these things. I did not envy him his devotion to Kurtz, though. He had not meditated over it. It came to him, and he accepted it with a sort of eager fatalism. I must say that to me it appeared about the most dangerous thing in every way he had come upon so far.

"They had come together unavoidably, like two ships becalmed near each other, and lay rubbing sides at last. I suppose Kurtz wanted an audience, because on a certain occasion, when encamped in the forest, they had talked all night, or more probably Kurtz had talked. 'We talked of everything,' he said, quite transported at the recollection. 'I forgot there was such a thing as sleep. The night did not seem to last an hour. Everything! Everything! . . . Of love, too.' 'Ah, he talked to you of love!' I said, much amused. 'It isn't what you think,' he cried, almost passionately. 'It was in general. He made me see things—things.'

"He threw his arms up. We were on deck at the time, and the headman of my wood-cutters, lounging near by, turned upon him his heavy and glittering eyes. I looked around, and I don't know why, but I assure you that never, never before, did this land, this river, this jungle, the very arch of this blazing sky, appear to me so hopeless and so dark, so impenetrable to human thought, so pitiless to human weakness. 'And, ever since, you have been with him, of course?' I said.

"On the contrary. It appears their intercourse had been very much broken by various causes. He had, as he informed me proudly, managed to nurse Kurtz through two illnesses (he alluded to it as you would to some risky feat), but as a rule Kurtz wandered alone, far in the depths of the forest. 'Very often coming to this station, I had to wait days and days before he would turn up,' he said. 'Ah, it was worth waiting for!—sometimes.' 'What was he doing? exploring or what?' I asked. 'Oh, yes, of course'; he had discovered lots of villages, a lake, too—he did not know exactly in what direction; it was dangerous to inquire too much—but mostly his expeditions had been for ivory. 'But he had no goods to trade with by that time,' I objected. 'There's a good lot of cartridges left even yet,' he answered, looking away. 'To speak plainly, he raided the country,' I said. He nodded. 'Not alone, surely!' He muttered something about the villages round that lake. 'Kurtz got the tribe to follow him, did he?' I suggested. He fidgeted a little. 'They adored him,' he said. The tone of these words was so extraordinary that I looked at him searchingly. It was curious to see his mingled eagerness and reluctance to speak of Kurtz. The man filled his life, occupied his thoughts, swayed his emotions. 'What can you expect?' he burst out; 'he came to them with thunder and lightning, you know—and they had never seen anything like it—and very terrible. He could be very terrible. You can't judge Mr. Kurtz as you

would an ordinary man. No, no, no! Now—just to
give you an idea—I don't mind telling you, he wanted
to shoot me, too, one day—but I don't judge him.'
'Shoot you!' I cried 'What for?' 'Well, I had a small
lot of ivory the chief of that village near my house
gave me. You see I used to shoot game for them.
Well, he wanted it, and wouldn't hear reason. He
declared he would shoot me unless I gave him the
ivory and then cleared out of the country, because
he could do so, and had a fancy for it, and there was
nothing on earth to prevent him killing whom he
jolly well pleased. And it was true, too. I gave him
the ivory. What did I care! But I didn't clear out.
No, no. I couldn't leave him. I had to be careful,
of course, till we got friendly again for a time. He
had his second illness then. Afterwards I had to
keep out of the way; but I didn't mind. He was
living for the most part in those villages on the lake.
When he came down to the river, sometimes he would
take to me, and sometimes it was better for me to be
careful. This man suffered too much. He hated all
this, and somehow he couldn't get away. When I had
a chance I begged him to try and leave while there was
time; I offered to go back with him. And he would
say yes, and then he would remain; go off on another
ivory hunt; disappear for weeks; forget himself
amongst these people—forget himself—you know.'
'Why! he's mad,' I said. He protested indignantly.
Mr. Kurtz couldn't be mad. If I had heard him talk,
only two days ago, I wouldn't dare hint at such a
thing. . . . I had taken up my binoculars while we
talked, and was looking at the shore, sweeping the

limit of the forest at each side and at the back of the
house. The consciousness of there being people in that
bush, so silent, so quiet—as silent and quiet as the
ruined house on the hill—made me uneasy. There was
no sign on the face of nature of this amazing tale that
was not so much told as suggested to me in desolate
exclamations, completed by shrugs, in interrupted
phrases, in hints ending in deep sighs. The woods
were unmoved, like a mask—heavy, like the closed
door of a prison—they looked with their air of hidden
knowledge, of patient expectation, of unapproachable
silence. The Russian was explaining to me that it was
only lately that Mr. Kurtz had come down to the
river, bringing along with him all the fighting men
of that lake tribe. He had been absent for several
months—getting himself adored, I suppose—and had
come down unexpectedly, with the intention to all
appearance of making a raid either across the river or
down stream. Evidently the appetite for more ivory
had got the better of the—what shall I say?—less
material aspirations. However he had got much worse
suddenly. 'I heard he was lying helpless, and so I
came up—took my chance,' said the Russian. 'Oh, he
is bad, very bad.' I directed my glass to the house.
There were no signs of life, but there was the ruined
roof, the long mud wall peeping above the grass,
with three little square window-holes, no two of the
same size; all this brought within reach of my hand,
as it were. And then I made a brusque movement, and
one of the remaining posts of that vanished fence
leaped up in the field of my glass. You remember I
told you I had been struck at the distance by certain

attempts at ornamentation, rather remarkable in the ruinous aspect of the place. Now I had suddenly a nearer view, and its first result was to make me throw my head back as if before a blow. Then I went carefully from post to post with my glass, and I saw my mistake. These round knobs were not ornamental but symbolic; they were expressive and puzzling, striking and disturbing—food for thought and also for vultures if there had been any looking down from the sky; but at all events for such ants as were industrious enough to ascend the pole. They would have been even more impressive, those heads on the stakes, if their faces had not been turned to the house. Only one, the first I had made out, was facing my way. I was not so shocked as you may think. The start back I had given was really nothing but a movement of surprise. I had expected to see a knob of wood there, you know. I returned deliberately to the first I had seen—and there it was, black, dried, sunken, with closed eyelids—a head that seemed to sleep at the top of that pole, and, with the shrunken dry lips showing a narrow white line of the teeth, was smiling, too, smiling continuously at some endless and jocose dream of that eternal slumber.

"I am not disclosing any trade secrets. In fact, the manager said afterwards that Mr. Kurtz's methods had ruined the district. I have no opinion on that point, but I want you clearly to understand that there was nothing exactly profitable in these heads being there. They only showed that Mr. Kurtz lacked restraint in the gratification of his various lusts, that there was something wanting in him—some small

matter which, when the pressing need arose, could not
be found under his magnificent eloquence. Whether
he knew of his deficiency himself I can't say. I think
the knowledge came to him at last—only at the very
last. But the wilderness had found him out early, and
had taken on him a terrible vegeance for the fantastic
invasion. I think it had whispered to him things about
himself which he did not know, things of which he
had no conception till he took counsel with this great
solitude—and the whisper had proved irresistibly fascinating. It echoed loudly within him because he was
hollow at the core. . . . I put down the glass, and
the head that had appeared near enough to be spoken
to seemed at once to have leaped away from me into
inaccessible distance.

"The admirer of Mr. Kurtz was a bit crestfallen. In
a hurried, indistinct voice he began to assure me he had
not dared to take these—say, symbols—down. He was
not afraid of the natives; they would not stir till Mr.
Kurtz gave the word. His ascendancy was extraordinary. The camps of the people surrounded the
place, and the chiefs came every day to see him. They
would crawl. . . . 'I don't want to know anything of
the ceremonies used when approaching Mr. Kurtz,'
I shouted. Curious, this feeling that came over me
that such details would be more intolerable than
those heads drying on the stakes under Mr. Kurtz's
windows. After all, that was only a savage sight, while
I seemed at one bound to have been transported into
some lightless region of subtle horrors, where pure,
uncomplicated savagery was a positive relief, being
something that had a right to exist—obviously—in the

sunshine. The young man looked at me with surprise. I suppose it did not occur to him that Mr. Kurtz was no idol of mine. He forgot I hadn't heard any of these splendid monologues on, what was it? on love, justice, conduct of life—or what not. If it had come to crawling before Mr. Kurtz, he crawled as much as the veriest savage of them all. I had no idea of the conditions, he said: these heads were the heads of rebels. I shocked him excessively by laughing. Rebels! What would be the next definition I was to hear? There had been enemies, criminals, workers—and these were rebels. Those rebellious heads looked very subdued to me on their sticks. 'You don't know how such a life tries a man like Kurtz,' cried Kurtz's last disciple. 'Well, and you?' I said. 'I! I! I am a simple man. I have no great thoughts. I want nothing from anybody. How can you compare me to . . . ?' His feelings were too much for speech, and suddenly he broke down. 'I don't understand,' he groaned. 'I've been doing my best to keep him alive, and that's enough. I had no hand in all this. I have no abilities. There hasn't been a drop of medicine or a mouthful of invalid food for months here. He was shamefully abandoned. A man like this, with such ideas. Shamefully! Shamefully! I—I—haven't slept for the last ten nights . . .'

"His voice lost itself in the calm of the evening. The long shadows of the forest had slipped downhill while we talked, had gone far beyond the ruined hovel, beyond the symbolic row of stakes. All this was in the gloom, while we down there were yet in the sunshine, and the stretch of the river abreast of the clearing glittered in a still and dazzling splendour, with a murky and overshadowed bend above and below. Not a living soul was seen on the shore. The bushes did not rustle.

"Suddenly round the corner of the house a group of men appeared, as though they had come up from the ground. They waded waist-deep in the grass, in a compact body, bearing an improvised stretcher in their midst. Instantly, in the emptiness of the landscape, a cry arose whose shrillness pierced the still air like a sharp arrow flying straight to the very heart of the land; and, as if by enchantment, streams of human beings—of naked human beings—with spears in their hands, with bows, with shields, with wild glances and savage movements, were poured into the clearing by the dark-faced and pensive forest. The bushes shook, the grass swayed for a time, and then everything stood still in attentive immobility.

" 'Now, if he does not say the right thing to them we are all done for,' said the Russian at my elbow. The knot of men with the stretcher had stopped, too, halfway to the steamer, as if petrified. I saw the man on the stretcher sit up, lank and with an uplifted arm, above the shoulders of the bearers. 'Let us hope that the man who can talk so well of love in general will find some particular reason to spare us this time,' I said. I resented bitterly the absurd danger of our situation, as if to be at the mercy of that atrocious phantom had been a dishonouring necessity. I could not hear a sound, but through my glasses I saw the thin arm extended commandingly, the lower jaw moving, the eyes of that apparition shining darkly far in its

bony head that nodded with grotesque jerks. Kurtz—
Kurtz—that means short in German—don't it? Well,
the name was as true as everything else in his life—
and death. He looked at least seven feet long. His
covering had fallen off, and his body emerged from it
pitiful and appalling as from a winding-sheet. I could
see the cage of his ribs all astir, the bones of his arm
waving. It was as though an animated image of death
carved out of old ivory had been shaking its hand with
menaces at a motionless crowd of men made of dark
and glittering bronze. I saw him open his mouth wide
—it gave him a weirdly voracious aspect, as though he
had wanted to swallow all the air, all the earth, all the
men before him. A deep voice reached me faintly. He
must have been shouting. He fell back suddenly. The
stretcher shook as the bearers staggered forward
again, and almost at the same time I noticed that the
crowd of savages was vanishing without any percepti-
ble movement of retreat, as if the forest that had
ejected these beings so suddenly had drawn them in
again as the breath is drawn in a long aspiration.

"Some of the pilgrims behind the stretcher carried
his arms—two shot-guns, a heavy rifle, and a light
revolver-carbine—the thunderbolts of that pitiful
Jupiter. The manager bent over him murmuring as
he walked beside his head. They laid him down in one
of the little cabins—just a room for a bed place and a
camp-stool or two, you know. We had brought his
belated correspondence, and a lot of torn envelopes
and open letters littered his bed. His hand roamed
feebly amongst these papers. I was struck by the fire
of his eyes and the composed languor of his expres-

sion. It was not so much the exhaustion of disease. He did not seem in pain. This shadow looked satiated and calm, as though for the moment it had had its fill of all the emotions.

"He rustled one of the letters, and looking straight in my face said, 'I am glad.' Somebody had been writing to him about me. These special recommendations were turning up again. The volume of tone he emitted without effort, almost without the trouble of moving his lips, amazed me. A voice! a voice! It was grave, profound, vibrating, while the man did not seem capable of a whisper. However, he had enough strength in him—factitious no doubt—to very nearly make an end of us, as you shall hear directly.

"The manager appeared silently in the doorway; I stepped out at once and he drew the curtain after me. The Russian, eyed curiously by the pilgrims, was staring at the shore. I followed the direction of his glance.

"Dark human shapes could be made out in the distance, flitting indistinctly against the gloomy border of the forest, and near the river two bronze figures, leaning on tall spears, stood in the sunlight under fantastic head-dresses of spotted skins, warlike and still in statuesque repose. And from right to left along the lighted shore moved a wild and gorgeous apparition of a woman.

"She walked with measured steps, draped in striped and fringed clothes, treading the earth proudly, with a slight jingle and flash of barbarous ornaments. She carried her head high; her hair was done in the shape of a helmet; she had brass leggings to the knee, brass wire gauntlets to the elbow, a crimson spot on her tawny cheek, innumerable necklaces of glass beads on her neck; bizarre things, charms, gifts of witch-men, that hung about her, glittered and trembled at every step. She must have had the value of several elephant tusks upon her. She was savage and superb, wild-eyed and magnificent; there was something ominous and stately in her deliberate progress. And in the hush that had fallen suddenly upon the whole sorrowful land, the immense wilderness, the colossal body of the fecund and mysterious life seemed to look at her, pensive, as though it had been looking at the image of its own tenebrous and passionate soul.

"She came abreast of the steamer, stood still, and faced us. Her long shadow fell to the water's edge. Her face had a tragic and fierce aspect of wild sorrow and of dumb pain mingled with the fear of some struggling, half-shaped resolve. She stood looking at us without a stir, and like the wilderness itself, with an air of brooding over an inscrutable purpose. A whole minute passed, and then she made a step forward. There was a low jingle, a glint of yellow metal, a sway of fringed draperies, and she stopped as if her heart had failed her. The young fellow by my side growled. The pilgrims murmured at my back. She looked at us all as if her life had depended upon the unswerving steadiness of her glance. Suddenly she opened her bared arms and threw them up rigid above her head, as though in an uncontrollable desire to touch the sky, and at the same time the swift shadows darted out on the earth, swept around on the river, gathering the steamer into a shadowy embrace. A formidable silence hung over the scene.

"She turned away slowly, walked on, following the bank, and passed into the bushes to the left. Once only her eyes gleamed back at us in the dusk of the thickets before she disappeared.

" 'If she had offered to come aboard I really think I would have tried to shoot her,' said the man of patches, nervously. 'I have been risking my life every day for the last fortnight to keep her out of the house. She got in one day and kicked up a row about those miserable rags I picked up in the storeroom to mend my clothes with. I wasn't decent. At least it must have been that, for she talked like a fury to Kurtz for an hour, pointing at me now and then. I don't understand the dialect of this tribe. Luckily for me, I fancy Kurtz felt too ill that day to care, or there would have been mischief. I don't understand. . . . No—it's too much for me. Ah, well, it's all over now.'

"At this moment I heard Kurtz's deep voice behind the curtain: 'Save me!—save the ivory, you mean. Don't tell me. Save *me*! Why, I've had to save you. You are interrupting my plans now. Sick! Sick! Not so sick as you would like to believe. Never mind. I'll carry my ideas out yet—I will return. I'll show you what can be done. You with your little peddling notions—you are interfering with me. I will return. I. . . .'

"The manager came out. He did me the honour to take me under the arm and lead me aside. 'He is very low, very low,' he said. He considered it necessary to sigh, but neglected to be consistently sorrowful. 'We have done all we could for him—haven't we? But there is no disguising the fact, Mr. Kurtz has done more harm than good to the Company. He did not see the time was not ripe for vigorous action. Cautiously, cautiously—that's my principle. We must be cautious yet. The district is closed to us for a time. Deplorable! Upon the whole, the trade will suffer. I don't deny there is a remarkable quantity of ivory—mostly fossil. We must save it, at all events—but look how precarious the position is—and why? Because the method is unsound.' 'Do you,' said I, looking at the shore, 'call it "unsound method?" ' 'Without doubt,' he exclaimed hotly. 'Don't you?' . . . 'No method at all,' I murmured after a while. 'Exactly,' he exulted. 'I anticipated this. Shows a complete want of judgment. It is my duty to point it out in the proper quarter.' 'Oh,' said I, 'that fellow—what's his name?—the brickmaker, will make a readable report for you.' He appeared confounded for a moment. It seemed to me I had never breathed an atmosphere so vile, and I turned mentally to Kurtz for relief—positively for relief. 'Nevertheless I think Mr. Kurtz is a remarkable man,' I said with emphasis. He started, dropped on me a cold heavy glance, said very quietly, 'he *was*,' and turned his back on me. My hour of favour was over; I found myself lumped along with Kurtz as a partisan of methods for which the time was not ripe: I was unsound! Ah! but it was something to have at least a choice of nightmares.

"I had turned to the wilderness really, not to Mr. Kurtz, who, I was ready to admit, was as good as buried. And for a moment it seemed to me as if I also were buried in a vast grave full of unspeakable secrets. I felt an intolerable weight oppressing my breast, the

smell of the damp earth, the unseen presence of vic-
torious corruption, the darkness of an impenetrable
night. . . . The Russian tapped me on the shoulder.
I heard him mumbling and stammering something
about 'brother seaman—couldn't conceal—knowledge
of matters that would affect Mr. Kurtz's reputation.'
I waited. For him evidently Mr. Kurtz was not in his
grave; I suspect that for him Mr. Kurtz was one of
the immortals. 'Well!' said I at last, 'speak out. As it
happens, I am Mr. Kurtz's friend—in a way.'

"He stated with a good deal of formality that had
we not been 'of the same profession,' he would have
kept the matter to himself without regard to consequences. 'He suspected there was an active ill-will towards him on the part of these white men that——'
'You are right,' I said, remembering a certain conversation I had overheard. 'The manager thinks you
ought to be hanged.' He showed a concern at this
intelligence which amused me at first. 'I had better
get out of the way quietly,' he said earnestly. 'I can do
no more for Kurtz now, and they would soon find
some excuse. What's to stop them? There's a military
post three hundred miles from here.' 'Well, upon my
word,' said I, 'perhaps you had better go if you have
any friends amongst the savages near by.' 'Plenty,' he
said. 'They are simple people—and I want nothing,
you know.' He stood biting his lip, then: 'I don't want
any harm to happen to these whites here, but of course
I was thinking of Mr. Kurtz's reputation—but you
are a brother seaman and——' 'All right,' said I, after
a time. 'Mr. Kurtz's reputation is safe with me.' I did
not know how truly I spoke.

"He informed me, lowering his voice, that it was Kurtz who had ordered the attack to be made on the steamer. 'He hated sometimes the idea of being taken away—and then again. . . . But I don't understand these matters. I am a simple man. He thought it would scare you away—that you would give it up, thinking him dead. I could not stop him. Oh, I had an awful time of it this last month.' 'Very well,' I said. 'He is all right now.' 'Ye-e-es,' he muttered, not very convinced apparently. 'Thanks,' said I; 'I shall keep my eyes open.' 'But quiet—eh?' he urged anxiously. 'It would be awful for his reputation if anybody here——' I promised a complete discretion with great gravity. 'I have a canoe and three black fellows waiting not very far. I am off. Could you give me a few Martini-Henry cartridges?' I could, and did, with proper secrecy. He helped himself, with a wink at me, to a handful of my tobacco. 'Between sailors—you know—good English tobacco.' At the door of the pilot-house he turned round—'I say, haven't you a pair of shoes you could spare?' He raised one leg. 'Look.' The soles were tied with knotted strings sandalwise under his bare feet. I rooted out an old pair, at which he looked with admiration before tucking it under his left arm. One of his pockets (bright red) was bulging with cartridges, from the other (dark blue) peeped 'Towson's Inquiry,' etc., etc. He seemed to think himself excellently well equipped for a renewed encounter with the wilderness. 'Ah! I'll never, never meet such a man again. You ought to have heard him recite poetry—his own, too, it was, he told me. Poetry!' He rolled his eyes at the recollection of these delights. 'Oh, he enlarged my mind!' 'Good-bye,' said I. He shook hands and vanished in the night. Sometimes I ask myself whether I had ever really seen him—whether it was possible to meet such a phenomenon! . . .

"When I woke up shortly after midnight his warning came to my mind with its hint of danger that seemed, in the starred darkness, real enough to make me get up for the purpose of having a look round. On the hill a big fire burned, illuminating fitfully a crooked corner of the station-house. One of the agents with a picket of a few of our blacks, armed for the purpose, was keeping guard over the ivory; but deep within the forest, red gleams that wavered, that seemed to sink and rise from the ground amongst confused columnar shapes of intense blackness, showed the exact position of the camp where Mr. Kurtz's adorers were keeping their uneasy vigil. The monotonous beating of a big drum filled the air with muffled shocks and a lingering vibration. A steady droning sound of many men chanting each to himself some weird incantation came out from the black, flat wall of the woods as the humming of bees comes out of a hive, and had a strange narcotic effect upon my half-awake senses. I believe I dozed off leaning over the rail, till an abrupt burst of yells, an overwhelming outbreak of a pent-up and mysterious frenzy, woke me up in a bewildered wonder. It was cut short all at once, and the low droning went on with an effect of audible and soothing silence. I glanced casually into the little cabin. A light was burning within, but Mr. Kurtz was not there.

"I think I would have raised an outcry if I had believed my eyes. But I didn't believe them at first—the thing seemed so impossible. The fact is I was completely unnerved by a sheer blank fright, pure abstract terror, unconnected with any distinct shape of physical danger. What made this emotion so overpowering was—how shall I define it?—the moral shock I received, as if something altogether monstrous, intolerable to thought and odious to the soul, had been thrust upon me unexpectedly. This lasted of course the merest fraction of a second, and then the usual sense of commonplace, deadly danger, the possibility of a sudden onslaught and massacre, or something of the kind, which I saw impending, was positively welcome and composing. It pacified me, in fact, so much that I did not raise an alarm.

"There was an agent buttoned up inside an ulster and sleeping on a chair on deck within three feet of me. The yells had not awakened him; he snored very slightly; I left him to his slumbers and leaped ashore. I did not betray Mr. Kurtz—it was ordered I should never betray him—it was written I should be loyal to the nightmare of my choice. I was anxious to deal with this shadow by myself alone—and to this day I don't know why I was so jealous of sharing with any one the peculiar blackness of that experience.

"As soon as I got on the bank I saw a trail—a broad trail through the grass. I remember the exultation with which I said to myself, 'He can't walk—he is crawling on all-fours—I've got him.' The grass was wet with dew. I strode rapidly with clenched fists. I fancy I had some vague notion of falling upon him and giving him a drubbing. I don't know. I had some imbecile thoughts. The knitting old woman with the cat obtruded herself upon my memory as a most improper person to be sitting at the other end of such an affair. I saw a row of pilgrims squirting lead in the air out of Winchesters held to the hip. I thought I would never get back to the steamer, and imagined myself living alone and unarmed in the woods to an advanced age. Such silly things—you know. And I remember I confounded the beat of the drum with the beating of my heart, and was pleased at its calm regularity.

"I kept to the track though—then stopped to listen. The night was very clear; a dark blue space, sparkling with dew and starlight, in which black things stood very still. I thought I could see a kind of motion ahead of me. I was strangely cocksure of everything that night. I actually left the track and ran in a wide semicircle (I verily believe chuckling to myself) so as to get in front of that stir, of that motion I had seen —if indeed I had seen anything. I was circumventing Kurtz as though it had been a boyish game.

"I came upon him, and, if he had not heard me coming, I would have fallen over him, too, but he got up in time. He rose, unsteady, long, pale, indistinct, like a vapour exhaled by the earth, and swayed slightly, misty and silent before me; while at my back the fires loomed between the trees, and the murmur of many voices issued from the forest. I had cut him off cleverly; but when actually confronting him I seemed to come to my senses, I saw the danger in its right proportion. It was by no means over yet. Suppose he began to shout? Though he could hardly stand, there was still plenty of vigour in his voice. 'Go away—hide yourself,' he said, in that profound tone. It was very awful. I glanced back. We were within thirty yards from the nearest fire. A black figure stood up, strode on long black legs, waving long black arms, across the glow. It had horns—antelope horns, I think —on its head. Some sorcerer, some witch-man, no doubt: it looked fiendlike enough. 'Do you know what you are doing?' I whispered. 'Perfectly,' he answered, raising his voice for that single word: it sounded to me far off and yet loud, like a hail through a speaking-trumpet. 'If he makes a row we are lost,' I thought to myself. This clearly was not a case for fisticuffs, even apart from the very natural aversion I had to beat that Shadow—this wandering and tormented thing. 'You will be lost,' I said—'utterly lost.' One gets sometimes such a flash of inspiration, you know. I did say the right thing, though indeed he could not have been more irretrievably lost than he was at this very moment, when the foundations of our intimacy were being laid—to endure—to endure—even to the end— even beyond.

" 'I had immense plans,' he muttered irresolutely. 'Yes,' said I; 'but if you try to shout I'll smash your head with——' There was not a stick or a stone near. 'I will throttle you for good,' I corrected myself. 'I was on the threshold of great things,' he pleaded, in a voice of longing, with a wistfulness of tone that made my blood run cold. 'And now for this stupid scoundrel——' 'Your success in Europe is assured in any case,' I affirmed steadily. I did not want to have the throttling of him, you understand—and indeed it

would have been very little use for any practical purpose. I tried to break the spell—the heavy, mute spell
of the wilderness—that seemed to draw him to its
pitiless breast by the awakening of forgotten and
brutal instincts, by the memory of gratified and monstrous passions. This alone, I was convinced, had
driven him out to the edge of the forest, to the bush,
towards the gleam of fires, the throb of drums, the
drone of weird incantations; this alone had beguiled
his unlawful soul beyond the bounds of permitted
aspirations. And, don't you see, the terror of the position was not in being knocked on the head—though I
had a very lively sense of that danger, too—but in
this, that I had to deal with a being to whom I could
not appeal in the name of anything high or low. I had,
even like the niggers, to invoke him—himself—his
own exalted and incredible degradation. There was
nothing either above or below him, and I knew it. He
had kicked himself loose of the earth. Confound the
man! he had kicked the very earth to pieces. He was
alone, and I before him did not know whether I stood
on the ground or floated in the air. I've been telling
you what we said—repeating the phrases we pronounced—but what's the good? They were common
everyday words—the familiar, vague sounds exchanged on every waking day of life. But what of
that? They had behind them, to my mind, the terrific
suggestiveness of words heard in dreams, of phrases
spoken in nightmares. Soul! If anybody ever struggled
with a soul, I am the man. And I wasn't arguing with
a lunatic either. Believe me or not, his intelligence was
perfectly clear—concentrated, it is true, upon himself

with horrible intensity, yet clear; and therein was my
only chance—barring, of course, the killing him there
and then, which wasn't so good, on account of unavoidable noise. But his soul was mad. Being alone in
the wilderness, it had looked within itself, and, by
heavens! I tell you, it had gone mad. I had—for my
sins, I suppose—to go through the ordeal of looking
into it myself. No eloquence could have been so
withering to one's belief in mankind as his final burst
of sincerity. He struggled with himself, too. I saw it—
I heard it. I saw the inconceivable mystery of a soul
that knew no restraint, no faith, and no fear, yet struggling blindly with itself. I kept my head pretty well;
but when I had him at last stretched on the couch, I
wiped my forehead, while my legs shook under me as
though I had carried half a ton on my back down that
hill. And yet I had only supported him, his bony arm
clasped round my neck—and he was not much heavier
than a child.

"When next day we left at noon, the crowd, of
whose presence behind the curtain of trees I had been
acutely conscious all the time, flowed out of the woods
again, filled the clearing, covered the slope with a
mass of naked, breathing, quivering, bronze bodies. I
steamed up a bit, then swung down stream, and two
thousand eyes followed the evolutions of the splashing, thumping, fierce river-demon beating the water
with its terrible tail and breathing black smoke into
the air. In front of the first rank, along the river,
three men, plastered with bright red earth from head
to foot, strutted to and fro restlessly. When we came
abreast again, they faced the river, stamped their feet,

nodded their horned heads, swayed their scarlet bodies; they shook towards the fierce river-demon a bunch of black feathers, a mangy skin with a pendent tail—something that looked like a dried gourd; they shouted periodically together strings of amazing words that resembled no sounds of human language; and the deep murmurs of the crowd, interrupted suddenly, were like the responses of some satanic litany.

"We had carried Kurtz into the pilot-house: there was more air there. Lying on the couch, he stared through the open shutter. There was an eddy in the mass of human bodies, and the woman with helmeted head and tawny cheeks rushed out to the very brink of the stream. She put out her hands, shouted something, and all that wild mob took up the shout in a roaring chorus of articulated, rapid, breathless utterance.

" 'Do you understand this?' I asked.

"He kept on looking out past me with fiery, longing eyes, with a mingled expression of wistfulness and hate. He made no answer, but I saw a smile, a smile of indefinable meaning, appearing on his colourless lips that a moment after twitched convulsively. 'Do I not?' he said slowly, gasping, as if the words had been torn out of him by a supernatural power.

"I pulled the string of the whistle, and I did this because I saw the pilgrims on deck getting out their rifles with an air of anticipating a jolly lark. At the sudden screech there was a movement of abject terror through that wedged mass of bodies. 'Don't! don't you frighten them away,' cried some one on deck disconsolately. I pulled the string time after time. They broke and ran, they leaped, they crouched, they swerved, they dodged the flying terror of the sound. The three red chaps had fallen flat, face down on the shore, as though they had been shot dead. Only the barbarous and superb woman did not so much as flinch, and stretched tragically her bare arms after us over the sombre and glittering river.

"And then that imbecile crowd down on the deck started their little fun, and I could see nothing more for smoke.

"The brown current ran swiftly out of the heart of darkness, bearing us down towards the sea with twice the speed of our upward progress; and Kurtz's life was running swiftly, too, ebbing, ebbing out of his heart into the sea of inexorable time. The manager was very placid, he had no vital anxieties now, he took us both in with a comprehensive and satisfied glance: the 'affair' had come off as well as could be wished. I saw the time approaching when I would be left alone of the party of 'unsound method.' The pilgrims looked upon me with disfavour. I was, so to speak, numbered with the dead. It is strange how I accepted this unforeseen partnership, this choice of nightmares forced upon me in the tenebrous land invaded by these mean and greedy phantoms.

"Kurtz discoursed. A voice! a voice! It rang deep to the very last. It survived his strength to hide in the magnificent folds of eloquence the barren darkness of his heart. Oh, he struggled! he struggled! The wastes of his weary brain were haunted by shadowy images now—images of wealth and fame revolving obse-

quiously round his unextinguishable gift of noble and
lofty expression. My Intended, my station, my career,
my ideas—these were the subjects for the occasional
utterances of elevated sentiments. The shade of the
original Kurtz frequented the bedside of the hollow
sham, whose fate it was to be buried presently in the
mould of primeval earth. But both the diabolic love
and the unearthly hate of the mysteries it had penetrated fought for the possession of that soul satiated
with primitive emotions, avid of lying fame, of sham
distinction, of all the appearances of success and power.

"Sometimes he was contemptibly childish. He desired to have kings meet him at railway-stations on his
return from some ghastly Nowhere, where he intended to accomplish great things. 'You show them
you have in you something that is really profitable,
and then there will be no limits to the recognition of
your ability,' he would say. 'Of course you must take
care of the motives—right motives—always.' The
long reaches that were like one and the same reach,
monotonous bends that were exactly alike, slipped
past the steamer with their multitude of secular trees
looking patiently after this grimy fragment of another world, the forerunner of change, of conquest,
of trade, of massacres, of blessings. I looked ahead—
piloting. 'Close the shutter,' said Kurtz suddenly one
day; 'I can't bear to look at this.' I did so. There was
a silence. 'Oh, but I will wring your heart yet!' he
cried at the invisible wilderness.

"We broke down—as I had expected—and had to
lie up for repairs at the head of an island. This delay
was the first thing that shook Kurtz's confidence. One

morning he gave me a packet of papers and a photo-
graph—the lot tied together with a shoe-string. 'Keep
this for me,' he said. 'This noxious fool' (meaning the
manager) 'is capable of prying into my boxes when I
am not looking.' In the afternoon I saw him. He was
lying on his back with closed eyes, and I withdrew
quietly, but I heard him mutter, 'Live rightly, die, die
. . .' I listened. There was nothing more. Was he
rehearsing some speech in his sleep, or was it a fragment of a phrase from some newspaper article? He
had been writing for the papers and meant to do so
again, 'for the furthering of my ideas. It's a duty.'

"His was an impenetrable darkness. I looked at him
as you peer down at a man who is lying at the bottom
of a precipice where the sun never shines. But I had
not much time to give him, because I was helping the
engine-driver to take to pieces the leaky cylinders, to
straighten a bent connecting-rod, and in other such
matters. I lived in an infernal mess of rust, filings,
nuts, bolts, spanners, hammers, ratchet-drills—things
I abominate, because I don't get on with them. I
tended the little forge we fortunately had aboard; I
toiled wearily in a wretched scrap-heap—unless I had
the shakes too bad to stand.

"One evening coming in with a candle I was startled to hear him say a little tremulously, 'I am lying
here in the dark waiting for death.' The light was
within a foot of his eyes. I forced myself to murmur,
'Oh, nonsense!' and stood over him as if transfixed.

"Anything approaching the change that came over
his features I have never seen before, and hope never
to see again. Oh, I wasn't touched. I was fascinated.

It was as though a veil had been rent. I saw on that ivory face the expression of sombre pride, of ruthless power; of craven terror—of an intense and hopeless despair. Did he live his life again in every detail of desire, temptation, and surrender during that supreme moment of complete knowledge? He cried in a whisper at some image, at some vision—he cried out twice, a cry that was no more than a breath:

" 'The horror! The horror!'

"I blew the candle out and left the cabin. The pilgrims were dining in the mess-room, and I took my place opposite the manager, who lifted his eyes to give me a questioning glance, which I successfully ignored. He leaned back, serene, with that peculiar smile of his sealing the unexpressed depths of his meanness. A continuous shower of small flies streamed upon the lamp, upon the cloth, upon our hands and faces. Suddenly the manager's boy put his insolent black head in the doorway, and said in a tone of scathing contempt:

" 'Mistah Kurtz—he dead.'

"All the pilgrims rushed out to see. I remained, and went on with my dinner. I believe that I was considered brutally callous. However, I did not eat much. There was a lamp in there—light, don't you know—and outside it was so beastly, beastly dark. I went no more near the remarkable man who had pronounced a judgment upon the adventures of his soul on this earth. The voice was gone. What else had been there? But I am of course aware that next day the pilgrims buried something in a muddy hole.

"And then they very nearly buried me.

"However, as you see, I did not go to join Kurtz
there and then. I did not. I remained to dream the
nightmare out to the end, and to show my loyalty to
Kurtz once more. Destiny. My destiny! Droll thing
life is—that mysterious arrangement of merciless logic
for a futile purpose. The most you can hope from it
is some knowledge of yourself—that comes too late—
a crop of unextinguishable regrets. I have wrestled
with death. It is the most unexciting contest you can
imagine. It takes place in an impalpable greyness,
with nothing underfoot, with nothing around, without
spectators, without clamour, without glory, without
the great desire of victory, without the great fear of
defeat, in a sickly atmosphere of tepid scepticism,
without much belief in your own right, and still less
in that of your adversary. If such is the form of ultimate wisdom, then life is a greater riddle than some
of us think it to be. I was within a hair's breadth of the
last opportunity for pronouncement, and I found with
humiliation that probably I would have nothing to
say. This is the reason why I affirm that Kurtz was a
remarkable man. He had something to say. He said
it. Since I had peeped over the edge myself, I understand better the meaning of his stare, that could not
see the flame of the candle, but was wide enough to
embrace the whole universe, piercing enough to pene-
trate all the hearts that beat in the darkness. He had
summed up—he had judged. 'The horror!' He was a
remarkable man. After all, this was the expression of
some sort of belief; it had candour, it had conviction,
it had a vibrating note of revolt in its whisper, it had
the appalling face of a glimpsed truth—the strange

commingling of desire and hate. And it is not my own extremity I remember best—a vision of greyness without form filled with physical pain, and a careless contempt for the evanescence of all things—even of this pain itself. No! It is his extremity that I seem to have lived through. True, he had made that last stride, he had stepped over the edge, while I had been permitted to draw back my hesitating foot. And perhaps in this is the whole difference; perhaps all the wisdom, and all truth, and all sincerity, are just compressed into that inappreciable moment of time in which we step over the threshold of the invisible. Perhaps! I like to think my summing-up would not have been a word of careless contempt. Better his cry—much better. It was an affirmation, a moral victory paid for by innumerable defeats, by abominable terrors, by abominable satisfactions. But it was a victory! That is why I have remained loyal to Kurtz to the last, and even beyond, when a long time after I heard once more, not his own voice, but the echo of his magnificent eloquence thrown to me from a soul as translucently pure as a cliff of crystal.

"No, they did not bury me, though there is a period of time which I remember mistily, with a shuddering wonder, like a passage through some inconceivable world that had no hope in it and no desire. I found myself back in the sepulchral city resenting the sight of people hurrying through the streets to filch a little money from each other, to devour their infamous cookery, to gulp their unwholesome beer, to dream their insignificant and silly dreams. They trespassed upon my thoughts. They were intruders whose knowledge of life was to me an irritating pretence, because I felt so sure they could not possibly know the things I knew. Their bearing, which was simply the bearing of commonplace individuals going about their business in the assurance of perfect safety, was offensive to me like the outrageous flauntings of folly in the face of a danger it is unable to comprehend. I had no particular desire to enlighten them, but I had some difficulty in restraining myself from laughing in their faces so full of stupid importance. I daresay I was not very well at that time. I tottered about the streets—there were various affairs to settle—grinning bitterly at perfectly respectable persons. I admit my behaviour was inexcusable, but then my temperature was seldom normal in these days. My dear aunt's endeavours to 'nurse up my strength' seemed altogether beside the mark. It was not my strength that wanted nursing, it was my imagination that wanted soothing. I kept the bundle of papers given me by Kurtz, not knowing exactly what to do with it. His mother had died lately, watched over, as I was told, by his Intended. A clean-shaved man, with an official manner and wearing gold-rimmed spectacles, called on me one day and made inquiries, at first circuitous, afterwards suavely pressing, about what he was pleased to denominate certain 'documents.' I was not surprised, because I had had two rows with the manager on the subject out there. I had refused to give up the smallest scrap out of that package, and I took the same attitude with the spectacled man. He became darkly menacing at last, and with much heat argued that the Company had the right to every bit of information about its 'territories.'

And said he, 'Mr. Kurtz's knowledge of unexplored regions must have been necessarily extensive and peculiar—owing to his great abilities and to the deplorable circumstances in which he had been placed: therefore——' I assured him Mr. Kurtz's knowledge, however extensive, did not bear upon the problems of commerce or administration. He invoked then the name of science. 'It would be an incalculable loss if,' etc., etc. I offered him the report on the 'Suppression of Savage Customs,' with the postscriptum torn off. He took it up eagerly, but ended by sniffing at it with an air of contempt. 'This is not what we had a right to expect,' he remarked. 'Expect nothing else,' I said. 'There are only private letters.' He withdrew upon some threat of legal proceedings, and I saw him no more; but another fellow, calling himself Kurtz's cousin, appeared two days later, and was anxious to hear all the details about his dear relative's last moments. Incidentally he gave me to understand that Kurtz had been essentially a great musician. 'There was the making of an immense success,' said the man, who was an organist, I believe, with lank grey hair flowing over a greasy coat-collar. I had no reason to doubt his statement; and to this day I am unable to say what was Kurtz's profession, whether he ever had any—which was the greatest of his talents. I had taken him for a painter who wrote for the papers, or else for a journalist who could paint—but even the cousin (who took snuff during the interview) could not tell me what he had been—exactly. He was a universal genius—on that point I agreed with the old chap, who thereupon blew his nose noisily into a large cotton handkerchief and withdrew in senile agitation, bearing off some family letters and memoranda without importance. Ultimately a journalist anxious to know something of the fate of his 'dear colleague' turned up. This visitor informed me Kurtz's proper sphere ought to have been politics 'on the popular side.' He had furry straight eyebrows, bristly hair cropped short, an eyeglass on a broad ribbon, and, becoming expansive, confessed his opinion that Kurtz really couldn't write a bit—'but heavens! how that man could talk. He electrified large meetings. He had faith—don't you see?—he had the faith. He could get himself to believe anything—anything. He would have been a splendid leader of an extreme party.' 'What party?' I asked. 'Any party,' answered the other. 'He was an—an—extremist.' Did I not think so? I assented. Did I know, he asked, with a sudden flash of curiosity, 'what it was that had induced him to go out there?' 'Yes,' said I, and forthwith handed him the famous Report for publication, if he thought fit. He glanced through it hurriedly, mumbling all the time, judged 'it would do,' and took himself off with this plunder.

"Thus I was left at last with a slim packet of letters and the girl's portrait. She struck me as beautiful —I mean she had a beautiful expression. I know that the sunlight can be made to lie, too, yet one felt that no manipulation of light and pose could have conveyed the delicate shade of truthfulness upon those features. She seemed ready to listen without mental reservation, without suspicion, without a thought for herself. I concluded I would go and give her back her

portrait and those letters myself. Curiosity? Yes; and
also some other feeling perhaps. All that had been
Kurtz's had passed out of my hands: his soul, his
body, his station, his plans, his ivory, his career. There
remained only his memory and his Intended—and I
wanted to give that up, too, to the past, in a way—to
surrender personally all that remained of him with
me to that oblivion which is the last word of our
common fate. I don't defend myself. I had no clear
perception of what it was I really wanted. Perhaps it
was an impulse of unconscious loyalty, or the fulfil-
ment of one of those ironic necessities that lurk in the
facts of human existence. I don't know. I can't tell.
But I went.

"I thought his memory was like the other memories of the dead that accumulate in every man's life—
a vague impress on the brain of shadows that had
fallen on it in their swift and final passage; but before
the high and ponderous door, between the tall houses
of a street as still and decorous as a well-kept alley in
a cemetery, I had a vision of him on the stretcher,
opening his mouth voraciously, as if to devour all the
earth with all its mankind. He lived then before me;
he lived as much as he had ever lived—a shadow in-
satiable of splendid appearances, of frightful realities;
a shadow darker than the shadow of the night, and
draped nobly in the folds of a gorgeous eloquence.
The vision seemed to enter the house with me—the
stretcher, the phantom-bearers, the wild crowd of
obedient worshippers, the gloom of the forests, the
glitter of the reach between the murky bends, the beat
of the drum, regular and muffled like the beating of a

heart—the heart of a conquering darkness. It was a moment of triumph for the wilderness, an invading and vengeful rush which, it seemed to me, I would have to keep back alone for the salvation of another soul. And the memory of what I had heard him say afar there, with the horned shapes stirring at my back, in the glow of fires, within the patient woods, those broken phrases came back to me, were heard again in their ominous and terrifying simplicity. I remembered his abject pleading, his abject threats, the colossal scale of his vile desires, the meanness, the torment, the tempestuous anguish of his soul. And later on I seemed to see his collected languid manner, when he said one day, 'This lot of ivory now is really mine. The Company did not pay for it. I collected it myself at a very great personal risk. I am afraid they will try to claim it as theirs though. H'm. It is a difficult case. What do you think I ought to do—resist? Eh? I want no more than justice.' . . . He wanted no more than justice—no more than justice. I rang the bell before a mahogany door on the first floor, and while I waited he seemed to stare at me out of the glassy panel—stare with that wide and immense stare embracing, condemning, loathing all the universe. I seemed to hear the whispered cry, 'The horror! The horror!'

"The dusk was falling. I had to wait in a lofty drawingroom with three long windows from floor to ceiling that were like three luminous and bedraped columns. The bent gilt legs and backs of the furniture shone in indistinct curves. The tall marble fireplace had a cold and monumental whiteness. A grand piano stood massively in a corner; with dark gleams on the flat surfaces like a sombre and polished sarcophagus. A high door opened—closed. I rose.

"She came forward, all in black, with a pale head, floating towards me in the dusk. She was in mourning. It was more than a year since his death, more than a year since the news came; she seemed as though she would remember and mourn forever. She took both my hands in hers and murmured, 'I had heard you were coming.' I noticed she was not very young—I mean not girlish. She had a mature capacity for fidelity, for belief, for suffering. The room seemed to have grown darker, as if all the sad light of the cloudy evening had taken refuge on her forehead. This fair hair, this pale visage, this pure brow, seemed surrounded by an ashy halo from which the dark eyes looked out at me. Their glance was guileless, profound, confident, and trustful. She carried her sorrowful head as though she were proud of that sorrow, as though she would say, 'I—I alone know how to mourn for him as he deserves.' But while we were still shaking hands, such a look of awful desolation came upon her face that I perceived she was one of those creatures that are not the playthings of Time. For her he had died only yesterday. And, by Jove! the impression was so powerful that for me, too, he seemed to have died only yesterday—nay, this very minute. I saw her and him in the same instant of time—his death and her sorrow—I saw her sorrow in the very moment of his death. Do you understand? I saw them together—I heard them together. She had said, with a deep catch of the breath, 'I have survived' while my strained ears seemed to hear distinctly, mingled with her tone of despairing regret, the summing up whisper of his eternal condemnation. I asked myself what I was doing there, with a sensation of panic in my heart as though I had blundered into a place of cruel and absurd mysteries not fit for a human being to behold. She motioned me to a chair. We sat down. I laid the packet gently on the little table, and she put her hand over it. . . . 'You knew him well,' she murmured, after a moment of mourning silence.

" 'Intimacy grows quickly out there,' I said. 'I knew him as well as it is possible for one man to know another.'

" 'And you admired him,' she said. 'It was impossible to know him and not to admire him. Was it?'

" 'He was a remarkable man,' I said, unsteadily. Then before the appealing fixity of her gaze, that seemed to watch for more words on my lips, I went on, 'It was impossible not to——'

" 'Love him,' she finished eagerly, silencing me into an appalled dumbness. 'How true! how true! But when you think that no one knew him so well as I! I had all his noble confidence. I knew him best.'

" 'You knew him best,' I repeated. And perhaps she did. But with every word spoken the room was growing darker, and only her forehead, smooth and white, remained illumined by the unextinguishable light of belief and love.

" 'You were his friend,' she went on. 'His friend,' she repeated, a little louder. 'You must have been, if he had given you this, and sent you to me. I feel I can speak to you—and oh! I must speak. I want you—you who have heard his last words—to know I have been worthy of him. . . . It is not pride. . . . Yes! I am proud to know I understood him better than any one on earth—he told me so himself. And since his mother died I have had no one—no one—to—to——'

"I listened. The darkness deepened. I was not even sure whether he had given me the right bundle. I rather suspect he wanted me to take care of another batch of his papers which, after his death, I saw the manager examining under the lamp. And the girl talked, easing her pain in the certitude of my sympathy; she talked as thirsty men drink. I had heard that her engagement with Kurtz had been disapproved by her people. He wasn't rich enough or something. And indeed I don't know whether he had not been a pauper all his life. He had given me some reason to infer that it was his impatience of comparative poverty that drove him out there.

" '. . . Who was not his friend who had heard him speak once?' she was saying. 'He drew men towards him by what was best in them.' She looked at me with intensity. 'It is the gift of the great,' she went on, and the sound of her low voice seemed to have the accompaniment of all the other sounds, full of mystery, desolation, and sorrow, I had ever heard—the ripple of the river, the soughing of the trees swayed by the wind, the murmurs of the crowds, the faint ring of incomprehensible words cried from afar, the whisper of a voice speaking from beyond the threshold of an eternal darkness. 'But you have heard him! You know!' she cried.

" 'Yes, I know,' I said with something like despair in my heart, but bowing my head before the faith that was in her, before that great and saving illusion that shone with an unearthly glow in the darkness, in the triumphant darkness from which I could not have defended her—from which I could not even defend myself.

" 'What a loss to me—to us!'—she corrected herself with beautiful generosity; then added in a murmur, 'To the world.' By the last gleams of twilight I could see the glitter of her eyes, full of tears—of tears that would not fall.

" 'I have been very happy—very fortunate—very proud,' she went on. 'Too fortunate. Too happy for a little while. And now I am unhappy for—for life.'

"She stood up; her fair hair seemed to catch all the remaining light in a glimmer of gold. I rose, too.

" 'And of all this,' she went on mournfully, 'of all his promise, and of all his greatness, of his generous mind, of his noble heart, nothing remains—nothing but a memory. You and I——'

" 'We shall always remember him,' I said hastily.

" 'No!' she cried. 'It is impossible that all this should be lost—that such a life should be sacrificed to leave nothing—but sorrow. You know what vast plans he had. I knew of them, too—I could not perhaps understand—but others knew of them. Something must remain. His words, at least, have not died.'

" 'His words will remain,' I said.

" 'And his example,' she whispered to herself. 'Men looked up to him—his goodness shone in every act. His example——'

" 'True,' I said; 'his example, too. Yes, his example. I forgot that.'

" 'But I do not. I cannot—I cannot believe—not yet. I cannot believe that I shall never see him again, that nobody will see him again, never, never, never.'

"She put out her arms as if after a retreating figure, stretching them back and with clasped pale hands across the fading and narrow sheen of the window. Never see him! I saw him clearly enough then. I shall see this eloquent phantom as long as I live, and I shall see her, too, a tragic and familiar Shade, resembling in this gesture another one, tragic also, and bedecked with powerless charms, stretching bare brown arms over the glitter of the infernal stream, the stream of darkness. She said suddenly very low, 'He died as he lived.'

" 'His end,' said I, with dull anger stirring in me, 'was in every way worthy of his life.'

" 'And I was not with him,' she murmured. My anger subsided before a feeling of infinite pity.

" 'Everything that could be done——' I mumbled.

" 'Ah, but I believed in him more than any one on earth—more than his own mother, more than—himself. He needed me! Me! I would have treasured every sigh, every word, every sign, every glance.'

"I felt like a chill grip on my chest. 'Don't,' I said, in a muffled voice.

" 'Forgive me. I—I have mourned so long in silence—in silence. . . . You were with him—to the last? I think of his loneliness. Nobody near to understand him as I would have understood. Perhaps no one to hear. . . .'

" 'To the very end,' I said, shakily. 'I heard his very last words. . . .' I stopped in a fright.

" 'Repeat them,' she murmured in a heart-broken tone. 'I want—I want—something—something—to—to live with.'

"I was on the point of crying at her, 'Don't you hear them?' The dusk was repeating them in a persistent whisper all around us, in a whisper that seemed to swell menacingly like the first whisper of a rising wind. 'The horror! The horror!'

" 'His last word—to live with,' she insisted. 'Don't you understand I loved him—I loved him—I loved him!'

"I pulled myself together and spoke slowly.

" 'The last word he pronounced was—your name.'

"I heard a light sigh and then my heart stood still, stopped dead short by an exulting and terrible cry, by the cry of inconceivable triumph and of unspeakable pain. 'I knew it—I was sure!' . . . She knew. She was sure. I heard her weeping; she had hidden her face in her hands. It seemed to me that the house would collapse before I could escape, that the heavens would fall upon my head. But nothing happened. The heavens do not fall for such a trifle. Would they have fallen, I wonder, if I had rendered Kurtz that justice which was his due? Hadn't he said he wanted only justice? But I couldn't. I could not tell her. It would have been too dark—too dark altogether. . . ."

Marlow ceased, and sat apart, indistinct and silent, in the pose of a meditating Buddha. Nobody moved for a time. "We have lost the first of the ebb," said the Director suddenly. I raised my head. The offing was barred by a black bank of clouds, and the tranquil waterway leading to the uttermost ends of the earth flowed sombre under an overcast sky—seemed to lead into the heart of an immense darkness.

THE SECRET
SHARER

I

On my right hand there were lines of fishing stakes resembling a mysterious system of half-submerged bamboo fences, incomprehensible in its division of the domain of tropical fishes, and crazy of aspect as if abandoned for ever by some nomad tribe of fishermen now gone to the other end of the ocean; for there was no sign of human habitation as far as the eye could reach. To the left a group of barren islets, suggesting ruins of stone walls, towers, and blockhouses, had its foundations set in a blue sea that itself looked solid, so still and stable did it lie below my feet; even the track of light from the westering sun shone smoothly, without that animated glitter which tells of an imperceptible ripple. And when I turned my head to take a parting glance at the tug which had just left us anchored outside the bar, I saw the straight line of the flat shore joined to the stable sea, edge to edge, with a perfect and unmarked closeness, in one leveled floor half brown, half blue under the enormous dome of the sky. Corresponding in their insignificance to the islets of the sea, two small clumps of trees, one on each side of the only fault in the impeccable joint, marked the mouth of the river Meinam we had just left on the first preparatory stage of our homeward journey; and, far back on the inland level, a larger and loftier mass, the grove surrounding the great Paknam pagoda, was the only thing on which the eye could rest from the vain task of exploring the monoto-

nous sweep of the horizon. Here and there gleams as
of a few scattered pieces of silver marked the windings
of the great river; and on the nearest of them, just
within the bar, the tug steaming right into the land became lost to my sight, hull and funnel and masts, as
though the impassive earth had swallowed her up
without an effort, without a tremor. My eye followed
the light cloud of her smoke, now here, now there,
above the plain, according to the devious curves of the
stream, but always fainter and farther away, till I
lost it at last behind the miter-shaped hill of the great
pagodas. And then I was left alone with my ship,
anchored at the head of the Gulf of Siam.

She floated at the starting point of a long journey,
very still in an immense stillness, the shadows of her
spars flung far to the eastward by the setting sun. At
that moment I was alone on her decks. There was not
a sound in her—and around us nothing moved, nothing lived, not a canoe on the water, not a bird in the
air, not a cloud in the sky. In this breathless pause at
the threshold of a long passage we seemed to be
measuring our fitness for a long and arduous enterprise, the appointed task of both our existences to be
carried out, far from all human eyes, with only sky
and sea for spectators and for judges.

There must have been some glare in the air to interfere with one's sight, because it was only just before
the sun left us that my roaming eyes made out beyond
the highest ridges of the principal islet of the group
something which did away with the solemnity of
perfect solitude. The tide of darkness flowed on
swiftly; and with tropical suddenness a swarm of

stars came out above the shadowy earth, while I lingered yet, my hand resting lightly on my ship's rail as if on the shoulder of a trusted friend. But, with all that multitude of celestial bodies staring down at one, the comfort of quiet communion with her was gone for good. And there were also disturbing sounds by this time—voices, footsteps forward; the steward flitted along the main-deck, a busily ministering spirit; a hand bell tinkled urgently under the poop deck. . . .

I found my two officers waiting for me near the supper table, in the lighted cuddy. We sat down at once, and as I helped the chief mate, I said:

"Are you aware that there is a ship anchored inside the islands? I saw her mastheads above the ridge as the sun went down."

He raised sharply his simple face, overcharged by a terrible growth of whisker, and emitted his usual ejaculations: "Bless my soul, sir! You don't say so!"

My second mate was a round-cheeked, silent young man, grave beyond his years, I thought; but as our eyes happened to meet I detected a slight quiver on his lips. I looked down at once. It was not my part to encourage sneering on board my ship. It must be said, too, that I knew very little of my officers. In consequence of certain events of no particular significance, except to myself, I had been appointed to the command only a fortnight before. Neither did I know much of the hands forward. All these people had been together for eighteen months or so, and my position was that of the only stranger on board. I mention this because it has some bearing on what is to follow. But what I felt most was my being a stranger to the ship; and if all the truth must be told, I was somewhat of a stranger to myself. The youngest man on board (barring the second mate), and untried as yet by a position of the fullest responsibility, I was willing to take the adequacy of the others for granted. They had simply to be equal to their tasks; but I wondered how far I should turn out faithful to that ideal conception of one's own personality every man sets up for himself secretly.

Meantime the chief mate, with an almost visible effect of collaboration on the part of his round eyes and frightful whiskers, was trying to evolve a theory of the anchored ship. His dominant trait was to take all things into earnest consideration. He was of a painstaking turn of mind. As he used to say, he "liked to account to himself" for practically everything that came in his way, down to a miserable scorpion he had found in his cabin a week before. The why and the wherefore of that scorpion—how it got on board and came to select his room rather than the pantry (which was a dark place and more what a scorpion would be partial to), and how on earth it managed to drown itself in the inkwell of his writing desk—had exercised him infinitely. The ship within the islands was much more easily accounted for; and just as we were about to rise from table he made his pronouncement. She was, he doubted not, a ship from home lately arrived. Probably she drew too much water to cross the bar except at the top of spring tides. Therefore she went into that natural harbor to wait for a few days in preference to remaining in an open roadstead.

"That's so," confirmed the second mate, suddenly, in his slightly hoarse voice. "She draws over twenty feet. She's the Liverpool ship *Sephora* with a cargo of coal. Hundred and twenty-three days from Cardiff."

We looked at him in surprise.

"The tugboat skipper told me when he came on board for your letters, sir," explained the young man. "He expects to take her up the river the day after tomorrow."

After thus overwhelming us with the extent of his information he slipped out of the cabin. The mate observed regretfully that he "could not account for that young fellow's whims." What prevented him telling us all about it at once, he wanted to know.

I detained him as he was making a move. For the last two days the crew had had plenty of hard work, and the night before they had very little sleep. I felt painfully that I—a stranger—was doing something unusual when I directed him to let all hands turn in without setting an anchor watch. I proposed to keep on deck myself till one o'clock or thereabouts. I would get the second mate to relieve me at that hour.

"He will turn out the cook and the steward at four," I concluded, "and then give you a call. Of course at the slightest sign of any sort of wind we'll have the hands up and make a start at once."

He concealed his astonishment. "Very well, sir." Outside the cuddy he put his head in the second mate's door to inform him of my unheard-of caprice to take a five hours' anchor watch on myself. I heard the other raise his voice incredulously—"What? The

Captain himself?" Then a few more murmurs, a door closed, then another. A few moments later I went on deck.

My strangeness, which had made me sleepless, had prompted that unconventional arrangement, as if I had expected in those solitary hours of the night to get on terms with the ship of which I knew nothing, manned by men of whom I knew very little more. Fast alongside a wharf, littered like any ship in port with a tangle of unrelated things, invaded by unrelated shore people, I had hardly seen her yet properly. Now, as she lay cleared for sea, the stretch of her main-deck seemed to me very fine under the stars. Very fine, very roomy for her size, and very inviting. I descended the poop and paced the waist, my mind picturing to myself the coming passage through the Malay Archipelago, down the Indian Ocean, and up the Atlantic. All its phases were familiar enough to me, every characteristic, all the alternatives which were likely to face me on the high seas—everything! . . . except the novel responsibility of command. But I took heart from the reasonable thought that the ship was like other ships, the men like other men, and that the sea was not likely to keep any special surprises expressly for my discomfiture.

Arrived at that comforting conclusion, I bethought myself of a cigar and went below to get it. All was still down there. Everybody at the after end of the ship was sleeping profoundly. I came out again on the quarterdeck, agreeably at ease in my sleeping suit on that warm breathless night, barefooted, a glowing cigar in my teeth, and, going forward, I was met by the profound silence of the fore end of the ship. Only as I passed the door of the forecastle I heard a deep, quiet, trustful sigh of some sleeper inside. And suddenly I rejoiced in the great security of the sea as compared with the unrest of the land, in my choice of that untempted life presenting no disquieting problems, invested with an elementary moral beauty by the absolute straightforwardness of its appeal and by the singleness of its purpose.

The riding light in the forerigging burned with a clear, untroubled, as if symbolic, flame, confident and bright in the mysterious shades of the night. Passing on my way aft along the other side of the ship, I observed that the rope side ladder, put over, no doubt, for the master of the tug when he came to fetch away our letters, had not been hauled in as it should have been. I became annoyed at this, for exactitude in some small matters is the very soul of discipline. Then I reflected that I had myself peremptorily dismissed my officers from duty, and by my own act had prevented the anchor watch being formally set and things properly attended to. I asked myself whether it was wise ever to interfere with the established routine of duties even from the kindest of motives. My action might have made me appear eccentric. Goodness only knew how that absurdly whiskered mate would "account" for my conduct, and what the whole ship thought of that informality of their new captain. I was vexed with myself.

Not from compunction certainly, but, as it were mechanically, I proceeded to get the ladder in myself. Now a side ladder of that sort is a light affair and

comes in easily, yet my vigorous tug, which should
have brought it flying on board, merely recoiled upon
my body in a totally unexpected jerk. What the devil!
. . . I was so astounded by the immovableness of
that ladder that I remained stockstill, trying to account for it to myself like that imbecile mate of mine.
In the end, of course, I put my head over the rail.

The side of the ship made an opaque belt of shadow
on the darkling glassy shimmer of the sea. But I saw
at once something elongated and pale floating very
close to the ladder. Before I could form a guess a faint
flash of phosphorescent light, which seemed to issue
suddenly from the naked body of a man, flickered in
the sleeping water with the elusive, silent play of summer lightning in a night sky. With a gasp I saw re-
vealed to my stare a pair of feet, the long legs, a broad
livid back immersed right up to the neck in a greenish
cadaverous glow. One hand, awash, clutched the bottom rung of the ladder. He was complete but for the
head. A headless corpse! The cigar dropped out of my
gaping mouth with a tiny plop and a short hiss quite
audible in the absolute stillness of all things under
heaven. At that I suppose he raised up his face, a
dimly pale oval in the shadow of the ship's side. But
even then I could only barely make out down there
the shape of his black-haired head. However, it was
enough for the horrid, frost-bound sensation which
had gripped me about the chest to pass off. The moment of vain exclamations was past, too. I only
climbed on the spare spar and leaned over the rail as
far as I could, to bring my eyes nearer to that mystery
floating alongside.

As he hung by the ladder, like a resting swimmer, the sea lightning played about his limbs at every stir; and he appeared in it ghastly, silvery, fishlike. He remained as mute as a fish, too. He made no motion to get out of the water, either. It was inconceivable that he should not attempt to come on board, and strangely troubling to suspect that perhaps he did not want to. And my first words were prompted by just that troubled incertitude.

"What's the matter?" I asked in my ordinary tone, speaking down to the face upturned exactly under mine.

"Cramp," it answered, no louder. Then slightly anxious, "I say, no need to call anyone."

"I was not going to," I said.

"Are you alone on deck?"

"Yes."

I had somehow the impression that he was on the point of letting go the ladder to swim away beyond my ken—mysterious as he came. But, for the moment, this being appearing as if he had risen from the bottom of the sea (it was certainly the nearest land to the ship) wanted only to know the time. I told him. And he, down there, tentatively:

"I suppose your captain's turned in?"

"I am sure he isn't," I said.

He seemed to struggle with himself, for I heard something like the low, bitter murmur of doubt. "What's the good?" His next words came out with a hesitating effort.

"Look here, my man. Could you call him out quietly?"

I thought the time had come to declare myself.

"*I* am the captain."

I heard a "By Jove!" whispered at the level of the water. The phosphorescence flashed in the swirl of the water all about his limbs, his other hand seized the ladder.

"My name's Leggatt."

The voice was calm and resolute. A good voice. The self-possession of that man had somehow induced a corresponding state in myself. It was very quietly that I remarked:

"You must be a good swimmer."

"Yes. I've been in the water practically since nine o'clock. The question for me now is whether I am to let go this ladder and go on swimming till I sink from exhaustion, or—to come on board here."

I felt this was no mere formula of desperate speech, but a real alternative in the view of a strong soul. I should have gathered from this that he was young; indeed, it is only the young who are ever confronted by such clear issues. But at the time it was pure intuition on my part. A mysterious communication was established already between us two—in the face of that silent, darkened tropical sea. I was young, too; young enough to make no comment. The man in the water began suddenly to climb up the ladder, and I hastened away from the rail to fetch some clothes.

Before entering the cabin I stood still, listening in the lobby at the foot of the stairs. A faint snore came through the closed door of the chief mate's room. The second mate's door was on the hook, but the darkness in there was absolutely soundless. He, too, was young and could sleep like a stone. Remained the steward, but he was not likely to wake up before he was called. I got a sleeping suit out of my room and, coming back on deck, saw the naked man from the sea sitting on the main hatch, glimmering white in the darkness, his elbows on his knees and his head in his hands. In a moment he had concealed his damp body in a sleeping suit of the same gray-stripe pattern as the one I was wearing and followed me like my double on the poop. Together we moved right aft, barefooted, silent.

"What is it?" I asked in a deadened voice, taking the lighted lamp out of the binnacle, and raising it to his face.

"An ugly business."

He had rather regular features; a good mouth; light eyes under somewhat heavy, dark eyebrows; a smooth, square forehead; no growth on his cheeks; a small, brown mustache, and a well-shaped, round chin. His expression was concentrated, meditative, under the inspecting light of the lamp I held up to his face; such as a man thinking hard in solitude might wear. My sleeping suit was just right for his size. A well-knit young fellow of twenty-five at most. He caught his lower lip with the edge of white, even teeth.

"Yes," I said, replacing the lamp in the binnacle. The warm, heavy tropical night closed upon his head again.

"There's a ship over there," he murmured.

"Yes, I know. The *Sephora*. Did you know of us?"

"Hadn't the slightest idea. I am the mate of her——" He paused and corrected himself. "I should say I *was*."

"Aha! Something wrong?"

"Yes. Very wrong indeed. I've killed a man."

"What do you mean? Just now?"

"No, on the passage. Weeks ago. Thirty-nine south. When I say a man——"

"Fit of temper," I suggested, confidently.

The shadowy, dark head, like mine, seemed to nod imperceptibly above the ghostly gray of my sleeping suit. It was, in the night, as though I had been faced by my own reflection in the depths of a somber and immense mirror.

"A pretty thing to have to own up to for a Conway boy," murmured my double, distinctly.

"You're a Conway boy?"

"I am," he said, as if startled. Then, slowly . . . "Perhaps you too——"

It was so; but being a couple of years older I had left before he joined. After a quick interchange of dates a silence fell; and I thought suddenly of my absurd mate with his terrific whiskers and the "Bless my soul—you don't say so" type of intellect. My double gave me an inkling of his thoughts by saying: "My father's a parson in Norfolk. Do you see me before a judge and jury on that charge? For myself I can't see the necessity. There are fellows that an angel from heaven—— And I am not that. He was one of those creatures that are just simmering all the time with a silly sort of wickedness. Miserable devils that have no business to live at all. He wouldn't do his duty and wouldn't let anybody else do theirs. But what's the good of talking! You know well enough the sort of ill-conditioned snarling cur——"

He appealed to me as if our experiences had been as identical as our clothes. And I knew well enough the pestiferous danger of such a character where there are no means of legal repression. And I knew well enough also that my double there was no homicidal ruffian. I did not think of asking him for details, and he told me the story roughly in brusque, disconnected sentences. I needed no more. I saw it all going on as though I were myself inside that other sleeping suit.

"It happened while we were setting a reefed fore-sail, at dusk. Reefed foresail! You understand the sort of weather. The only sail we had left to keep the ship running; so you may guess what it had been like for days. Anxious sort of job, that. He gave me some of his cursed insolence at the sheet. I tell you I was overdone with this terrific weather that seemed to have no end to it. Terrific, I tell you—and a deep ship. I believe the fellow himself was half crazed with funk. It was no time for gentlemanly reproof, so I turned round and felled him like an ox. He up and at me. We closed just as an awful sea made for the ship. All hands saw it coming and took to the rigging, but I had him by the throat, and went on shaking him like a rat, the men above us yelling, 'Look out! look out!' Then a crash as if the sky had fallen on my head. They say that for over ten minutes hardly anything was to be seen of the ship—just the three masts and a bit of the forecastle head and of the poop all awash driving along in a smother of foam. It was a miracle that they found us, jammed together behind the forebits. It's clear that I meant business, because I was holding him by the throat still when they picked us up. He was black in the face. It was too much for them. It seems they rushed us aft together, gripped as we were, screaming 'Murder!' like a lot of lunatics, and broke into the cuddy. And the ship running for her life, touch and go all the time, any minute her last in a sea fit to turn your hair gray only a-looking at it. I understand that the skipper, too, started raving like the rest of them. The man had been deprived of sleep for more than a week, and to have this sprung on him at the height of a furious gale nearly drove him out of his mind. I wonder they didn't fling me overboard after getting the carcass of their precious shipmate out of my fingers. They had rather a job to separate us, I've been told. A sufficiently fierce story to make an old judge and a respectable jury sit up a bit. The first thing I heard when I came to myself was the maddening howling of that endless gale, and on that the voice of the old man. He was hanging on to my bunk, staring into my face out of his sou'wester.

" 'Mr. Leggatt, you have killed a man. You can act no longer as chief mate of this ship.' "

His care to subdue his voice made it sound monotonous. He rested a hand on the end of the skylight to steady himself with, and all that time did not stir a limb, so far as I could see. "Nice little tale for a quiet tea party," he concluded in the same tone.

One of my hands, too, rested on the end of the skylight; neither did I stir a limb, so far as I knew. We stood less than a foot from each other. It occurred to me that if old "Bless my soul—you don't say so" were to put his head up the companion and catch sight of us, he would think he was seeing double, or imagine himself come upon a scene of weird witch-craft; the strange captain having a quiet confabulation by the wheel with his own gray ghost. I became very much concerned to prevent anything of the sort. I heard the other's soothing undertone.

"My father's a parson in Norfolk," it said. Evi-dently he had forgotten he had told me this impor-tant fact before. Truly a nice little tale.

"You had better slip down into my stateroom now," I said, moving off stealthily. My double followed my movements; our bare feet made no sound; I let him in, closed the door with care, and, after giving a call to the second mate, returned on deck for my relief.

"Not much sign of any wind yet," I remarked when he approached.

"No, sir. Not much," he assented, sleepily, in his hoarse voice, with just enough deference, no more, and barely suppressing a yawn.

"Well, that's all you have to look out for. You have got your orders."

"Yes, sir."

I paced a turn or two on the poop and saw him take up his position face forward with his elbow in the rat-lines of the mizzen rigging before I went below. The mate's faint snoring was still going on peacefully. The cuddy lamp was burning over the table on which stood a vase with flowers, a polite attention from the ship's provision merchant—the last flowers we should see for the next three months at the very least. Two

bunches of bananas hung from the beam symmetri-
cally, one on each side of the rudder casing. Everything was as before in the ship—except that two of
her captain's sleeping suits were simultaneously in use,
one motionless in the cuddy, the other keeping very
still in the captain's stateroom.

It must be explained here that my cabin had the
form of the capital letter L, the door being within the
angle and opening into the short part of the letter. A
couch was to the left, the bed place to the right; my
writing desk and the chronometers' table faced the
door. But anyone opening it, unless he stepped right
inside, had no view of what I call the long (or vertical) part of the letter. It contained some lockers sur-
mounted by a bookcase; and a few clothes, a thick
jacket or two, caps, oilskin coat, and such like, hung on
hooks. There was at the bottom of that part a door
opening into my bathroom, which could be entered
also directly from the saloon. But that way was never
used.

The mysterious arrival had discovered the advantage of this particular shape. Entering my room,
lighted strongly by a big bulkhead lamp swung on
gimbals above my writing desk, I did not see him anywhere till he stepped out quietly from behind the
coats hung in the recessed part.

"I heard somebody moving about, and went in
there at once," he whispered.

I, too, spoke under my breath.

"Nobody is likely to come in here without knocking
and getting permission."

He nodded. His face was thin and the sunburn

faded, as though he had been ill. And no wonder. He had been, I heard presently, kept under arrest in his cabin for nearly seven weeks. But there was nothing sickly in his eyes or in his expression. He was not a bit like me, really; yet, as we stood leaning over my bed place, whispering side by side, with our dark heads together and our backs to the door, anybody bold enough to open it stealthily would have been treated to the uncanny sight of a double captain busy talking in whispers with his other self.

"But all this doesn't tell me how you came to hang on to our side ladder," I inquired, in the hardly audible murmurs we used, after he had told me something more of the proceedings on board the *Sephora* once the bad weather was over.

"When we sighted Java Head I had had time to think all those matters out several times over. I had six weeks of doing nothing else, and with only an hour or so every evening for a tramp on the quarter-deck."

He whispered, his arms folded on the side of my bed place, staring through the open port. And I could imagine perfectly the manner of this thinking out— a stubborn if not a steadfast operation; something of which I should have been perfectly incapable.

"I reckoned it would be dark before we closed with the land," he continued, so low that I had to strain my hearing near as we were to each other, shoulder touching shoulder almost. "So I asked to speak to the old man. He always seemed very sick when he came to see me—as if he could not look me in the face. You know, that foresail saved the ship. She was too deep to have run long under bare poles. And it was I that

managed to set it for him. Anyway, he came. When I
had him in my cabin—he stood by the door looking at
me as if I had the halter round my neck already—I
asked him right away to leave my cabin door unlocked
at night while the ship was going through Sunda
Straits. There would be the Java coast within two or
three miles, off Angier Point. I wanted nothing more.
I've had a prize for swimming my second year in the
Conway."

"I can believe it," I breathed out.

"God only knows why they locked me in every
night. To see some of their faces you'd have thought
they were afraid I'd go about at night strangling people. Am I a murdering brute? Do I look it? By Jove!
If I had been he wouldn't have trusted himself like
that into my room. You'll say I might have chucked
him aside and bolted out, there and then—it was dark
already. Well, no. And for the same reason I wouldn't
think of trying to smash the door. There would have
been a rush to stop me at the noise, and I did not
mean to get into a confounded scrimmage. Somebody
else might have got killed—for I would not have
broken out only to get chucked back, and I did not
want any more of that work. He refused, looking
more sick than ever. He was afraid of the men, and
also of that old second mate of his who had been
sailing with him for years—a gray-headed old humbug; and his steward, too, had been with him devil
knows how long—seventeen years or more—a dog-
matic sort of loafer who hated me like poison, just
because I was the chief mate. No chief mate ever
made more than one voyage in the *Sephora*, you

know. Those two old chaps ran the ship. Devil only knows what the skipper wasn't afraid of (all his nerve went to pieces altogether in that hellish spell of bad weather we had)—of what the law would do to him —of his wife, perhaps. Oh, yes! she's on board. Though I don't think she would have meddled. She would have been only too glad to have me out of the ship in any way. The 'brand of Cain' business, don't you see. That's all right. I was ready enough to go off wandering on the face of the earth—and that was price enough to pay for an Abel of that sort. Anyhow, he wouldn't listen to me. 'This thing must take its course. I represent the law here.' He was shaking like a leaf. 'So you won't?' 'No!' 'Then I hope you will be able to sleep on that,' I said, and turned my back on him. 'I wonder that *you* can,' cries he, and locks the door.

"Well after that, I couldn't. Not very well. That was three weeks ago. We have had a slow passage through the Java Sea; drifted about Carimata for ten days. When we anchored here they thought, I suppose, it was all right. The nearest land (and that's five miles) is the ship's destination; the consul would soon set about catching me; and there would have been no object in bolting to these islets there. I don't suppose there's a drop of water on them. I don't know how it was, but tonight that steward, after bringing me my supper, went out to let me eat it, and left the door unlocked. And I ate it—all there was, too. After I had finished I strolled out on the quarter-deck. I don't know that I meant to do anything. A breath of fresh air was all I wanted, I believe. Then a sudden temptation came over me. I kicked off my slippers and was in the water before I had made up my mind fairly. Somebody heard the splash and they raised an awful hullabaloo. 'He's gone! Lower the boats! He's committed suicide! No, he's swimming.' Certainly I was swimming. It's not so easy for a swimmer like me to commit suicide by drowning. I landed on the nearest islet before the boat left the ship's side. I heard them pulling about in the dark, hailing, and so on, but after a bit they gave up. Everything quieted down and the anchorage became as still as death. I sat down on a stone and began to think. I felt certain they would start searching for me at daylight. There was no place to hide on those stony things—and if there had been, what would have been the good? But now I was clear of that ship, I was not going back. So after a while I took off all my clothes, tied them up in a bundle with a stone inside, and dropped them in the deep water on the outer side of that islet. That was suicide enough for me. Let them think what they liked, but I didn't mean to drown myself. I meant to swim till I sank—but that's not the same thing. I struck out for another of these little islands, and it was from that one that I first saw your riding light. Something to swim for. I went on easily, and on the way I came upon a flat rock a foot or two above water. In the daytime, I dare say, you might make it out with a glass from your poop. I scrambled up on it and rested myself for a bit. Then I made another start. That last spell must have been over a mile."

His whisper was getting fainter and fainter, and all the time he stared straight out through the porthole, in which there was not even a star to be seen. I had not interrupted him. There was something that made comment impossible in his narrative, or perhaps in himself; a sort of feeling, a quality, which I can't find a name for. And when he ceased, all I found was a futile whisper: "So you swam for our light?"

"Yes—straight for it. It was something to swim for. I couldn't see any stars low down because the coast was in the way, and I couldn't see the land, either. The water was like glass. One might have been swimming in a confounded thousand-feet deep cistern with no place for scrambling out anywhere; but what I didn't like was the notion of swimming round and round like a crazed bullock before I gave out; and as I didn't mean to go back . . . No. Do you see me being hauled back, stark naked, off one of these little islands by the scruff of the neck and fighting like a wild beast? Somebody would have got killed for certain, and I did not want any of that. So I went on. Then your ladder——"

"Why didn't you hail the ship?" I asked, a little louder.

He touched my shoulder lightly. Lazy footsteps came right over our heads and stopped. The second mate had crossed from the other side of the poop and might have been hanging over the rail for all we knew.

"He couldn't hear us talking—could he?" My double breathed into my very ear, anxiously.

His anxiety was in answer, a sufficient answer, to the question I had put to him. An answer containing all the difficulty of that situation. I closed the porthole quietly, to make sure. A louder word might have been overheard.

"Who's that?" he whispered then.

"My second mate. But I don't know much more of the fellow than you do."

And I told him a little about myself. I had been appointed to take charge while I least expected anything of the sort, not quite a fortnight ago. I didn't know either the ship or the people. Hadn't had the time in port to look about me or size anybody up. And as to the crew, all they knew was that I was appointed to take the ship home. For the rest, I was almost as much of a stranger on board as himself, I said. And at the moment I felt it most acutely. I felt that it would take very little to make me a suspect person in the eyes of the ship's company.

He had turned about meantime; and we, the two strangers in the ship, faced each other in identical attitudes.

"Your ladder——" he murmured, after a silence. "Who'd have thought of finding a ladder hanging over at night in a ship anchored out here! I felt just then a very unpleasant faintness. After the life I've been leading for nine weeks, anybody would have got out of condition. I wasn't capable of swimming round as far as your rudder chains. And, lo and behold! there was a ladder to get hold of. After I gripped it I said to myself, 'What's the good?' When I saw a man's head looking over I thought I would swim away presently and leave him shouting—in whatever language it was. I didn't mind being looked at. I—I liked it. And then you speaking to me so quietly—as if you had expected me—made me hold on a little longer. It had been a confounded lonely time—I don't mean while swimming. I was glad to talk a little to somebody that didn't belong to the *Sephora*. As to asking for the captain, that was a mere impulse. It could have been no use, with all the ship knowing about me and the other people pretty certain to be round here in the morning. I don't know—I wanted to be seen, to talk with somebody, before I went on. I don't know what I would have said. . . . 'Fine night, isn't it?' or something of the sort."

"Do you think they will be round here presently?" I asked with some incredulity.

"Quite likely," he said, faintly.

He looked extremely haggard all of a sudden. His head rolled on his shoulders.

"H'm. We shall see then. Meantime get into that bed," I whispered. "Want help? There."

It was a rather high bed place with a set of drawers underneath. This amazing swimmer really needed the lift I gave him by seizing his leg. He tumbled in, rolled over on his back, and flung one arm across his eyes. And then, with his face nearly hidden, he must have looked exactly as I used to look in that bed. I gazed upon my other self for a while before drawing across carefully the two green serge curtains which ran on a brass rod. I thought for a moment of pinning them together for greater safety, but I sat down on the couch, and once there I felt unwilling to rise and hunt for a pin. I would do it in a moment. I was extremely tired, in a peculiarly intimate way, by the strain of stealthiness, by the effort of whispering and

the general secrecy of this excitement. It was three
o'clock by now and I had been on my feet since nine,
but I was not sleepy; I could not have gone to sleep. I
sat there, fagged out, looking at the curtains, trying to
clear my mind of the confused sensation of being in
two places at once, and greatly bothered by an exasperating knocking in my head. It was a relief to dis-
cover suddenly that it was not in my head at all, but
on the outside of the door. Before I could collect myself the words "Come in" were out of my mouth, and
the steward entered with a tray, bringing in my morning coffee. I had slept, after all, and I was so frightened that I shouted, "This way! I am here, steward,"
as though he had been miles away. He put down the
tray on the table next the couch and only then said,
very quietly, "I can see you are here, sir." I felt him
give me a keen look, but I dared not meet his eyes
just then. He must have wondered why I had drawn
the curtains of my bed before going to sleep on the
couch. He went out, hooking the door open as usual.

I heard the crew washing decks above me. I knew I
would have been told at once if there had been any
wind. Calm, I thought, and I was doubly vexed. Indeed, I felt dual more than ever. The steward reappeared suddenly in the doorway. I jumped up from
the couch so quickly that he gave a start.

"What do you want here?"

"Close your port, sir—they are washing decks."

"It is closed," I said, reddening.

"Very well, sir." But he did not move from the
doorway and returned my stare in an extraordinary,
equivocal manner for a time. Then his eyes wavered,

all his expression changed, and in a voice unusually gentle, almost coaxingly:

"May I come in to take the empty cup away, sir?"

"Of course!" I turned my back on him while he popped in and out. Then I unhooked and closed the door and even pushed the bolt. This sort of thing could not go on very long. The cabin was as hot as an oven, too. I took a peep at my double, and discovered that he had not moved, his arm was still over his eyes; but his chest heaved; his hair was wet; his chin glistened with perspiration. I reached over him and opened the port.

"I must show myself on deck," I reflected.

Of course, theoretically, I could do what I liked, with no one to say nay to me within the whole circle of the horizon; but to lock my cabin door and take the key away I did not dare. Directly I put my head out of the companion I saw the group of my two officers, the second mate barefooted, the chief mate in long India-rubber boots, near the break of the poop, and the steward halfway down the poop ladder talking to them eagerly. He happened to catch sight of me and dived, the second ran down on the main-deck shouting some order or other, and the chief mate came to meet me, touching his cap.

There was a sort of curiosity in his eye that I did not like. I don't know whether the steward had told them that I was "queer" only, or downright drunk, but I know the man meant to have a good look at me. I watched him coming with a smile which, as he got into point-blank range, took effect and froze his very whiskers. I did not give him time to open his lips.

"Square the yards by lifts and braces before the hands go to breakfast."

It was the first particular order I had given on board that ship; and I stayed on deck to see it executed, too. I had felt the need of asserting myself without loss of time. That sneering young cub got taken down a peg or two on that occasion, and I also seized the opportunity of having a good look at the face of every foremast man as they filed past me to go to the after braces. At breakfast time, eating nothing myself, I presided with such frigid dignity that the two mates were only too glad to escape from the cabin as soon as decency permitted; and all the time the dual working of my mind distracted me almost to the point of insanity. I was constantly watching myself, my secret self, as dependent on my actions as my own personality, sleeping in that bed, behind that door which faced me as I sat at the head of the table. It was very much like being mad, only it was worse because one was aware of it.

I had to shake him for a solid minute, but when at last he opened his eyes it was in the full possession of his senses with an inquiring look.

"All's well so far," I whispered. "Now you must vanish into the bathroom."

He did so, as noiseless as a ghost, and then I rang for the steward, and facing him boldly, directed him to tidy up my stateroom while I was having my bath —"and be quick about it." As my tone admitted of no excuses, he said, "Yes, sir," and ran off to fetch his dustpan and brushes. I took a bath and did most of my dressing, splashing, and whistling softly for the steward's edification, while the secret sharer of my life stood drawn up bolt upright in that little space, his face looking very sunken in daylight, his eyelids lowered under the stern, dark line of his eyebrows drawn together by a slight frown.

When I left him there to go back to my room the steward was finishing dusting. I sent for the mate and engaged him in some insignificant conversation. It was, as it were, trifling with the terrific character of his whiskers; but my object was to give him an opportunity for a good look at my cabin. And then I could at last shut, with a clear conscience, the door of my stateroom and get my double back into the recessed part. There was nothing else for it. He had to sit still on a small folding stool, half smothered by the heavy coats hanging there. We listened to the steward going into the bathroom out of the saloon, filling the water bottles there, scrubbing the bath, setting things to rights, whisk, bang, clatter—out again into the saloon—turn the key—click. Such was my scheme for keeping my second self invisible. Nothing better could be contrived under the circumstances. And there we sat; I at my writing desk ready to appear busy with some papers, he behind me out of sight of the door. It would not have been prudent to talk in daytime; and I could not have stood the excitement of that queer sense of whispering to myself. Now and then, glancing over my shoulder, I saw him far back there, sitting rigidly on the low stool, his bare feet close together, his arms folded, his head hanging on his breast—and perfectly still. Anybody would have taken him for me.

I was fascinated by it myself. Every moment I had to glance over my shoulder. I was looking at him when a voice outside the door said:

"Beg pardon, sir."

"Well!" . . . I kept my eyes on him, and so when the voice outside the door announced, "There's a ship's boat coming our way, sir," I saw him give a start—the first movement he had made for hours. But he did not raise his bowed head.

"All right. Get the ladder over."

I hesitated. Should I whisper something to him? But what? His immobility seemed to have been never disturbed. What could I tell him he did not know already? . . . Finally I went on deck.

II

The skipper of the *Sephora* had a thin red whisker all round his face, and the sort of complexion that goes with hair of that color; also the particular, rather smeary shade of blue in the eyes. He was not exactly a showy figure; his shoulders were high, his stature but middling—one leg slightly more bandy than the other. He shook hands, looking vaguely around. A spiritless tenacity was his main characteristic, I judged. I behaved with a politeness which seemed to disconcert him. Perhaps he was shy. He mumbled to me as if he were ashamed of what he was saying; gave his name (it was something like Archbold—but at this distance of years I hardly am sure), his ship's name, and a few other particulars of that sort, in the manner of a criminal making a reluctant and doleful confession. He had had terrible weather on the passage out —terrible—terrible—wife aboard, too.

By this time we were seated in the cabin and the steward brought in a tray with a bottle and glasses. "Thanks! No." Never took liquor. Would have some water, though. He drank two tumblerfuls. Terrible thirsty work. Ever since daylight had been exploring the islands round his ship.

"What was that for—fun?" I asked, with an appearance of polite interest.

"No!" He sighed. "Painful duty."

As he persisted in his mumbling and I wanted my double to hear every word, I hit upon the notion of informing him that I regretted to say I was hard of hearing.

"Such a young man, too!" he nodded, keeping his smeary blue, unintelligent eyes fastened upon me. "What was the cause of it—some disease?" he inquired, without the least sympathy and as if he thought that, if so, I'd got no more than I deserved.

"Yes; disease," I admitted in a cheerful tone which seemed to shock him. But my point was gained, because he had to raise his voice to give me his tale. It is not worth while to record that version. It was just over two months since all this had happened, and he had thought so much about it that he seemed completely muddled as to its bearings, but still immensely impressed.

"What would you think of such a thing happening on board your own ship? I've had the *Sephora* for these fifteen years. I am a well-known shipmaster."

He was densely distressed—and perhaps I should have sympathized with him if I had been able to detach my mental vision from the unsuspected sharer of my cabin as though he were my second self. There he was on the other side of the bulkhead, four or five feet from us, no more, as we sat in the saloon. I looked politely at Captain Archbold (if that was his name), but it was the other I saw, in a gray sleeping suit, seated on a low stool, his bare feet close together, his arms folded, and every word said between us falling into the ears of his dark head bowed on his chest.

"I have been at sea now, man and boy, for seven-and-thirty years, and I've never heard of such a thing happening in an English ship. And that it should be my ship. Wife on board, too."

I was hardly listening to him.

"Don't you think," I said, "that the heavy sea which you told me, came aboard just then might have killed the man? I have seen the sheer weight of a sea kill a man very neatly, by simply breaking his neck."

"Good God!" he uttered, impressively, fixing his smeary blue eyes on me. "The sea! No man killed by the sea ever looked like that." He seemed positively scandalized at my suggestion. And as I gazed at him certainly not prepared for anything original on his part, he advanced his head close to mine and thrust his tongue out at me so suddenly that I couldn't help starting back.

After scoring over my calmness in this graphic way he nodded wisely. If I had seen the sight, he assured me, I would never forget it as long as I lived. The weather was too bad to give the corpse a proper sea burial. So next day at dawn they took it up on the poop, covering its face with a bit of bunting; he read a short prayer, and then, just as it was, in its oilskins and long boots, they launched it amongst those mountainous seas that seemed ready every moment to swallow up the ship herself and the terrified lives on board of her.

"That reefed foresail saved you," I threw in.

"Under God—it did," he exclaimed fervently. "It was by a special mercy, I firmly believe, that it stood some of those hurricane squalls."

"It was the setting of that sail which——" I began.

"God's own hand in it," he interrupted me. "Nothing less could have done it. I don't mind telling you that I hardly dared give the order. It seemed impossible that we could touch anything without losing it, and then our last hope would have been gone."

The terror of that gale was on him yet. I let him go on for a bit, then said, casually—as if returning to a minor subject:

"You were very anxious to give up your mate to the shore people, I believe?"

He was. To the law. His obscure tenacity on that point had in it something incomprehensible and a little awful; something, as it were, mystical, quite apart from his anxiety that he should not be suspected of "countenancing any doings of that sort." Seven-and-thirty virtuous years at sea, of which over twenty of immaculate command, and the last fifteen in the *Sephora*, seemed to have laid him under some pitiless obligation.

"And you know," he went on, groping shame-facedly amongst his feelings, "I did not engage that young fellow. His people had some interest with my owners. I was in a way forced to take him on. He looked very smart, very gentlemanly, and all that. But do you know—I never liked him, somehow. I am a plain man. You see, he wasn't exactly the sort for the chief mate of a ship like the *Sephora*."

I had become so connected in thoughts and impressions with the secret sharer of my cabin that I felt as if I, personally, were being given to understand that I, too, was not the sort that would have done for the chief mate of a ship like the *Sephora*. I had no doubt of it in my mind.

"Not at all the style of man. You understand," he insisted, superfluously, looking hard at me.

I smiled urbanely. He seemed at a loss for a while.

"I suppose I must report a suicide."

"Beg pardon?"

"Sui-cide! That's what I'll have to write to my owners directly I get in."

"Unless you manage to recover him before tomorrow," I assented, dispassionately. . . . "I mean, alive."

He mumbled something which I really did not catch, and I turned my ear to him in a puzzled manner. He fairly bawled:

"The land—I say, the mainland is at least seven miles off my anchorage."

"About that."

My lack of excitement, of curiosity, of surprise, of any sort of pronounced interest, began to arouse his distrust. But except for the felicitous pretense of deafness I had not tried to pretend anything. I had felt utterly incapable of playing the part of ignorance properly, and therefore was afraid to try. It is also certain that he had brought some ready-made suspicions with him, and that he viewed my politeness as a strange and unnatural phenomenon. And yet how else could I have received him? Not heartily! That was impossible for psychological reasons, which I need not state here. My only object was to keep off his inquiries. Surlily? Yes, but surliness might have provoked a point-blank question. From its novelty to him and from its nature, punctilious courtesy was the manner best calculated to restrain the man. But there was the danger of his breaking through my defense bluntly. I could not, I think, have met him by a direct lie, also for psychological (not moral) reasons. If he had only known how afraid I was of his putting my feeling of identity with the other to the test! But, strangely enough—(I thought of it only afterwards) —I believe that he was not a little disconcerted by the reverse side of that weird situation, by something in me that reminded him of the man he was seeking— suggested a mysterious similitude to the young fellow he had distrusted and disliked from the first.

However that might have been, the silence was not very prolonged. He took another oblique step.

"I reckon I had no more than a two-mile pull to your ship. Not a bit more."

"And quite enough, too, in this awful heat," I said.

Another pause full of mistrust followed. Necessity, they say, is mother of invention, but fear, too, is not

barren of ingenious suggestions. And I was afraid he
would ask me point-blank for news of my other self.

"Nice little saloon, isn't it?" I remarked, as if noticing for the first time the ways his eyes roamed from
one closed door to the other. "And very well fitted
out, too. Here, for instance," I continued, reaching
over the back of my seat negligently and flinging the
door open, "is my bathroom."

He made an eager movement, but hardly gave it a
glance. I got up, shut the door of the bathroom, and
invited him to have a look round, as if I were very
proud of my accommodation. He had to rise and be
shown round, but he went through the business without any raptures whatever.

"And now we'll have a look at my stateroom," I
declared, in a voice as loud as I dared to make it,
crossing the cabin to the starboard side with purposely
heavy steps.

He followed me in and gazed around. My intelligent double had vanished. I played my part.

"Very convenient—isn't it?"

"Very nice. Very comf . . ." He didn't finish and
went out brusquely as if to escape from some un-
righteous wiles of mine. But it was not to be. I had
been too frightened not to feel vengeful; I felt I had
him on the run, and I meant to keep him on the run.
My polite insistence must have had something menacing in it, because he gave in suddenly. And I did not
let him off a single item; mate's room, pantry, store-
rooms, the very sail locker which was also under the
poop—he had to look into them all. When at last

I showed him out on the quarter-deck he drew a long, spiritless sigh, and mumbled dismally that he must really be going back to his ship now. I desired my mate, who had joined us, to see to the captain's boat.

The man of whiskers gave a blast on the whistle which he used to wear hanging round his neck, and yelled, *"Sephora's* away!" My double down there in my cabin must have heard, and certainly could not feel more relieved than I. Four fellows came running out from somewhere forward and went over the side, while my own men, appearing on deck too, lined the rail. I escorted my visitor to the gangway ceremoniously, and nearly overdid it. He was a tenacious beast. On the very ladder he lingered, and in that unique, guiltily conscientious manner of sticking to the point:

"I say . . . you . . . you don't think that——"

I covered his voice loudly:

"Certainly not. . . . I am delighted. Good-by."

I had an idea of what he meant to say, and just saved myself by the privilege of defective hearing. He was too shaken generally to insist, but my mate, close witness of that parting, looked mystified and his face took on a thoughtful cast. As I did not want to appear as if I wished to avoid all communication with my officers, he had the opportunity to address me.

"Seems a very nice man. His boat's crew told our chaps a very extraordinary story, if what I am told by the steward is true. I suppose you had it from the captain, sir?"

"Yes. I had a story from the captain."

"A very horrible affair—isn't it, sir?"

"It is."

"Beats all these tales we hear about murders in Yankee ships."

"I don't think it beats them. I don't think it resembles them in the least."

"Bless my soul—you don't say so! But of course I've no acquaintance whatever with American ships, not I, so I couldn't go against your knowledge. It's horrible enough for me. . . . But the queerest part is that those fellows seemed to have some idea the man was hidden aboard here. They had really. Did you ever hear of such a thing?"

"Preposterous—isn't it?"

We were walking to and fro athwart the quarter-deck. No one of the crew forward could be seen (the day was Sunday), and the mate pursued:

"There was some little dispute about it. Our chaps took offense. 'As if we would harbor a thing like that,' they said. 'Wouldn't you like to look for him in our coal-hole?' Quite a tiff. But they made it up in the end. I suppose he did drown himself. Don't you, sir?"

"I don't suppose anything."

"You have no doubt in the matter, sir?"

"None whatever."

I left him suddenly. I felt I was producing a bad impression, but with my double down there it was most trying to be on deck. And it was almost as trying to be below. Altogether a nerve-trying situation. But on the whole I felt less torn in two when I was with him. There was no one in the whole ship whom I dared take into my confidence. Since the hands had got to know his story, it would have been impossible to pass him off for anyone else, and an accidental discovery was to be dreaded now more than ever. . . .

The steward being engaged in laying the table for dinner, we could talk only with our eyes when I first went down. Later in the afternoon we had a cautious try at whispering. The Sunday quietness of the ship was against us; the stillness of air and water around her was against us; the elements, the men were against us—everything was against us in our secret partnership; time itself—for this could not go on forever. The very trust in Providence was, I suppose, denied to his guilt. Shall I confess that this thought cast me down very much? And as to the chapter of accidents which counts for so much in the book of success, I could only hope that it was closed. For what favorable accident could be expected?

"Did you hear everything?" were my first words as soon as we took up our position side by side, leaning over my bed place.

He had. And the proof of it was his earnest whisper, "The man told you he hardly dared to give the order."

I understood the reference to be to that saving foresail.

"Yes. He was afraid of it being lost in the setting."

"I assure you he never gave the order. He may think he did, but he never gave it. He stood there with me on the break of the poop after the main topsail blew away, and whimpered about our last hope—positively whimpered about it and nothing else—and the night coming on! To hear one's skipper go on like that in such weather was enough to drive any fellow out of his mind. It worked me up into a sort of desperation. I just took it into my own hands and went away from him, boiling, and—— But what's the use telling you? *You* know! . . . Do you think that if I had not been pretty fierce with them I should have got the men to do anything? Not It! The bo's'n perhaps? Perhaps! It wasn't a heavy sea—it was a sea gone mad! I suppose the end of the world will be something like that; and a man may have the heart to see it coming once and be done with it—but to have to face it day after day—— I don't blame anybody. I was precious little better than the rest. Only—I was an officer of that old coal wagon, anyhow——"

"I quite understand," I conveyed that sincere assurance into his ear. He was out of breath with whispering; I could hear him pant slightly. It was all very simple. The same strung-up force which had given twenty-four men a chance, at least, for their lives, had, in a sort of recoil, crushed an unworthy mutinous existence.

But I had no leisure to weigh the merits of the matter—footsteps in the saloon, a heavy knock. "There's enough wind to get under way with, sir." Here was the call of a new claim upon my thoughts and even upon my feelings.

"Turn the hands up," I cried through the door. "I'll be on deck directly."

I was going out to make the acquaintance of my ship. Before I left the cabin our eyes met—the eyes of the only two strangers on board. I pointed to the recessed part where the little campstool awaited him and laid my finger on my lips. He made a gesture—

somewhat vague—a little mysterious, accompanied by a faint smile, as if of regret.

This is not the place to enlarge upon the sensations of a man who feels for the first time a ship move under his feet to his own independent word. In my case they were not unalloyed. I was not wholly alone with my command; for there was that stranger in my cabin. Or rather, I was not completely and wholly with her. Part of me was absent. That mental feeling of being in two places at once affected me physically as if the mood of secrecy had penetrated my very soul. Before an hour had elapsed since the ship had begun to move, having occasion to ask the mate (he stood by my side) to take a compass bearing of the pagoda, I caught myself reaching up to his ear in whispers. I say I caught myself, but enough had escaped to startle the man. I can't describe it otherwise than by saying that he shied. A grave, preoccupied manner, as though he were in possession of some perplexing intelligence, did not leave him henceforth. A little later I moved away from the rail to look at the compass with such a stealthy gait that the helmsman noticed it—and I could not help noticing the unusual roundness of his eyes. These are trifling instances, though it's to no commander's advantage to be suspected of ludicrous eccentricities. But I was also more seriously affected. There are to a seaman certain words, gestures, that should in given conditions come as naturally, as instinctively as the winking of a menaced eye. A certain order should spring on to his lips without thinking; a certain sign should get itself made, so to speak, without reflection. But all unconscious alertness had aban-

doned me. I had to make an effort of will to recall
myself back (from the cabin) to the conditions of the
moment. I felt that I was appearing an irresolute commander to those people who were watching me more
or less critically.

And, besides, there were the scares. On the second
day out, for instance, coming off the deck in the afternoon (I had straw slippers on my bare feet) I stopped
at the open pantry door and spoke to the steward. He
was doing something there with his back to me. At
the sound of my voice he nearly jumped out of his
skin, as the saying is, and incidentally broke a cup.

"What on earth's the matter with you?" I asked,
astonished.

He was extremely confused. "Beg your pardon,
sir. I made sure you were in your cabin."

"You see I wasn't."

"No, sir. I could have sworn I had heard you moving in there not a moment ago. It's most extraordinary . . . very sorry, sir."

I passed on with an inward shudder. I was so identified with my secret double that I did not even mention the fact in those scanty, fearful whispers we exchanged. I suppose he had made some slight noise of
some kind or other. It would have been miraculous
if he hadn't at one time or another. And yet, haggard
as he appeared, he looked always perfectly self-con-
trolled, more than calm—almost invulnerable. On my
suggestion he remained almost entirely in the bathroom, which, upon the whole, was the safest place.
There could be really no shadow of an excuse for
anyone ever wanting to go in there, once the steward

had done with it. It was a very tiny place. Sometimes he reclined on the floor, his legs bent, his head sustained on one elbow. At others I would find him on the campstool, sitting in his gray sleeping suit and with his cropped dark hair like a patient, unmoved convict. At night I would smuggle him into my bed place, and we would whisper together, with the regular footfalls of the officer of the watch passing and repassing over our heads. It was an infinitely miserable time. It was lucky that some tins of fine preserves were stowed in a locker in my stateroom; hard bread I could always get hold of; and so he lived on stewed chicken, *pâté de foie gras*, asparagus, cooked oysters, sardines—on all sorts of abominable sham delicacies out of tins. My early-morning coffee he always drank; and it was all I dared do for him in that respect.

Every day there was the horrible maneuvering to go through so that my room and then the bathroom should be done in the usual way. I came to hate the sight of the steward, to abhor the voice of that harmless man. I felt that it was he who would bring on the disaster of discovery. It hung like a sword over our heads.

The fourth day out, I think (we were then working down the east side of the Gulf of Siam, tack for tack, in light winds and smooth water)—the fourth day, I say, of this miserable juggling with the unavoidable, as we sat at our evening meal, that man, whose slightest movement I dreaded, after putting down the dishes ran up on deck busily. This could not be dangerous. Presently he came down again; and then it appeared that he had remembered a coat of mine which I had thrown over a rail to dry after having been wetted in a shower which had passed over the ship in the afternoon. Sitting stolidly at the head of the table I became terrified at the sight of the garment on his arm. Of course he made for my door. There was no time to lose.

"Steward," I thundered. My nerves were so shaken that I could not govern my voice and conceal my agitation. This was the sort of thing that made my terrifically whiskered mate tap his forehead with his forefinger. I had detected him using that gesture while talking on deck with a confidential air to the carpenter. It was too far to hear a word, but I had no doubt that this pantomime could only refer to the strange new captain.

"Yes, sir," the pale-faced steward turned resignedly to me. It was this maddening course of being shouted at, checked without rhyme or reason, arbitrarily chased out of my cabin, suddenly called into it, sent flying out of his pantry on incomprehensible errands, that accounted for the growing wretchedness of his expression.

"Where are you going with that coat?"

"To your room, sir."

"Is there another shower coming?"

"I'm sure I don't know, sir. Shall I go up again and see, sir?"

"No! never mind."

My object was attained, as of course my other self in there would have heard everything that passed. During this interlude my two officers never raised their eyes off their respective plates; but the lip of that confounded cub, the second mate, quivered visibly.

I expected the steward to hook my coat on and come out at once. He was very slow about it; but I dominated my nervousness sufficiently not to shout after him. Suddenly I became aware (it could be heard plainly enough) that the fellow for some reason or other was opening the door of the bathroom. It was the end. The place was literally not big enough to swing a cat in. My voice died in my throat and I went stony all over. I expected to hear a yell of surprise and terror, and made a movement, but had not the strength to get on my legs. Everything remained still. Had my second self taken the poor wretch by the throat? I don't know what I could have done next moment if I had not seen the steward come out of my room, close the door, and then stand quietly by the sideboard.

"Saved," I thought. "But, no! Lost! Gone! He was gone!"

I laid my knife and fork down and leaned back in my chair. My head swam. After a while, when sufficiently recovered to speak in a steady voice, I instructed my mate to put the ship round at eight o'clock himself.

"I won't come on deck," I went on. "I think I'll turn in, and unless the wind shifts I don't want to be disturbed before midnight. I feel a bit seedy."

"You did look middling bad a little while ago," the chief mate remarked without showing any great concern.

They both went out, and I stared at the steward

clearing the table. There was nothing to be read on that wretched man's face. But why did he avoid my eyes, I asked myself. Then I thought I should like to hear the sound of his voice.

"Steward!"

"Sir!" Startled as usual.

"Where did you hang up that coat?"

"In the bathroom, sir." The usual anxious tone. "It's not quite dry yet, sir."

For some time longer I sat in the cuddy. Had my double vanished as he had come? But of his coming there was an explanation, whereas his disappearance would be inexplicable. . . . I went slowly into my dark room, shut the door, lighted the lamp, and for a time dared not turn round. When at last I did I saw him standing bolt-upright in the narrow recessed part. It would not be true to say I had a shock, but an irresistible doubt of his bodily existence flitted through my mind. Can it be, I asked myself, that he is not visible to other eyes than mine? It was like being haunted. Motionless, with a grave face, he raised his hands slightly at me in a gesture which meant clearly, "Heavens! what a narrow escape!" Narrow indeed. I think I had come creeping quietly as near insanity as any man who has not actually gone over the border. That gesture restrained me, so to speak.

The mate with the terrific whiskers was now putting the ship on the other tack. In the moment of profound silence which follows upon the hands going to their stations I heard on the poop his raised voice: "Hard alee!" and the distant shout of the order repeated on the main-deck. The sails, in that light breeze, made but a faint fluttering noise. It ceased. The ship was coming round slowly: I held my breath in the renewed stillness of expectation; one wouldn't have thought that there was a single living soul on her decks. A sudden brisk shout, "Mainsail haul!" broke the spell, and in the noisy cries and rush overhead of the men running away with the main brace we two, down in my cabin, came together in our usual position by the bed place.

He did not wait for my question. "I heard him fumbling here and just managed to squat myself down in the bath," he whispered to me. "The fellow only opened the door and put his arm in to hang the coat up. All the same——"

"I never thought of that," I whispered back, even more appalled than before at the closeness of the shave, and marveling at that something unyielding in his character which was carrying him through so finely. There was no agitation in his whisper. Whoever was being driven distracted, it was not he. He was sane. And the proof of his sanity was continued when he took up the whispering again.

"It would never do for me to come to life again."

It was something that a ghost might have said. But what he was alluding to was his old captain's reluctant admission of the theory of suicide. It would obviously serve his turn—if I had understood at all the view which seemed to govern the unalterable purpose of his action.

"You must maroon me as soon as ever you can get amongst these islands off the Cambodge shore," he went on.

"Maroon you! We are not living in a boy's adventure tale," I protested. His scornful whispering took me up.

"We aren't indeed! There's nothing of a boy's tale in this. But there's nothing else for it. I want no more. You don't suppose I am afraid of what can be done to me? Prison or gallows or whatever they may please. But you don't see me coming back to explain such things to an old fellow in a wig and twelve respectable tradesmen, do you? What can they know whether I am guilty or not—or of *what* I am guilty, either? That's my affair. What does the Bible say? 'Driven off the face of the earth.' Very well, I am off the face of the earth now. As I came at night so I shall go."

"Impossible!" I murmured. "You can't."

"Can't? . . . Not naked like a soul on the Day of Judgment. I shall freeze on to this sleeping suit. The Last Day is not yet—and . . . you have understood thoroughly. Didn't you?"

I felt suddenly ashamed of myself. I may say truly that I understood—and my hesitation in letting that man swim away from my ship's side had been a mere sham sentiment, a sort of cowardice.

"It can't be done now till next night," I breathed out. "The ship is on the off-shore tack and the wind may fail us."

"As long as I know that you understand," he whispered. "But of course you do. It's a great satisfaction to have got somebody to understand. You seem to have been there on purpose." And in the same whisper, as if we two whenever we talked had to say things to each other which were not fit for the world to hear, he added, "It's very wonderful."

We remained side by side talking in our secret way—but sometimes silent or just exchanging a whispered word or two at long intervals. And as usual he stared through the port. A breath of wind came now and again into our faces. The ship might have been moored in dock, so gently and on an even keel she slipped through the water, that did not murmur even at our passage, shadowy and silent like a phantom sea.

At midnight I went on deck, and to my mate's great surprise put the ship round on the other tack. His terrible whiskers flitted round me in silent criticism. I certainly should not have done it if it had been only a question of getting out of that sleepy gulf as quickly as possible. I believe he told the second mate, who relieved him, that it was a great want of judgment. The other only yawned. That intolerable cub shuffled about so sleepily and lolled against the rails in such a slack, improper fashion that I came down on him sharply.

"Aren't you properly awake yet?"

"Yes, sir! I am awake."

"Well, then, be good enough to hold yourself as if you were. And keep a lookout. If there's any current we'll be closing with some islands before daylight."

The east side of the gulf is fringed with islands, some solitary, others in groups. On the blue background of the high coast they seem to float on silvery patches of calm water, arid and gray, or dark green and rounded like clumps of evergreen bushes, with the larger ones, a mile or two long, showing the out-

lines of ridges, ribs of gray rock under the dank mantle
of matted leafage. Unknown to trade, to travel,
almost to geography, the manner of life they harbor
is an unsolved secret. There must be villages—settlements of fishermen at least—on the largest of them,
and some communication with the world is probably
kept up by native craft. But all that forenoon, as we
headed for them, fanned along by the faintest of
breezes, I saw no sign of man or canoe in the field of
the telescope I kept on pointing at the scattered group.

At noon I gave no orders for a change of course,
and the mate's whiskers became much concerned and
seemed to be offering themselves unduly to my notice.
At last I said:

"I am going to stand right in. Quite in—as far as I
can take her."

The stare of extreme surprise imparted an air of
ferocity also to his eyes, and he looked truly terrific
for a moment.

"We're not doing well in the middle of the gulf,"
I continued, casually. "I am going to look for the land
breezes tonight."

"Bless my soul! Do you mean, sir, in the dark
amongst the lot of all them islands and reefs and
shoals?"

"Well—if there are any regular land breezes at all
on this coast one must get close inshore to find them,
mustn't one?"

"Bless my soul!" he exclaimed again under his
breath. All that afternoon he wore a dreamy, contem-
plative appearance which in him was a mark of per-
plexity. After dinner I went into my stateroom as if I

meant to take some rest. There we two bent our dark heads over a half-unrolled chart lying on my bed.

"There," I said. "It's got to be Koh-ring. I've been looking at it ever since sunrise. It has got two hills and a low point. It must be inhabited. And on the coast opposite there is what looks like the mouth of a biggish river—with some towns, no doubt, not far up. It's the best chance for you that I can see."

"Anything. Koh-ring let it be."

He looked thoughtfully at the chart as if surveying chances and distances from a lofty height—and following with his eyes his own figure wandering on the blank land of Cochin-China, and then passing off that piece of paper clean out of sight into uncharted regions. And it was as if the ship had two captains to plan her course for her. I had been so worried and restless running up and down that I had not had the patience to dress that day. I had remained in my sleeping suit, with straw slippers and a soft floppy hat. The closeness of the heat in the gulf had been most oppressive, and the crew were used to seeing me wandering in that airy attire.

"She will clear the south point as she heads now," I whispered into his ear. "Goodness only knows when, though, but certainly after dark. I'll edge her in to half a mile, as far as I may be able to judge in the dark——"

"Be careful," he murmured, warningly—and I realized suddenly that all my future, the only future for which I was fit, would perhaps go irretrievably to pieces in any mishap to my first command.

I could not stop a moment longer in the room. I

motioned him to get out of sight and made my way on the poop. That unplayful cub had the watch. I walked up and down for a while thinking things out, then beckoned him over.

"Send a couple of hands to open the two quarter-deck ports," I said, mildly.

He acutally had the impudence, or else so forgot himself in his wonder at such an incomprehensible order, as to repeat:

"Open the quarter-deck ports! What for, sir?"

"The only reason you need concern yourself about is because I tell you to do so. Have them open wide and fastened properly."

He reddened and went off, but I believe made some jeering remark to the carpenter as to the sensible practice of ventilating a ship's quarter-deck. I know he popped into the mate's cabin to impart the fact to him because the whiskers came on deck, as it were by chance, and stole glances at me from below—for signs of lunacy or drunkenness, I suppose.

A little before supper, feeling more restless than ever, I rejoined, for a moment, my second self. And to find him sitting so quietly was surprising, like something against nature, inhuman.

I developed my plan in a hurried whisper.

"I shall stand in as close as I dare and then put her round. I will presently find means to smuggle you out of here into the sail locker, which communicates with the lobby. But there is an opening, a sort of square for hauling the sails out, which gives straight on the quarter deck and which is never closed in fine weather, so as to give air to the sails. When the ship's way is deadened in stays and all the hands are aft at the main braces you will have a clear road to slip out and get overboard through the open quarter-deck port. I've had them both fastened up. Use a rope's end to lower yourself into the water so as to avoid a splash—you know. It could be heard and cause some beastly complication."

He kept silent for a while, then whispered, "I understand."

"I won't be there to see you go," I began with an effort. "The rest . . . I only hope I have understood, too."

"You have. From first to last"—and for the first time there seemed to be a faltering, something strained in his whisper. He caught hold of my arm, but the ringing of the supper bell made me start. He didn't though; he only released his grip.

After supper I didn't come below again till well past eight o'clock. The faint, steady breeze was loaded with dew; and the wet, darkened sails held all there was of propelling power in it. The night, clear and starry, sparkled darkly, and the opaque, lightless patches shifting slowly against the low stars were the drifting islets. On the port bow there was a big one more distant and shadowily imposing by the great space of sky it eclipsed.

On opening the door I had a back view of my very own self looking at a chart. He had come out of the recess and was standing near the table.

"Quite dark enough," I whispered.

He stepped back and leaned against my bed with a level, quiet glance. I sat on the couch. We had nothing to say to each other. Over our heads the officer of the watch moved here and there. Then I heard him move quickly. I knew what that meant. He was making for the companion; and presently his voice was outside my door.

"We are drawing in pretty fast, sir. Land looks rather close."

"Very well," I answered. "I am coming on deck directly."

I waited till he was gone out of the cuddy, then rose. My double moved too. The time had come to exchange our last whispers, for neither of us was ever to hear each other's natural voice.

"Look here!" I opened a drawer and took out three sovereigns. "Take this anyhow. I've got six and I'd give you the lot, only I must keep a little money to buy some fruit and vegetables for the crew from native boats as we go through Sunda Straits."

He shook his head.

"Take it," I urged him, whispering desperately. "No one can tell what——"

He smiled and slapped meaningly the only pocket of the sleeping jacket. It was not safe, certainly. But I produced a large old silk handkerchief of mine, and tying the three pieces of gold in a corner, pressed it on him. He was touched, I supposed, because he took it at last and tied it quickly round his waist under the jacket, on his bare skin.

Our eyes met; several seconds elapsed, till, our glances still mingled, I extended my hand and turned the lamp out. Then I passed through the cuddy, leaving the door of my room wide open. . . . "Steward!"

He was still lingering in the pantry in the greatness of his zeal, giving a rub-up to a plated cruet stand the last thing before going to bed. Being careful not to wake up the mate, whose room was opposite, I spoke in an undertone.

He looked round anxiously. "Sir!"

"Can you get me a little hot water from the galley?"

"I am afraid, sir, the galley fire's been out for some time now."

"Go and see."

He flew up the stairs.

"Now," I whispered, loudly, into the saloon—too loudly, perhaps, but I was afraid I couldn't make a sound. He was by my side in an instant—the double captain slipped past the stairs—through a tiny dark passage . . . a sliding door. We were in the sail locker, scrambling on our knees over the sails. A sudden thought struck me. I saw myself wandering barefooted, bareheaded, the sun beating on my dark poll. I snatched off my floppy hat and tried hurriedly in the dark to ram it on my other self. He dodged and fended off silently. I wonder what he thought had come to me before he understood and suddenly desisted. Our hands met gropingly, lingered united in a steady, motionless clasp for a second. . . . No word was breathed by either of us when they separated.

I was standing quietly by the pantry door when the steward returned.

"Sorry, sir. Kettle barely warm. Shall I light the spirit lamp?"

"Never mind."

I came out on deck slowly. It was now a matter of conscience to shave the land as close as possible—for now he must go overboard whenever the ship was put in stays. Must! There could be no going back for him. After a moment I walked over to leeward and my heart flew into my mouth at the nearness of the land on the bow. Under any other circumstances I would not have held on a minute longer. The second mate had followed me anxiously.

I looked on till I felt I could command my voice.

"She will weather," I said then in a quiet tone.

"Are you going to try that, sir?" he stammered out incredulously.

I took no notice of him and raised my tone just enough to be heard by the helmsman.

"Keep her good full."

"Good full, sir."

The wind fanned my cheek, the sails slept, the world was silent. The strain of watching the dark loom of the land grow bigger and denser was too much for me. I had shut my eyes—because the ship must go closer. She must! The stillness was intolerable. Were we standing still?

When I opened my eyes the second view started my heart with a thump. The black southern hill of Koh-ring seemed to hang right over the ship like a towering fragment of the ever-lasting night. On that enormous mass of blackness there was not a gleam to be seen, not a sound to be heard. It was gliding irresistibly towards us and yet seemed already within reach of the hand. I saw the vague figures of the watch grouped in the waist, gazing in awed silence.

"Are you going on, sir?" inquired an unsteady voice at my elbow.

I ignored it. I had to go on.

"Keep her full. Don't check her way. That won't do now," I said, warningly.

"I can't see the sails very well," the helmsman answered me, in strange, quavering tones.

Was she close enough? Already she was, I won't say in the shadow of the land, but in the very blackness of it, already swallowed up as it were, gone too close to be recalled, gone from me altogether.

"Give the mate a call," I said to the young man who stood at my elbow as still as death. "And turn all hands up."

My tone had a borrowed loudness reverberated from the height of the land. Several voices cried out together: "We are all on deck, sir."

Then stillness again, with the great shadow gliding closer, towering higher, without a light, without a sound. Such a hush had fallen on the ship that she might have been a bark of the dead floating in slowly under the very gate of Erebus.

"My God! Where are we?"

It was the mate moaning at my elbow. He was thunderstruck, and as it were deprived of the moral support of his whiskers. He clapped his hands and absolutely cried out, "Lost!"

"Be quiet," I said, sternly.

He lowered his tone, but I saw the shadowy gesture of his despair. "What are we doing here?"

"Looking for the land wind."

He made as if to tear his hair, and addressed me recklessly.

"She will never get out. You have done it, sir. I knew it'd end in something like this. She will never weather, and you are too close now to stay. She'll drift ashore before she's round. O my God!"

I caught his arm as he was raising it to batter his poor devoted head, and shook it violently.

"She's ashore already," he wailed, trying to tear himself away.

"Is she? . . . Keep good full there!"

"Good full, sir," cried the helmsman in a frightened, thin, childlike voice.

I hadn't let go the mate's arm and went on shaking it. "Ready about, do you hear? You go forward"—shake—"and stop there"—shake—"and hold your noise"—shake—"and see these head-sheets properly overhauled"—shake, shake—shake.

And all the time I dared not look towards the land lest my heart should fail me. I released my grip at last and he ran forward as if fleeing for dear life.

I wondered what my double there in the sail locker thought of this commotion. He was able to hear everything—and perhaps he was able to understand why, on my conscience, it had to be thus close—no less. My first order "Hard alee!" re-echoed ominously under the towering shadow of Koh-ring as if I had shouted in a mountain gorge. And then I watched the land intently. In that smooth water and light wind it was impossible to feel the ship coming-to. No! I could not feel her. And my second self was making now ready to ship out and lower himself overboard. Perhaps he was gone already . . . ?

The great black mass brooding over our very mastheads began to pivot away from the ship's side silently. And now I forgot the secret stranger ready to depart, and remembered only that I was a total stranger to the ship. I did not know her. Would she do it? How was she to be handled?

I swung the mainyard and waited helplessly. She was perhaps stopped, and her very fate hung in the balance, with the black mass of Koh-ring like the gate of the everlasting night towering over her taffrail. What would she do now? Had she way on her yet? I stepped to the side swiftly, and on the shadowy water I could see nothing except a faint phosphorescent flash revealing the glassy smoothness of the sleeping surface. It was impossible to tell—and I had not learned yet the feel of my ship. Was she moving? What I needed was something easily seen, a piece of paper, which I could throw overboard and watch. I had nothing on me. To run down for it I didn't dare. There was no time. All at once my strained, yearning stare distinguished a white object floating within a yard of the ship's side. White on the black water. A phosphorescent flash passed under it. What was that thing? . . . I recognized my own floppy hat. It must have fallen off his head . . . and he didn't bother. Now I had what I wanted—the saving mark for my eyes. But I hardly thought of my other self, now gone from the ship, to be hidden forever from all friendly faces, to be a fugitive and a vagabond on the earth, with no brand of the curse on his sane forehead to stay a slaying hand . . . too proud to explain.

And I watched the hat—the expression of my sudden pity for his mere flesh. It had been meant to save his homeless head from the dangers of the sun. And now—behold—it was saving the ship, by serving me for a mark to help out the ignorance of my strangeness. Ha! It was drifting forward, warning me just in time that the ship had gathered sternway.

"Shift the helm," I said in a low voice to the seaman standing still like a statue.

The man's eyes glistened wildly in the binnacle light as he jumped round to the other side and spun round the wheel.

I walked to the break of the poop. On the overshadowed deck all hands stood by the forebraces waiting for my order. The stars ahead seemed to be gliding from right to left. And all was so still in the world that I heard the quiet remark, "She's round," passed in a tone of intense relief between two seamen.

"Let go and haul."

The foreyards ran round with a great noise, amidst cheery cries. And now the frightful whiskers made themselves heard giving various orders. Already the ship was drawing ahead. And I was alone with her. Nothing! no one in the world should stand now between us, throwing a shadow on the way of silent knowledge and mute affection, the perfect communion of a seaman with his first command.

Walking to the taffrail, I was in time to make out,

on the very edge of a darkness thrown by a towering black mass like the very gateway of Erebus—yes, I was in time to catch an evanescent glimpse of my white hat left behind to mark the spot where the secret sharer of my cabin and of my thoughts, as though he were my second self, had lowered himself into the water to take his punishment: a free man, a proud swimmer striking out for a new destiny.

JOSEPH CONRAD:
A BIOGRAPHICAL SKETCH

Joseph Conrad, christened Józef Teodor Konrad Nalecz Korzeniowski, was born on the 3rd of December, 1857, in a part of Russia which had once belonged to Poland. His father and mother were ardent Polish patriots, resenting bitterly the partition of Poland between "the German learned pig" and "the Russian mangy dog." In many ways the growing boy—an only child—was disturbingly affected by his family's political misfortunes. At four he saw his father, a member of the landed gentry and a writer of considerable reputation, arrested as an agitator for Polish freedom and exiled to the cold regions north of Moscow. At seven he wept at the death of his young mother, who had insisted on accompanying her husband into exile, taking her son with her, and had succumbed to the resulting privations. At eleven, after seeing his father suffer for years from neglect and the resultant depression, he walked behind his coffin in the large procession in Cracow that was honoring a martyr to what seemed a hopeless cause. Thus, though Conrad retained many happy memories of his parents and relatives, he always grieved over the fate of his loved ones and of his native land.

It is not surprising that, after a few years of formal schooling in Cracow, the orphaned teen-ager left his ancestral home forever. He had concluded that there was no future for a Pole in occupied Poland; in rebellion he turned his back on the cold north for the warm Mediterranean at Marseilles and chose the life of a sailor without ever having seen the sea. Not only was he escaping from political tensions and from unstimulating schooling, but he was seeking economic independence and adventure—

the adventure he had read about in his favorite books by
Victor Hugo, Captain Marryat, and James Fenimore
Cooper. Although his Polish relatives looked upon his
becoming a common sailor as a denigration of his cultural
and social background, the French merchant marine was
a reasonable place for him to turn. He did not intend to
remain a common sailor; he merely planned to use the
sea as a road to richer experience. He chose French ships
to sail in because French was a second language for him,
as it was for most cultivated Poles; because France was a
favored country for his people; and because his uncle,
who had become a sort of foster father, had connections
in the shipping industry in the Mediterranean port.

The four years Conrad spent at Marseilles and in
French ships were exciting and happy ones. He quickly
got a job sailing to the West Indies, and on his second
voyage it appears that he was involved in extra-legal activities in a Latin-American country where a revolution
was being fomented. He later drew on these experiences
in one of his greatest novels, *Nostromo*. Back in Marseilles, where he had many friends, he became involved in
smuggling guns to the supporters of the unsuccessful pre-
tender to the Spanish throne, Don Carlos VII. If we take
such writings as *The Mirror of the Sea* and *The Arrow
of Gold* as basically autobiographical (as Conrad said we
should) we must assume that he wrecked his smuggling
craft, *The Tremolino*, on the Spanish coast and escaped
with difficulty to France. There he had a love affair with
a Basque adventuress, also a Carlist, named Doña Rita,
"with the volatile little soul of a sparrow dressed in fine
Parisian feathers, which had the risk of coming off dis-
concertingly at unexpected moments." Over Rita he is
supposed to have fought a pistol duel with a Captain
Blunt, an American. He wounded Blunt, who in turn
put a bullet through Conrad's body just above the heart.
When his uncle reached the wounded hero, both Rita and
Blunt had disappeared. Conrad told his solicitous but outraged relative that he had lost all his money gambling at

Monte Carlo and had tried to commit suicide; he said nothing about the duel. Perhaps there actually was a romantic duel, perhaps only an abortive suicide; either action would account for the end of Conrad's adventures in France.

At any rate, Conrad's next job was on a British ship with a home port in Suffolk. Much has been made of this shift in flags, because, of course, if Conrad had not become an English sailor he probably would never have become an English novelist. He appears to have made the change partly because a berth on the *Mavis* was the most available job, partly because he was nearly twenty-one, when he would be subject to military service with the Russians if they could get hold of him. While the French line with which he had been working operated under an international agreement to honor such commitments, British ships refused to recognize any such obligation. Moreover, by learning English quickly, which, as a good linguist Conrad knew he could do, and by applying himself diligently in the British merchant marine, he probably could get his captain's papers in the not too distant future and in addition arrange for naturalization as a British subject. This would not only put him out of danger of seizure by the Russians but would allow him to visit his relatives in occupied Poland without fear of trouble. That he had made a wise choice and had settled down a good deal since his Rita-*Tremolino* days was proved by events. In 1886 he passed his examinations for master mariner and in that same year was naturalized as a British subject.

Between the time he left Marseilles to the time he quit the *Adowa*, his last ship—some dozen years—Conrad served on British vessels in various capacities ranging from able seaman to captain. Most of these were sailing ships, though for an important period he was second mate of a steamer, the *Vidar*, owned by an Arab but flying the British flag, which plied between Singapore and various jungle ports in Borneo. He got his first view of the Orient on an old barque, *The Palestine*, that burned and sank off the coast of Java, giving him the background for his novelette *Youth*. He also served on ships in the Eastern wool trade and on a fast passenger clipper to Australia. He saw much of the Malay archipelago, where many of his stories are laid. His only sea command was the *Otago*, which he took over in Bangkok after the former captain's death. It is as the skipper of the *Otago* that he pictures himself in *The Secret Sharer*. The background for *Heart of Darkness*, however, comes from an interlude in Conrad's service in the British merchant marine, when, as the result of a romantic impulse, he made arrangements with the Belgians to go into the Congo to pilot a river boat, "a sardine can with a stern wheel." His short stay in the Congo did much to undermine his health, a fact which undoubtedly contributed to his giving up the sea as an occupation a few years later. However, by then he had nearly completed his first novel, *Almayer's Folly*; it was becoming increasingly clear that the son of a university-trained aristocrat who had written poetry and plays, as well as translating works by de Vigny, Hugo, and Shakespeare into Polish, was going to be an artist in words just as he had been a man of action on the sea.

The rest of Joseph Conrad's story is that of careful craftsman in fiction and a noted stylist in English. Although he wrote slowly, partly because of his temperament and partly because English was an acquired tongue for him (he never learned to speak without a pronounced accent), he produced a considerable number of distinguished works. From his first book he used "Joseph Conrad" as his writing name, realizing that two of his given names were preferable to the foreign-sounding Korzeniowski, which had been consistently but variously misspelled on the sailing papers of British ships. Almost equally skillful in the short story and the novel, he specialized in adventure stories, most of them laid in exotic places or on the sea, but adventure stories in which characters were realistic and moral probing and psychological portrayal were constantly present. For years he had a very limited audience, and it was not until he wrote *Chance*, after twenty years spent in producing sixteen notable volumes, that he achieved popular success. Earlier he had difficulty living on his writing, even after his income was augmented by a Civil List pension from the British government. He married happily and helped bring up two sons. He lived modestly, preferring country homes, particularly in Kent. He was fortunate in making close friends of other important writers such as John Galsworthy, Stephen Crane, Ford Madox Ford, and Henry James. He made a few trips out of England, the most important of which were a return to his Polish homeland at the outbreak of World War I and a short visit to New York late in his life (he had become so popular in America that he was almost mobbed by well-wishers). In the year of his death, he turned down a knighthood offered by George V. He was never a very healthy man; he suffered almost constantly from indigestion and gout, and his discomfort was increased by his hypochondria and tendency towards melancholia. However, he experienced no long painful illness at the end but died almost literally at his desk in 1924, when he was sixty-six years old.

CRITICAL
SUPPLEMENT

SOURCES AND COMPOSITION

The Crime which Suggested *The Secret Sharer:*
The Times [London], Friday, August 4, 1882

CENTRAL CRIMINAL COURT, *August 3.*
(*Before* Mr. JUSTICE STEPHEN.)

John Anderson, 31, seaman [alias Sidney Smith], was indicted for the wilful murder of John Francis.

Mr. Poland and Mr. Montagu Williams prosecuted for the Treasury; Mr. Edward Clark, Q.C., and Mr. Besley appeared for the defence.

The accused, it appeared, was chief mate on board a tea clipper called the Cutty Sark, which sailed from the port of London in May, 1880. The deceased, who was a coloured man, shipped as an able seaman, and it was stated that he soon afterwards incurred the displeasure of the prisoner in consequence of his incompetency. About the 9th or 10th of August, 1880, the vessel had just rounded the Cape, and at a quarter to 9 o'clock the prisoner was in command of the watch. The night was dark and dirty, and the watch was occupied in hauling the sail round. The deceased not being competent to perform seaman's duty, had been placed on the forecastle on the look out. The watch on hauling the ropes found that the "fore lazy tack" was fastened, and the prisoner called out to the deceased to let the tack go. The deceased replied, "Very well," or, according to the prisoner's version, "Go to the devil." Immediately afterwards the deceased let go the lazy tack, but instead of doing so as an able seaman would, he let the end go overboard. The prisoner said, "That ———————————— has done that out of spite." The deceased retorted, "Well, you told me to let it go," and the prisoner exclaimed, "I will come on the forecastle and heave you overboard, you nigger." The deceased replied,

"If you come up here I have got the capstan bar waiting for you." The prisoner then went on to the forecastle and was seen to raise the capstan bar, with which he struck the deceased on the head. The blow knocked the man over the forecastle on to the deck, and he never spoke again. The prisoner said to the watch, "Did you see that nigger lift the capstan bar to me," but the men replied that they did not. The prisoner said, "He will lift no more capstan bars to me, for I have knocked him down," and he added, "I have knocked him down like a bullock; he never gave a kick." The account given by the prisoner was that he did it in self-defence. The captain of the vessel attended to the deceased, but he remained insensible till the following day, when he expired from the injuries he received, and was buried at sea. Before the arrival of the ship at Anjer the accused, with the connivance of the captain, made his escape. The vessel proceeded thence to Singapore, and during the passage the captain committed suicide by jumping overboard, having previously dropped into the sea the capstan bar used by the prisoner. At Singapore the matter was reported to a magistrate, who, in due course, instituted an inquiry. The prisoner was arrested in London.

It was stated in cross-examination that the deceased man Francis had on several occasions threatened the prisoner's life, and once he sharpened his knife upon the grindstone for the purpose of carrying his threat into execution.

Mr. EDWARD CLARKE, addressing his Lordship at the close of the case, submitted that the evidence could not sustain the Court charging the prisoner with murder.

Mr. JUSTICE STEPHEN concurred; and

Mr. CLARKE said that, in those circumstances, he could not resist a verdict of manslaughter. The learned counsel addressed the Court in mitigation of punishment, pointing out that the vessel had been under-manned, and that at the time in question the accused had had an important manoeuvre to perform with respect to the sail. The deceased behaved in an insolent and "lubberly" manner, and it was absolutely necessary that the prisoner should assert his authority.

Numerous witnesses were then called on the part of the defence to show that the prisoner bore an excellent character and was a man whose disposition was humane and kindly.

The jury, by his Lordship's direction, then returned a verdict of manslaughter against the accused.

Mr. JUSTICE STEPHEN, in passing sentence, told the prisoner he had considered the case with anxious attention and with very great pain, because the evidence which had been given showed that he was a man of good character generally speaking and of humane disposition. He was happy to be able to give full weight to the evidence given in his favour. The deceased had certainly acted in a manner which was calculated to make the prisoner very angry, but it must be clearly understood that the taking of human life by brutal violence, whether on sea or on land, whether the life be that of a black or a white man, was a dreadful crime, and deserving of exemplary punishment. He sentenced the prisoner to seven years' penal servitude.

Conrad's Experiences in the Congo *
Jocelyn Baines

He [Conrad] arrived in Brussels in the last week of April [1890] to find that there was an end to procrastination. The Company had just heard that one of its steamer captains had been killed by the Africans and had decided to appoint Conrad in his place. He immediately set about hectic preparations for his departure, having to

* From Jocelyn Baines, *Joseph Conrad*. New York, McGraw-Hill (1960), pp. 110–119.

make two journeys between London and Brussels in the course of a few days. In "Heart of Darkness" Conrad describes Marlow's last days in Europe, his final visit to the Company's offices in the rue Brédérode, his medical inspection by the macabrely facetious doctor and his farewell to his aunt. He then went by rail from Brussels to Bordeaux, whence he sailed for Boma on the *Ville de Maceio* in the second week of May, apparently taking with him what he had written of *Almayer's Folly*. . . .

Conrad disembarked from the *Ville de Maceio* at Boma and continued on a smaller boat to Matadi about forty miles up the Congo and the highest navigable point, where he arrived on 13 June.

At this date it was an important station, with 170 European inhabitants and four factories—English, Portuguese, Dutch and French—as well as the Sanford Exploring Expedition's buildings, which had been taken over by SACHC [*Société Anonyme pour le Commerce du Haut-Congo*]. Work was also in progress on a railroad which was to run from Matadi to Kinshasa. . . .

While at Matadi Conrad started to keep a diary which has been preserved. In the first entry he wrote:

Feel considerably in doubt about the future. Think just now that my life amongst the people (white) around here cannot be very comfortable. Intend avoid acquaintances as much as possible.

And in the next entry:

Prominent characteristic of the social life here; people speaking ill of each other.

This impression is echoed by Marlow in "Heart of Darkness".

The Congo had without question attracted a mixed assortment of whites. The most sinister and ruthless group consisted of those lured by the vision of immense riches, who were determined to make their packet and then get out before the climate killed them; then there were misfits, like Carlier in "An Outpost of Progress", or men who for some reason had found it advisable to leave Europe for an area where it did not much matter if their pasts caught up with them. But there were also tough adventurers who were tempted by the magnitude and novelty of the challenge which such an enterprise presented, and ardent missionaries enticed by the number of souls available for conversion. Finally there were men, impatient with the humdrum routine of highly organised civilised life, who were constantly attracted by the unknown and felt that they could only express themselves amid the freedom of unsubdued humanity and nature; among them were Conrad himself and Roger Casement, the only man from the whole Congo episode of whom Conrad spoke with any enthusiasm. He wrote in his diary:

Made the acquaintance of Mr. Roger Casement, which I should consider as a great pleasure under any circumstances and now it becomes a positive piece of luck. Thinks, speaks well, most intelligent and very sympathetic.

* * * * * * * * * * * * *

After just over a fortnight at Matadi—"an eternity" to Marlow—where he filled in some of the time packing ivory into cases, Conrad and a M. Harou left on 28 June with a caravan and thirty-one carriers on a 200-mile trek to another of the Company's stations at Kinshasa on Stanley Pool.

The journey must have been an ordeal. The party travelled on what were little more than tracks through fairly open but rough, hilly country, a landscape which Conrad described at first as "gray-yellowish (dry grass) with reddish patches (soil) and clumps of dark green vegetation scattered sparsely about", and a few days later as "a confused wilderness of hills, landslips on their sides showing red". There were numerous ravines carrying streams or rivers into the Congo, and at a later stage of the journey—presumably the caravan had been left behind—at least one river to be crossed by canoe. After a cold night spent battling with mosquitoes they would set out shortly after dawn when the mists were still hovering and the sky was overcast and tramp through deserted country, except for an occasional native market, the gruesome sight of the decaying corpse of an African, or the distant beating of drums. At about midday, when the temperature was becoming too hot for travel, they would stop at a camping-place which was often dirty and without an adequate supply of water; it was a relief to come upon the clean and comfortable Protestant Mission at Sutili, where they were entertained by Mrs Percy Comber.

Conrad's white co-traveller, Harou, whom he described in "Heart of Darkness" as "not a bad chap, but rather too fleshy and with the exasperating habit of fainting on the hot hillsides, miles away from the least bit of shade and water", was constantly ill from the start. He was immensely heavy and the need to have him carried much of the way in a hammock caused frequent rows with the carriers. Although he was ill at Manyanga and several other times confessed to feeling seedy, Conrad's own health seems to have held out remarkably well.

Here are some of the more interesting or typical entries in his diary:

Thursday, 3rd July. Left at 6 a.m. after a good night's rest. Crossed a low range of hills and entered a broad valley, or rather plain, with a break in the middle. Met an off[icer] of the State inspecting. A few minutes afterwards saw at a camp[ing] place the dead body of a Backongo. Shot? Horrid smell. . . .

Noticed Palma Christi—Oil Palm. Very straight, tall and thick trees in some places. Name not known to me. . . .

Bird notes charming. One especially a flute-like note. Another kind of 'boom' ressembling [*sic*] the very distant baying of a hound. Saw only pigeons and a few green parroquets. Very small and not many. No birds of prey seen by me.

These notes are interesting because Conrad very seldom refers to objects of natural history in his work and Richard Curle states that he "practically never showed the slightest interest" in such things.

Friday, 4th July. . . . Saw another dead body lying by the path in an attitude of meditative repose. . . . At night when the moon rose heard shouts and drumming in distant villages. Passed a bad night.

Saturday, 5th July. . . . Today fell into a muddy puddle— Beastly! The fault of the man that carried me. After camp[ing] went to a small stream bathed and washed clothes. Getting jolly well sick of this fun.

Monday, 7th July. Left at 6 after good night's rest, on the road to Inkandu, which is some distance past Lukunga Govt. station. Route very accidented. Succession of round steep hills. At times walking along the crest of a chain of hills. Just before Lukunga our carriers took a wide sweep to the southward till the station bore N[orth]. Walking through long grass for 1½ hours. Crossed a river about 100 feet wide and 4 deep.

After another ½-hour's walk through manioc plantations in good order rejoined our route to the E[astward] of Lukunga sta[tion], walking along an undulating plain towards the Inkandu market on a hill. Hot, thirsty and tired. At eleven arrived on the mket place. About 200 people. No water. No camp[ing] place. After remaining for one hour left in search of a resting place. Row of carriers. No water. At last about 1½ p.m. camped on an exposed hill side near a muddy creek. No shade. Tent on a slope. Sun heavy. Wretched.

Direction N.E. by N.—Distance 22 miles.

Night miserably cold. No sleep. Mosquitos.

Tuesday, 29th. . . . On the road today passed a skeleton tied up to a post. Also white man's grave—no name—heap of stones in the form of a cross. Health good now.

Thursday, 31st. . . . From 9 a.m. infernally hot day. Harou very little better. Self rather seedy. Bathed.

Then, on the last day before reaching Kinshasa (when the first notebook ends):

Friday, 1st of August, 1890. . . . Harou not very well. Mosquitos—frogs—beastly! Glad to see the end of this stupid tramp. Feel rather seedy. Sun rose red. Very hot day. Wind S[outh].

The journey had lasted thirty-six days, including a halt of seventeen at Manyanga.

At Kinshasa Conrad's sense of foreboding was given tangible confirmation. The Company's steamer, *Florida*, of which he was supposed to take command had been badly damaged and was at the moment undergoing repairs. However, he was not kept hanging about but was immediately attached as supernumerary to another of the Company's steamers, the *Roi des Belges*, in order to learn the river. The *Roi des Belges* was about to leave for Stanley Falls with Camille Delcommune, who had just been made acting-director of SACHC in the Congo, and one of its objects was to collect the Company's agent named Georges Antoine Klein who was seriously ill.

.   .   .   .

During the voyage on the *Roi des Belges* the captain became ill and Conrad was put temporarily in command. *Mouvement Géographique* singled out this voyage as having been done in particularly good time; nonetheless Klein, like Kurtz, died on the way back. Conrad used the voyage as the basis for that described in "Heart of Darkness" and the correspondence between the names Kurtz and Klein is obvious; in the manuscript of the story Conrad starts by writing Klein and then changes to Kurtz; but it is not known how closely Kurtz is modelled on the activities and character of Klein. Conrad described "Heart of Darkness" as "experience pushed a little (and only very little) beyond the actual facts of the case", and this story only differs significantly from several other accounts of events in the Congo in the intensity with which the experiences are realised; there is nothing improbable in the portrait of Kurtz.

On 24 September, the day of his return to Kinshasa, Conrad wrote to Maria Tyszka that he was very busy preparing for a new expedition, on the river Kassaï, which might mean an absence of more than ten months. This was the expedition of Alexandre Delcommune, Camille's elder brother, and Conrad had been designated to command the steamer when he was engaged by the Company in Brussels. . . . When he discovered that he would not be given the command of the steamer destined to carry Alexandre Delcommune's expedition he realised that his position was intolerable and gave up. He was also ill. . . .

. . . .

Conrad has described his last journey down the Congo in *A Personal Record*:

I got round the turn [between Kinshasa and Léopoldville] more or less alive, though I was too sick to care whether I did or not, and, always with *Almayer's Folly* amongst my diminishing baggage, I arrived at that delectable capital Boma, where before the departure of the steamer which was to take me home I had the time to wish myself dead over and over again with perfect sincerity.

He probably did not realise at the time to what extent these four months in the Congo had affected his health. It had never been very strong and the Congo climate permanently undermined it so that for the rest of his life he was dogged by recurrent fever and gouty symptoms. Nor was his body alone affected. It would be absurd to attribute his long periods of despair to the Congo experience—there had been enough previous experiences to confirm an innately gloomy disposition—and his remark to Garnett that "before the Congo I was a mere animal" is an obvious exaggeration. But "An Outpost of Progress", for all its irony and macabre humour and "Heart of Darkness", with its tone of outraged humanism and its consciousness of evil, show how deeply he was affected emotionally by the sight of such human baseness and degradation; moreover his Congo experience devastatingly exposed the cleavage between human pretensions and practice, a consciousness of which underlies Conrad's philosophy of life.

The Making of *Heart of Darkness* *
John Dozier Gordan

Little is known of the history of the last short story
Conrad wrote before he completed *Lord Jim*. The idea
was in his mind when he visited Garnett at the Cearne in
the late summer of 1898. He gave his host "in detail a
very full synopsis of what he intended to write. To my
surprise," Garnett remembered, "when I saw the printed
version I found that about a third of the most striking
incidents had been replaced by others of which he had
said nothing at all. The effect of the written narrative
was no less sombre than the spoken, and the end was
more consummate; but I regretted the omission of various
scenes, one of which described the hero lying sick to death
in a native hut, tended by an old negress who brought him
water from day to day, when he had been abandoned by
all the Belgians." The impetus for writing came under
especially flattering circumstances. The Blackwoods were
sufficiently impressed by "Karain" and "Youth" to request
a contribution for the one thousand issue of *Maga* in
February, 1899.

Apparently he promised the story for November,
1898; on January 6, 1899, he mentioned that he was
"fort occupé au milieu d'un travail qui attend et que l'on
attend de moi avec impatience puisqu'il devait être fini en
Novembre. . . ." The story seems to have been finished
around the middle of January for he wrote on January
12, "I am finishing in a frightful hurry a story for
B'wood and it's an immense effort." Richard Curle remembered "Conrad telling me that its 40,000 words

---

* From John Dozier Gordan, *Joseph Conrad, the Making of a
Novelist*. Cambridge, Mass., Harvard University Press (1940),
pp. 266–268.

occupied only about a month in writing." All that can be said of the composition of "Heart of Darkness" is that it was probably written between the middle of December, 1898, and the middle of January, 1899. This story and "An Outpost of Progress" were, according to the author, who neglected to mention his jungle fever, "all the spoil I brought out from the center of Africa, where, really, I had no sort of business."

The story ran under the title of "The Heart of Darkness" in *Blackwood's Magazine* for February, March, and April, 1899, and was republished as "Heart of Darkness" in *Youth: A Narrative and Two Other Stories*. When the first installment appeared, Conrad was delighted to hear from Cunninghame Graham that he liked it but cautioned his friend: "I am simply in the seventh heaven to find you like the 'H. of D.' so far. You bless me indeed. Mind you don't curse me by and bye for the very same thing. There are two more instalments in which the idea is so wrapped up in secondary notions that you,—even you!—may miss it." His fear of the obscurity of the story reappeared years later when he thanked Garnett on December 22, 1902, for his review of the collection *Youth* in the *Academy:* "And your brave attempt to grapple with the fogginess of H of D, to explain what I myself tried to shape blindfold, as it were, has touched me profoundly." Yet Conrad was well aware of the savage power of the story. He described it once as "histoire farouche d'un journaliste qui devient chef de station à l'intérieur et se fait adorer par une tribu de sauvages. Ainsi décrit le sujet a l'air rigolo, mais il ne l'est pas."

CONTEMPORARY REVIEWS

From *The Times Literary Supplement*
London, December 12, 1902

Telling tales, just spinning yarns, has gone out of fashion since the novel has become an epitome of everything a man has to say about anything. The three stories in YOUTH of Joseph Conrad (Blackwood, 6s.) are in this reference a return to an earlier taste. The yarns are of the sea, told with an astonishing zest; and given with vivid accumulation of detail and iterative persistency of emphasis on the quality of character and scenery. The method is exactly the opposite of Mr. Kipling's. It is a little precious; one notes a tasting of the quality of phrases and an occasional indulgence in poetic rhetoric. But the effect is not unlike Mr. Kipling's. In the first story, "Youth," the colour, the atmosphere of the East is brought out as in a picture. The concluding scene of the "Heart of Darkness" is crisp and brief enough for Flaubert, but the effect—a woman's ecstatic belief in a villain's heroism—is reached by an indulgence in the picturesque horror of the villain, his work and his surroundings, which is pitiless in its insistence, and quite extravagant according to the canons of art. But the power, the success in conveying the impression vividly, without loss of energy is undoubted and is refreshing. "The End of the Tether," the last of the three, is the longest and best. Captain Whalley is racy of the sea, and an embodiment of its finest traditions; and the pathos of his long-drawn wrestle with the anger of circumstances is poignant to the end. Mr. Conrad should have put him in the forefront of the book. There are many readers who would not get beyond the barren and not very pretty philosophy of "Youth"; more who might feel they had had enough horror at the end of "The Heart of Darkness." But they would miss a great deal if they did not reach "The End of the Tether." It has this further advantage over the other two tales, that it is much less clever, much less precious.

From *The Nation*
New York, June 11, 1903

[Conrad's] latest volume, entitled *Youth,* places him unmistakably among the best imaginative writers of his period. Objectively, the tales are realistic, sometimes violently realistic like Kipling's, but the record of action of particular things done and suffered is united with the universally human by a great imagination and a temperamental impressionability rich as Pierre Loti's, yet saved from sickliness by an Anglo-Saxon sanity. . . . The enchantment worked by Mr. Conrad's imagination is the elevation of all sorts of facts, the common and unusual, the sordid and picturesque, the heroic and ignoble, to an atmosphere charged with emotion at a very high pitch. . . .

"Heart of Darkness" vibrates with loathing of a land where primeval nature assumes the functions of a vengeful fate, and either kills invaders of her awful solitudes or reduces them to the condition of brutes. It is a dreadful and fascinating tale, full as any of Poe's of mystery and haunting terrors, yet with a substantial basis of reality that no man who had not lived as well as dreamed could conjure into existence. . . .

From *The Independent*
New York, March 6, 1913

The second tale [*The Secret Sharer*] is also of a captain. New to his ship and the officers under him, he is alone on deck one night, when out of the dark water emerges a swimmer from a vessel two miles away. This apparition confesses that he has been technically guilty of murder, tho not in any moral sense, whereupon the captain smuggles him into his cabin and conceals him there for several days until the ship is within a swimmer's reach of shore. Mr. Conrad has created a situation of tension thru character rather than incident. There are, to be sure, details of discovery barely averted, but in the main the stress is upon the captain's moods, fears and loyalty to his strange cabin-mate.

The keynote verse on the title page of this volume [*'Twixt Land and Sea*] declares that "life is a tragic folly." Here, as in almost all Conrad, the emphasis is on the tragic. But all who have enjoyed his other tales of hot blood and tropic seas, will enjoy this book, done with the author's measured artistic touch.

MODERN CRITICAL EVALUATIONS

Control of Point of View through
the Use of Marlow *
Joseph Warren Beach

. . . Conrad's eloquence is most frequently resorted
to in his earliest stories, before he had hit upon devices for
"making us see" more structural and less dependent on
mere style. In the course of his later writing he found a
considerable variety of such devices for bringing the subject into focus. To begin with, there are the various tech-
niques for identifying the author (and so the reader) with
the principal actor, making him feel his suspense, his
curiosities, his irritations, putting him at the same point of
view, physically and morally, as the character.

This method came very natural to Conrad in a good
many of his stories which are hardly more than tran-
scripts of his personal experience. "The Shadow-Line"
(1917), for example, is a first-person account, with only
insignificant variations from fact, of Conrad's voyage
from Bangkok to Singapore in the bark *Otago,* his first
command.

Something of the same thing is true of tales like
"Youth" and "Heart of Darkness" (1902), although
Conrad in these cases provided a special framework for
his stories. Experiences which were his own—almost literally exact throughout in "Youth," somewhat more
worked up and highlighted in "Heart of Darkness"—he
attributes to a Captain Marlow. He has the captain nar-
rate his adventures orally to a group of men. The author
describes the place and conditions under which the stories

* From Joseph Warren Beach, *The Twentieth Century Novel:
Studies in Technique.* New York, The Century Co. (1932), pp.
342-344.

were told, thus furnishing a sort of stage for his little drama. And so they are provided in advance with a certain emotional tone, which goes far to give them artistic unity and precision of effect. Moreover, their being told by word of mouth to a group of sympathetic but matter-of-fact listeners, necessarily affects the style, somewhat chastening Conrad's Orientalism, making it seem, so far as it lingers still, a peculiarity of Captain Marlow's temperament, and altogether contributing to the plausibility, the verisimilitude—a most important consideration in the art of making us "see."

"Heart of Darkness" is a much more difficult artistic achievement than "Youth," much more of an effort of the creative imagination. It was based on Conrad's voyage to the head-waters of the Congo and his personal impressions of the geographical and social conditions of that exploited country. Many of the characters were taken from life. Kurtz was suggested by one Klein, the company's agent at Stanley Falls. But what Marlow made of Kurtz and his way of doing it, that is the story.

Kurtz is a personal embodiment, a dramatization, of all that Conrad felt of futility, degradation, and horror in what the Europeans in the Congo called "progress," which meant the exploitation of the natives by every variety of cruelty and treachery known to greedy man. Kurtz was to Marlow, penetrating this country, a name, constantly recurring in people's talk, for cleverness and enterprise. But there were slight intimations, growing stronger as Marlow drew near to the heart of darkness, of traits and practices so abhorrent to all our notions of decency, honor, and humanity, that the enterprising trader gradually takes on the proportions of a ghastly and almost supernatural monster, symbol for Marlow of the general spirit of this European undertaking. The blackness and mystery of his character tone in with the savage mystery of the Congo, and they develop *pari passu* with the atmosphere of shadowy horror.

This development is conducted cumulatively by insensible degrees, by carefully calculated releases of new items, new intimations; and all this process is *controlled* through the consciousness of Marlow. Thus we have a triumph of atmospheric effect produced with the technique of the limited point of view, a story in a class with "The Fall of the House of Usher" and "The Turn of the Screw."

"Adjectival Insistence" in *Heart of Darkness* *
F. R. Leavis

Heart of Darkness is, by common consent, one of Conrad's best things. . . . The details and circumstances of the voyage to and up the Congo are present to us as if we were making the journey ourselves and (chosen for record as they are by a controlling imaginative purpose) they carry specificities of emotion and suggestion with them. . . . By means of this art of vivid essential record, in terms of things seen and incidents experienced by a main agent in the narrative, and particular contacts and exchanges with other human agents, the overwhelming sinister and fantastic "atmosphere" is engendered. Ordinary greed, stupidity and moral squalor are made to look like behaviour in a lunatic asylum against the vast and oppressive mystery of the surroundings, rendered potently in terms of sensation. This mean lunacy, which we are made to feel as at the same time normal and insane, is brought out by contrast with the fantastically secure innocence of the young harlequin-costumed Russian ("son of an arch-priest . . . Government of Tambov"), the introduction to whom is by the way of that copy of Towser's (or Towson's) *Inquiry into Some Points of Seamanship*, symbol of tradition, sanity, and the moral idea,

* From F. R. Leavis, *The Great Tradition*. New York, New York University Press (1963), pp. 212, 213, 215–216.

found lying, an incongruous mystery, in the dark heart of Africa.

Of course, . . . the author's comment cannot be said to be wholly implicit. Nevertheless, it is not separable from the thing rendered, but seems to emerge from the vibration of this as part of the tone. At least, this is Conrad's art at its best. There are, however, places in *Heart of Darkness* where we become aware of comment as an interposition, and worse, as an intrusion, at times an exasperating one. Hadn't he, we find ourselves asking, overworked "inscrutable," "inconceivable," "unspeakable" and that kind of word already?—yet still they recur. Is anything added to the oppressive mysteriousness of the Congo by such sentences as:

"It was the stillness of an implacable force brooding over an inscrutable intention."?

The same vocabulary, the same adjectival insistence upon inexpressible and incomprehensible mystery, is applied to the evocation of human profundities and spiritual horrors; to magnifying a thrilled sense of the unspeakable potentialities of the human soul. The actual effect is not to magnify but rather to muffle.

The Night Journey in *The Secret Sharer* and *Heart of Darkness* *
Albert J. Guerard

"A Smile of Fortune" and even the charming "Youth" may not belong with the best of Conrad. But "Heart of Darkness" and "The Secret Sharer" and *The Shadow Line* belong not only with that best. Historically speaking,

* From Albert J. Guerard, *Conrad the Novelist*. Cambridge, Mass., Harvard University Press (1958), pp. 14–16, 21–22, 24–25, 37–39.

they are among the first and best—one is tempted to say only—symbolist masterpieces in English fiction. The sea voyages and the one great Congo journey are unmistakably journeys within, and journeys through a darkness.

The matter may come to seem dark indeed, so a brief forewarning is necessary. The term and concept of the *night journey*, borrowed from anthropology and now gaining some currency in criticism, will appear several times in the following pages. By it I refer to the archetypal myth dramatized in much great literature since the Book of Jonah: the story of an essentially solitary journey involving profound spiritual change in the voyager. In its classical form the journey is a descent into the earth, followed by a return to light. Sometimes the dream is literally an illuminating dream (as with Don Quixote's experience in the well); more often it is dramatized through an actual voyage and movement through space. A familiar variant concerns passage through a tunnel or other dark place; another describes descent to the depths of the sea. It is assumed that this myth, like any powerful and universal dream, has some other meaning than one of literal adventure, though this other meaning is often unintended. *We dream this dream because we are the people we are; because our conscious and unconscious lives alike have certain psychic needs.* The nature of the vision may vary; so too may vary the nature of the change and rebirth experienced.

But very often the dream appears to be about the introspective process itself: about a risky descent into the preconscious or even unconscious; about a restorative return to the primitive sources of being and an advance through temporary regression. Psychologists have their different geographies of the unconscious, they too using or creating myths and symbolic figures to suggest unseen realities. Not all would agree that the male shadow, female anima, and occult mandala have as definite an existence as Jung implies, and not all would agree with him that integration of the personality is impossible without a full descent into the unconscious. But nearly all would agree that an unconscious exists.

It therefore should go without saying that a powerful successful dreaming of the night journey is itself likely to be unconscious to some extent; the dreamer may have no clear awareness of the nature of his dream. I suspect the myth of the night journey is unusually conscious in "The Secret Sharer," slightly less conscious in "Heart of Darkness," still less conscious in *The Shadow Line*. Psychologically speaking, "Youth" offers no real night journey at all.

. . . .

"On my right hand there were lines of fishing-stakes resembling a mysterious system of half-submerged bamboo fences, incomprehensible in its division of the domain of tropical fishes . . ." The strange first paragraph of "The Secret Sharer," with its dream landscape of ill-defined boundaries between land, air, and sea, prepares us for this most frankly psychological of Conrad's shorter works. Even at a quite explicit level it is the story of a personality test: "I wondered how far I should turn out faithful to that ideal conception of one's own personality every man sets up for himself secretly." The narrator-captain is insecure at the start; he looks forward to leaving "the unrest of the land." The story moves from his sense of being stranger to his ship, and to himself, to a final mature confidence and integration: "And I was alone with her. Nothing! no one in the world should stand now between us, throwing a shadow on the way of silent knowledge and mute affection, the perfect communication of a seaman with his first command." This is the end of the experience. But he must give up, almost at its beginning, his illusion of the sea's great security and "untempted life." For the temptation appears on the very next page in the guise of Leggatt, fugitive from the *Sephora* because he had killed a member of his crew.

Whatever test occurs, or whatever change in the narrator's personality, must be due to his relationship with Leggatt. For that relationship is the whole story.

.   .   .   .

This then is the situation in its purely human and material terms—a situation Conrad will dramatize again and again: the act of sympathetic identification with a suspect or outlaw figure, and the ensuing conflict between loyalty to the individual and loyalty to the community. It is, at our first response, a dramatic outward relationship. But as double Leggatt is also very inwardly a secret self. He provokes a crippling division of the narrator's personality, and one that interferes with his seamanship. On the first night the captain intends to pin together the curtains across the bed in which Leggatt is lying. But he cannot. He is too tired, in "a peculiarly intimate way." He feels less "torn in two" when he is with Leggatt in the cabin, but this naturally involves neglect of his duties. As for other times—"I was constantly watching myself, my secret self, as dependent on my actions as my own personality, sleeping in that bed, behind that door which faced me as I sat at the head of the table." He loses all "unconscious alertness," his relations with the other officers become more strained, and in the navigational crisis of Koh-ring he realizes that he does not know how to handle his ship. He has been seriously disoriented, and even begins to doubt Leggatt's bodily existence. "I think I had come creeping quietly as near insanity as any man who has not actually gone over the border." The whispering communion of the narrator and his double—of the seaman-self and some darker, more interior, and outlaw self—must have been necessary and rewarding, since the story ends as positively as it does. But it is obvious to both men that the arrangement cannot be permanent. Nor would it do for Leggatt *to come back to life* in his own guise.

The narrator therefore takes his ship close to the land, so that Leggatt can escape and swim to the island of Koh-ring. But he takes the ship much closer to that reefed shore than necessary. He is evidently compelled to take an extreme risk in payment for his experience. "It was now a matter of conscience to shave the land as close as possible . . . perhaps he [Leggatt] was able to understand why, on my conscience, it had to be thus close—no less." Before they separate he gives Leggatt three pieces of gold and forces his hat on him, to protect him from the tropic sun. And this act of "sudden pity for his mere flesh" saves the ship. At the critical moment when the captain must know whether the ship is moving, in that darkness as of the gateway of Erebus, he sees his hat, a saving mark, floating on the water. Now he can give the order to shift the helm; the ship at last moves ahead and is saved. The final sentence refers to Leggatt: "the secret sharer of my cabin and of my thoughts, as though he were my second self, had lowered himself into the water to take his punishment: a free man, a proud swimmer striking out for a new destiny." Leggatt is perhaps a free man in several senses, but not least in the sense that he has escaped the narrator's symbolizing projection. He has indeed become "mere flesh," is no longer a "double." And the hat floating on the black water now defines a necessary separateness.

* * * * * * * * * * * * * *

. . . It is time to recognize that the story ["Heart of Darkness"] is not primarily about Kurtz or about the brutality of Belgian officials but about Marlow its narrator. To what extent it also expresses the Joseph Conrad a biographer might conceivably recover, who in 1898 still felt a debt must be paid for his Congo journey and who paid it by the writing of this story, is doubtless an insoluble question. I suspect two facts (of a possible several hundred) are important. First, that going to the Congo was the enactment of a childhood wish associated with the disapproved childhood ambition to go to sea, and that this belated enactment was itself profoundly disapproved, in 1890, by the uncle and guardian. It was another gesture of a man bent on throwing his life away. But even more important may be the guilt of complicity, just such a guilt as many novelists of the Second World War have been obliged to work off. What Conrad thought of the expedition of the Katanga Company of 1890–1892 is accurately reflected in his remarks on the "Eldorado Exploring Expedition" of "Heart of Darkness": "It was reckless without hardihood, greedy without audacity, and cruel without courage . . . with no more moral purpose at the back of it than there is in burglars breaking into a safe." Yet Conrad hoped to obtain command of the expedition's ship even after he had returned from the initiatory voyage dramatized in his novel. Thus the adventurous Conrad and Conrad the novelist may have experienced collision. But the collision, again as with so many novelists of the second war, could well have been deferred and retrospective, not felt intensely at the time.

So much for the elusive Conrad of the biographers and of the "Congo Diary." Substantially and in its central emphasis "Heart of Darkness" concerns Marlow (projection to whatever great or small degree of a more irrecoverable Conrad) and his journey toward and through certain facets or potentialities of self. F. R. Leavis seems to regard him as a narrator only, providing a "specific and concretely realized point of view." But Marlow reiterates often enough that he is recounting a spiritual voyage of self-discovery. He remarks casually but crucially that he did not know himself before setting out, and that he likes work for the chance it provides to "find yourself . . . what no other man can ever know." The Inner Station "was the farthest point of navigation and the culminating point of my experience." At a material and rather superficial level, the journey is through the temptation of atavism. It is a record of "remote kinship" with the "wild and passionate uproar," of a "trace of a response" to it, of a final rejection of the "fascination of the abomination." And why should there not be the trace of a response? "The mind of man is capable of anything —because everything is in it, all the past as well as all the future." Marlow's temptation is made concrete through his exposure to Kurtz, a white man and sometime idealist who had fully responded to the wilderness: a potential and fallen self. "I had turned to the wilderness really, not to Mr. Kurtz." At the climax Marlow follows Kurtz ashore, confounds the beat of the drum with the beating of his heart, goes through the ordeal of looking into Kurtz's "mad soul," and brings him back to the ship. He returns to Europe a changed and more knowing man. Ordinary people are now "intruders whose knowledge of life was to me an irritating pretence, because I felt so sure they could not possibly know the things I knew."

On this literal plane, and when the events are so abstracted from the dream-sensation conveying them, it is hard to take Marlow's plight very seriously. Will he, the busy captain and moralizing narrator, also revert to savagery, go ashore for a howl and a dance, indulge unspeakable lusts? The late Victorian reader (and possibly Conrad himself) could take this more seriously than we; could literally believe not merely in a Kurtz's deterioration through months of solitude but also in the sudden reversions to the "beast" of naturalistic fiction. Insofar as Conrad does want us to take it seriously and literally, we must admit the nominal triumph of a currently accepted but false psychology over his own truer intuitions. But the triumph is only nominal. For the personal narrative is unmistakably authentic, which means that it explores something truer, more fundamental, and distinctly less material: the night journey into the unconscious, and confrontation of an entity within the self. "I flung one shoe overboard, and became aware that that was exactly what I had been looking forward to—a talk with Kurtz."

It little matters what, in terms of psychological symbolism, we call this double or say he represents: whether the Freudian id or the Jungian shadow or more vaguely the outlaw. And I am afraid it is impossible to say where Conrad's conscious understanding of his story began and ended. The important thing is the introspective plunge and the powerful dream seem true; and are therefore inevitably moving.

The Detribalization of Kurtz and the Second-Rate Helmsman *
Harold R. Collins

Civilizing savages is not such a simple affair as the early imperialists supposed. Africans "reclaimed" from the supports and restraints of their old social orders and unable to live by white standards may become less satisfactory human beings than raw, uncivilized savages. Since Joseph Conrad's time the process of detribalization has gained momentum in Africa; the impact of white civilization has produced a multitude of "unstable fools" and worse—disorganized, derelict personalities wandering between the lost primitive culture and white civilization. A close study of the relations of Kurtz, the cannibals, and the second-rate helmsman in "Heart of Darkness" shows some implications often overlooked and reminds us that the Conradian theme of moral isolation has a much wider application in the story than is generally supposed.

* * * * * * * * * * * * *

The "athletic black belonging to some coast tribe" is not a good helmsman. He is an "unstable kind of fool,"

* From Harold R. Collins, "Kurtz, the Cannibals, and the Second-Rate Helmsman." *The Western Humanities Review* (Autumn, 1954), pp. 299-310.

steering "with no end of swagger" while his white man is at his side, but "instantly the prey of an abject funk" the moment he is alone. When Kurtz's "adorers" attack the steamer, he prances about, "stamping his feet, champing his mouth, like a reined-in horse." He leaves the wheel to open the shutter on the land side, fire off the Martini-Henry, and yell at the shore—and gets himself speared for his reckless folly.

Explaining his helmsman's fatal imprudence, Marlow anticipates his comments on the degradation of Kurtz. "Poor fool! If he had only let that shutter alone. He had no restraint, no restraint—just like Kurtz—a tree swayed in the wind." The helmsman has been tested, as the cannibals are tested, as Kurtz has been tested. The cannibals, tormented by hunger, have refrained from eating the pilgrims. Kurtz, in "utter solitude without a policeman" and "utter silence, where no warning voice of a kind neighbor can be heard," has "lacked restraint in the gratification of his various lusts," has taken a "high seat among the devils of the land." The helmsman almost wrecks the tinpot steamer, endangers the lives of the passengers, and throws his life away; when the fixed standards of conduct of his profession require steady steering, he can not resist the temptation to caper as though he were dancing an old-fashioned African war dance and to help the pilgrims squirt lead into the bush; when he should show his mettle, he merely "shows off."

The helmsman is not dignified and dependable like the cannibals, the "raw bush natives." Anyone at all familiar with modern anthropological studies of the process of "detribalization" and more recent fiction dealing with Africa will be struck by the fact that Conrad is representing "detribalized" natives in the characters of the prisoners' guard, the ill-conditioned manager's boy, and the second-rate helmsman; he is representing Africans who have been deprived of their traditional beliefs and standards of conduct without having assumed, or being able to assume, those of the white men. The manager's boy and the helmsman have come from coast tribes. Africans from the coast would be much more likely to be partially civilized, be "mission boys," in the white settlers' contemptuous phrase, than would those living upriver, for on the coast white men have long had "factories," or trading posts, and the first missions were established there. We may recall Marlow's ironical comments on these partially civilized Africans: "One of the reclaimed" (the guard), "an improved specimen" (the fireman), "an overfed young negro" (the manager's boy), "thought the world of himself" (the helmsman). In "weaning those ignorant millions from their horrid ways," the Belgian emissaries of light have produced, not dark-skinned gentleman, but vain creatures whose ways are seldom perfectly agreeable.

. . . .

Probably we would be quite safe in classing the second-rate helmsman with those Conradian characters that the critics have called "isolates." He has been deprived of the restraints and consolations of a social order, as Kurtz has been. And like Kurtz he lacks that "inner strength," that saving "definite belief" which may save the man thus deprived.

Anyone who doubts that Conrad's helmsman is silly and irresponsible because he is "one of the reclaimed" should read the African novels of Alan Paton, Joyce Cary, and Elspeth Huxley. Some of the milder cases of detribalization remind us of Conrad's helmsman. Akande Tom, in Cary's *The African Witch* (1936) thinks very well of himself. When he is decked out in a white linen suit, a check cloth cap, black sun goggles, and red morocco slippers, he struts about the native quarters of a Nigerian town with the ridiculous bravado characteristic of half-civilized Africans. Since he is dressed, or conceives that he is dressed, like a white man, he feels that he has "become one with the white man's ju-ju." The title character in Cary's *Mister Johnson* tries his District Officer's patience with his inept work as a clerk; but he's wonderfully proud of his work, especially his handwriting: when he thinks he has written a perfect capital S, he leaps from his chair and laughs triumphantly. He doesn't dance at his work like Conrad's helmsman, but he keeps his District Officer awake nights with his noisy parties at which he entertains his friends with gin, drum music, and his improvisations in song and dance.

Conrad's mentioning of the "rascally grin" on the guard's face and of the impudence and insolence of the manager's boy clearly indicates he realized that the "reclaimed" Africans often had more serious shortcomings than vanity and instability. The African novels of Paton, Cary, and Huxley represent the moral disintegration of tribeless Africans. They illustrate Arthur Jarvis' statement on the "breaking of the tribes," in Paton's *Cry, the Beloved Country* (1948): "The old tribal system was, for all its superstition and witchcraft, a moral system. Our natives today produce criminals and prostitutes and drunkards, not because it is their nature to do so, but because their simple system of order and tradition has been destroyed. It was destroyed by the impact of our civilization." . . .

We have noticed that important motives in "Heart of Darkness" connect the white men with the Africans. Conrad knew that the white men who come to Africa professing to bring progress and light to "darkest Africa" have themselves been deprived of the sanctions of their European social orders; they also have been alienated from the old tribal ways. Thrown upon their own inner spiritual resources—like detribalized natives—they may be utterly damned by their greed, their sloth, and their hypocrisy into moral insignificance, as were the pilgrims, or they may be so corrupted by their absolute power over the Africans that some Marlow will need to lay their memory among the "dead cats of civilization."

Ecology in *Heart of Darkness* *
Leo Gurko

Conrad not only perceives nature through his senses, but is aware of the profound parallelisms that link it with men. The ecological side of his art consists of demonstrating these parallelisms according to the demands of the particular scene. In his early period this demonstration reached its climax in the baffling and powerful story, "Heart of Darkness." Marlow['s] . . . account of a journey up the Congo in fascinated search of a Belgian trader named Kurtz begins and ends on the Thames, with his four interlocutors sprawled on the deck of a yawl waiting in the gathering darkness for the tide to turn. The process of suturing nature with the mood of Marlow's African experience begins at once. "The sea-reach of the Thames stretched before us like the beginning of an interminable waterway," a waterway, we are informed a few paragraphs farther on, "leading to the uttermost ends of the earth." This continuum of nature, in which the rivers of the earth flow into one another indissolubly so that what happens on the Thames happens on the Congo also, is reinforced by the comment "the sea and the sky were welded together without a joint." The theme of all experience being one experience, transcending time and space, underlies the story, and appears in several variations. One variation on the theme is historical, one imperialist, one personal, and all rest on a vision of the earth as a single, interpenetrating whole. Conrad continuously evokes this idea by his fusions of landscape. Again the fusion is not manufactured to suit the purpose of his fiction, but a quality of nature organic to it which the author asks us to be aware of.

* From Leo Gurko, *Joseph Conrad: Giant in Exile.* New York, The Macmillan Co. (1962), pp. 148–153.

The historical note allies itself to the double movement of the tides. In Elizabethan times the Drakes and Franklins sailed from the light of England into the darkness of unknown seas, returning with the "round flanks" of their ships bulging with treasure. Nineteen centuries ago the incoming tide brought the Romans from the light of Rome into the darkness of England where decent young citizens in togas no doubt felt "the utter savagery" of the country closing round them. Modern imperialism is no different from ancient. "The conquest of the earth, which mostly means the taking it away from those who have a different complexion or slightly flatter noses than ourselves, is not a pretty thing when you look into it too much." Whereupon Marlow proceeds to look into it. He goes to Brussels, a city like "a whited sepulchre," headquarters of the Congo trade, to apply for a post as captain of a river steamer. He is hired at once to replace a man just killed in a skirmish with natives over two black hens. The natives flee their village in terror, and in time grass grows through the ribs of the dead man. The Brussels street where the company is located has grass sprouting between the stones, and in the anteroom of the office sit two women (the two black hens) knitting black wool. The repetition of sensory details and of symbolic analogues—in this instance the grass and the woman-hen concord—lends the story a central pulsation and reinforces the theme of indissolubility that lies at its heart.

The darkness of Africa has bleached Brussels into a sepulchral whiteness. Other death images of imperialism appear. On the trip down, Marlow's ship passes a French man-of-war firing into the empty bush. No sign of life is visible anywhere but "there she was, incomprehensible, firing into a continent. . . . There was a touch of insanity in the proceeding . . . not dissipated by somebody on board assuring me earnestly there was a camp of natives—he called them enemies!—hidden out of sight somewhere." After landing at the mouth of the Congo,

Marlow runs into a grove filled with dying Negroes, too broken in health to work on their chain gangs any longer. Farther on, at the Central Station, he meets the manager and his henchmen, crassly devoted to extracting as much ivory as possible out of the country: "To tear treasure out of the bowels of the earth was their desire, with no more moral purpose at the back of it than there is in burglars breaking into a safe." Their naked rapacity fills Marlow with loathing, and this quickens his interest in Kurtz, who came to Africa with the "higher" aim of civilizing the natives and whom even his enemies acknowledge to be remarkable. He, too, is an imperialist trader (he sends out record-breaking quantities of ivory) but of a different sort, and Marlow is now confronted with "a choice of nightmares," between the systems of values represented by the manager and by Kurtz. The imperialist theme merges with the personal, and Marlow the observer-traveler now changes into Marlow the moral participant.

   .   .   .   .

If the historical theme expands into the imperialist, the imperialist into the personal, all of them are held aloft by the frame of external nature rooted at the bottom of the story. The Congo appears as "an immense snake uncoiled, with its head in the sea, its body at rest curving over a vast country, and its tail lost in the depth of the land." Its banks are lined with contorted mangroves; the water exudes the smell of primeval mud. And the wilderness in back waits in silence for the departure of rapacious men, a silence that "went home to one's very heart." For those outsiders who linger in it too long, or invade it too deeply, it is sure to wreak a terrible vengeance by exposing them, as it does Kurtz, to unbearable temptations. In the end it stamps the very flesh with its imprimatur, so that Kurtz's bald skull looked exactly like an ivory ball. The Thames, which seems at the start to be a waterway leading to the uttermost ends of the earth, merges into the Congo, which flows not so much in space as in time, "travelling back to the earliest beginnings of the world." The perils of such a journey are highlighted by the wreckage en route: an undersized railway truck lying on its back with its wheels in the air, looking "as dead as the carcass of some animal," the steamer Marlow drags up from the bottom, resembling "the carcass of some big river animal"; finally Kurtz himself, "lying at the bottom of a precipice where the sun never shines," a precipice into which Marlow himself nearly falls but is saved at the last moment.

All the while, Marlow tells this story, which he announces as "the farthest point of navigation and the culminating point of my experience," looking like a Buddha dressed in European clothes. The combination of east and west underlines the universality of his theme, linking the Thames and the Congo, Africa and Europe, the ancient Romans and latter-day British, streets in Brussels and mud paths in the heart of the wilderness. Kurtz as a pan-European figure, not simply a Belgian, is emphasized by the details of his parentage: "His mother was half-English, his father was half-French. All Europe contributed to the making of Kurtz." The spear, which to the astonishment of the natives "went quite easy between the shoulder-blades" of the white captain whom Marlow replaces, is the same spear which later passes through the body of the black helmsman, to the astonishment of Marlow himself. He compares the far-off drums of Africa to "the sound of bells in a Christian country." The disappearance of the Africans before the onslaught of the white men is described in terms of the emptying of farms in England "if a lot of mysterious niggers armed with all kinds of fearful weapons suddenly took to travelling on the road between Deal and Gravesend, catching the yokels right and left to carry heavy loads for them."

Throughout, Marlow pronounces the kinship between the howling, screaming Congolese and the rest of humanity, climaxed by the look given him by the dying

Negro helmsman, a look creating a "subtle bond" between them: "And the intimate profundity of the look
he gave me when he received his hurt remains to this day
in my memory—like a claim of distant kinship affirmed
in a supreme moment." The match which the Buddha-
like Marlow lights in the Thames night toward the end
of his tale affirms not only the contrast between light and
darkness but the flow between them, a flow establishing
their subtle bond. The earth itself, with its rivers and
continents, its jungles, seas, and peoples, covering its immense range in space and time, supplies "Heart of Darkness" with an ultimate source of reference. Behind the
movement and symbolism of the story lies its ecology.
Leaving the protective comforts of civilization for his
plunge into barbaric darkness, Marlow learns to make
his way about in it, to distinguish its noble and ignoble
qualities, and by exposing himself to its pressures, he em-
braces the indivisibility of experience, reflected at every
point by the indivisibility of the earth itself in all its mani-
festations. He and it are in the end "welded together
without a joint."

SUGGESTIONS FOR
FURTHER READING

SELECTED WORKS BY JOSEPH CONRAD

The Nigger of the "Narcissus," 1897
Lord Jim, 1900
Youth, 1902
Typhoon, 1903
Nostromo, 1904
The Secret Agent, 1907
Under Western Eyes, 1911
A Personal Record, 1912
Chance, 1913
Victory, 1915
The Shadow-Line, 1917
The Arrow of Gold, 1919

BOOKS ABOUT CONRAD

Baines, Jocelyn. *Joseph Conrad: a Critical Biography,* New York, 1960.

Gordan, John D. *Joseph Conrad: the Making of a Novelist,* Cambridge, Mass., 1940.

Guerard, Albert J. *Conrad the Novelist,* Cambridge, Mass., 1958.

Gurko, Leo. *Joseph Conrad: Giant in Exile,* New York, 1962.

Hewitt, Douglas. *Conrad: a Reassessment,* Cambridge, England, 1952.

Jean-Aubry, G. *Joseph Conrad: Life and Letters,* New York, 1927.

————. *The Sea Dreamer: a Definitive Biography of Joseph Conrad,* New York, 1957.

Leavis, F. R. *The Great Tradition,* New York, 1963.

Moser, Thomas C. *Joseph Conrad: Achievement and Decline*, Cambridge, Mass., 1957.

Zabel, Morton D. *The Viking Portable Conrad*, New York, 1947.

ARTICLES ABOUT *The Secret Sharer*

Benson, Carl. "Conrad's Two Stories of Initiation," *PMLA*, LXIX (March, 1954), pp. 46–56.

Leiter, Louis H. "Echo Structures: Conrad's 'The Secret Sharer,'" *Twentieth Century Literature*, V (January, 1960), pp. 159–175.

Mudrick, Marvin. "Conrad and the Terms of Modern Criticism," *The Hudson Review*, VII (Autumn, 1954) pp. 419–426.

Stallman, R. W. "Conrad and 'The Secret Sharer,'" *Accent*, IX (Spring, 1949), pp. 131–143.

ARTICLES ABOUT *Heart of Darkness*

Collins, Harold R. "Kurtz, the Cannibals, and the Second-Rate Helmsman," *Western Humanities Review*, VII (Autumn, 1954), pp. 299–310.

Dean, Leonard F. "Tragic Pattern in Conrad's 'Heart of Darkness,'" *College English*, VI (November, 1944), pp. 100–104.

Evans, Robert O. "Conrad's Underworld," *Modern Fiction Studies*, II (May, 1956), pp. 56–62.

Feder, Lillian. "Marlow's Descent into Hell," *Nineteenth Century Fiction*, IX (March, 1955), pp. 280–292.

Stein, W. B. "The Lotus Posture and *Heart of Darkness*," *Modern Fiction Studies*, II (Winter, 1956–57), pp. 167–170.

Thale, Jerome. "Marlow's Quest," *University of Toronto Quarterly*, XXIV, (July, 1955), pp. 351–358.

Williams, George. "The Turn of the Tide in *Heart of Darkness*," *Modern Fiction Studies*, IX (Summer, 1963), pp. 171–173.

THE NAMES THAT SPELL GREAT LITERATURE

Choose from today's most renowned world authors—every one an important addition to your personal library.

Hermann Hesse

☐	13956	MAGISTER LUDI	$2.95
☐	13523	DEMIAN	$2.25
☐	11978	THE JOURNEY TO THE EAST	$1.95
☐	12529	SIDDHARTHA	$2.25
☐	12758	BENEATH THE WHEEL	$2.25
☐	12509	NARCISSUS AND GOLDMUND	$2.50
☐	13174	STEPPENWOLF	$2.25
☐	11510	ROSSHALDE	$1.95

Alexander Solzhenitsyn

☐	10111	THE FIRST CIRCLE	$2.50
☐	13441	ONE DAY IN THE LIFE OF IVAN DENISOVICH	$2.50
☐	2997	AUGUST 1914	$2.50
☐	13720	CANCER WARD	$3.95

Jerzy Kosinski

☐	14117	STEPS	$2.50
☐	13619	THE PAINTED BIRD	$2.50
☐	2613	COCKPIT	$2.25
☐	11899	BLIND DATE	$2.50
☐	13843	BEING THERE	$2.50

Doris Lessing

☐	13433	THE SUMMER BEFORE THE DARK	$2.95
☐	13675	THE GOLDEN NOTEBOOK	$3.95
☐	13967	THE FOUR-GATED CITY	$3.95
☐	11717	BRIEFING FOR A DESCENT INTO HELL	$2.25

André Schwarz-Bart

☐	12510	THE LAST OF THE JUST	$2.95

Buy them at your local bookstore or use this handy coupon for ordering:

Bantam Books, Inc., Dept. EDG, 414 East Golf Road, Des Plaines, Ill. 60016

Please send me the books I have checked above. I am enclosing $_____ (please add $1.00 to cover postage and handling). Send check or money order —no cash or C.O.D.'s please.

Mr/Mrs/Miss _____

Address _____

City _____ State/Zip _____

EDG—4/80

Please allow four to six weeks for delivery. This offer expires 10/80.

START A COLLECTION

With Bantam's fiction anthologies, you can begin almost anywhere. Choose from science fiction, classic literature, modern short stories, mythology, and more—all by both new and established writers in America and around the world.

READ TOMORROW'S LITERATURE—TODAY

The best of today's writing bound for tomorrow's classics.

Bantam Book Catalog

Here's your up-to-the-minute listing of over 1,400 titles by your favorite authors.

This illustrated, large format catalog gives a description of each title. For your convenience, it is divided into categories in fiction and non-fiction——gothics, science fiction, westerns, mysteries, cookbooks, mysticism and occult, biographies, history, family living, health, psychology, art.

So don't delay——take advantage of this special opportunity to increase your reading pleasure.

Just send us your name and address and 50¢ (to help defray postage and handling costs).